Catch to Release

Lacey Schmidt

Catch to Release

Lacey Schmidt

Affinity
eBook Press
NZ
2016

Catch to Release

Affinity E-Book Press NZ LTD
Canterbury, New Zealand

1st Edition

ISBN: 978-0-908351-99-2

Editor: Angela Koenig
Proof Editor: Alexis Smith
Cover Design: Irish Dragon Designs

Acknowledgments

Thank you to my soul mate, lovely wife, and personal hero, Laura. Thank you to my other perpetual heroes, Mom and Dad; and to my biological, in-law, and chosen siblings for standing by me no matter what.

Thank you to the authors and women of Affinity.

Thank you to my brilliant and patient business partners for their continuous encouragement of my second, secret career in noveling.

Finally, thank you to all of the wonderful kids who included me in a meaningful part of their lives (Kyla, Hannah Beth, Victoria, Jacob, Lucy, Patrick, Peyton, Parker, Alex, Ian, Taylor, Nathan, Hannah Marie, and Liam). You guys really taught me the ultimate premise of this novel: the best way to keep someone safe is to love them well. When we are well loved, we take better care of ourselves, and we don't put ourselves in harm's way trying to get love.

Dedication

To those brave and crazy enough to love through the hurt and absurdities. Indubitable compassion saves our faith in humanity. Despite atrocities like the senseless massacre that occurred in June 2016 at Pulse in Orlando, Florida, love heals.

Table of Contents

Chapter One - Bang, Bang. Got Me Good 1
Chapter Two - Stage Rfitht, Stage Right................ 4
Chapter Three - Attachement Disorders............... 16
Chapter Four - Lead Balloon Boom....................... 21
Chapter Five - Discarded Mail................................ 25
Chapter Six - Dream Class 39
Chapter Seven -A Bad Bomb Target...................... 50
Chapter Eight -Checks and Assurances................. 79
Chapter Nine -Button Pushing............................... 84
Chapter Ten -Conspicuous is a Word.................. 90
Chapter Eleven -Playing with the Dolls... 96
Chapter Twelve -One Part Paranoia......................112
Chapter Thirteen -Right as Might for a Rainy... .122
Chapter Fourteen -Post-Dozer Doldrums 124
Chapter Fifteen -Blue Blooked Counsel... 132
Chapter Sixteen -The Security Assessment. 143
Chapter Seventeen -Thanksgiving 152
Chapter Eighteen -Down and Dirty Blues 162
Chapter Nineteen -Yuletide Gala Going...............171
Chapter Twenty -Hurl 183
Chapter Twenty-one -Waiting Room Winks 189
Chapter Twenty-two -Since We're Here Anyway 196
Chapter Twenty-three -A Nearer Menace 206
Chapter Twenty-four -New Year's Eve Regrets....212
Chapter Twenty-five -Down Beats.........................218

Chapter Twenty-six -Bay Bound.............................224
Chapter Twenty-seven -Slap Iron...........................232
Chapter Twenty-eight -Release.............................248
Chapter Twenty-nine -To Catch.............................257
Chapter Thirty -Legalities.................................270
Chapter Thirty-one -Alternate Plans......................289
Chapter Thirty-two -Healing...............................304
Chapter Thirty-three -Catch to Release.................315
About the Author...319
Other Books from Affinity eBook Press.................320

Also by Lacey Schmidt

A Walk Away

Love's Luck

The Nightshade Lexicon

Chapter One

Bang, Bang. Got Me Good

Addison Weller pushed open the underground garage access door beneath the courthouse and glanced over everything before she ushered the Honorable John Errington through the door ahead of her. The fine hairs on the back of her neck stood up. She listened and heard only the hum of the industrial heating system, but a prescient tingle tapped lightly over her spine. Reaching her left hand inside her jacket, she put the tips of her fingers on the butt of her FN 5.7 pistol. She placed her right hand lightly on the back of the Honorable John Errington.

A solitary businessman watched them from over the hood of a black sedan forty feet to their left. Weller noticed he was immaculate in a navy suit, white shirt, and pale blue tie. His face was smooth and regular as milk, until he reached inside his jacket. One of his brown eyes darkened and squinted in an aim as he pulled out a Sig Sauer P299.

Weller drew her heavy FN 5.7 smoothly. Her left forefinger brushed the safety off as she slid her gun over the crisp linen of her suit vest with a soft rasp. She tossed her head to clear away a dark brown wisp of hair in her sightline. She leveled the gun. Adjusting her own aim to the poor lighting and the lack of breeze underground, she strained to hear over the adrenaline roaring in her ears. With one long, sure step forward, she brought her own body between Errington and the Sig Sauer's speeding bullet before firing her own weapon.

The two shots fired so quickly that John Errington wondered if he was dreaming them. For a brief second he thought to protest when Weller pushed him to the oily ground in front of a black BMW. Then Weller's stillness rested heavy on his back, and her weight behind her forearm spread across the back of his shoulders. He listened carefully to hear her breathing. He heard silence.

"Weller?" Errington shifted his face off the floor just enough to talk.

Under the tunnel of parked cars, he saw a man in a navy suit, arm outstretched but still holding a smoking gun, and a pool of velvet blood creeping over the oily floor. The man blinked at Errington as their eyes met, but the man didn't make any other movements. Errington watched a sigh fall from the man's lips to the floor. He swallowed, and asked again, "Weller?"

Weller's weight lifted with such speed that Errington

was too stunned to sit up.

He heard the steel door to the garage bang open and lifted his head to watch Weller wheel around to face the door with her FN 5.7 aimed and ready.

Errington let out a long shaky breath. One of Weller's team members, the exceedingly tall one with short brown hair, filled the doorway.

Errington rose to his knees as Weller lowered her weapon, and he heard her request, "Wimberly, call 911, and then call Jim O'Rourke at the Chicago DSS field office and tell him we've eliminated a hitman. He'll get the investigation rolling."

Errington stood and watched Wimberly nod before leaving to comply with his boss's request.

Weller offered a hand up. "Would you like to see if your phone charger is still in the car now?"

Errington tried to swallow the leaden fear bubbling in his stomach, but only managed to throw up on the floor between his wingtip shoes.

Chapter Two

Stage Fright, Stage Right

Shay Greenaura played the guitar like most people played a piano, with all ten fingers intimately involved. She thought of her guitar as another woman with a driving pulse that she could bend. The cheers of the seven thousand or so souls watching her play rushed over and around her like waves washing against stones at the sound of every clear note she struck. Sweat stung her eyes and she tossed her head to free the tangle of blond curls sticking to her forehead. She sang out the closing note and leaned into the tightening of every muscle in her small body. Her voice broke free and clear beyond the roar of the crowd for a last, lingering second. Wolf whistles and cheering rolled over the stage. She was already drunk with the calm, wonderful weariness of giving all of herself to her passion, her music.

Thirty feet away at the edge of the stage, a solitary man in a horde of exuberant women watched Shay touch the hands of her fans and smile at each one as she walked off the stage. The man eyed the crunchy-granola hippie chick next to him and decided she would do fine. *All of these liberated, self-righteous women ultimately just want to go home and be given some order, some direction, to soften the chaos of freedom.* He would seduce her first, as he knew she believed she wanted to be seduced. Then when she learned to trust him, he would ram order into her with each hammer of his cock and beat her to the edge of senseless before he silenced her life into eternal order. He smiled to himself and smoothed one hand over the Greenaura logo on his T-shirt. He would use the hippie chick for today. *But, one day...one day soon...Shay Greenaura will be my bitch.* That thought made him hard in his jeans. He caught the blue eyes of the petite blond hippie chick with a shy nodding smile calculated to earn her interest.

†

Gloved hands pattered on a keyboard in a dim public library just minutes before closing time on a rainy Tuesday. A YouTube video of Shay's latest concert rolled on in a minimized window, while in a larger desktop window, Shay's blue eyes crinkled with a grin in a candid still shot. The photo was a nice close-up of Shay in pajamas, at home on a winter night, snuggled up on the sofa with her daughter, Iva. The pleased photographer slashed a warning over the photo in *Jack-the-Ripper-horror* font, "I WILL KILL IVA. SLOWLY.

SO YOU CAN WATCH." The photographer saved the creation to a jump drive, careful to erase the file properties, pocketed the drive, and erased all history folders before leaving the library.

†

"This is the Chasten Scorn show coming at you live on Talk Time Satellite Radio. We are all ready to ridicule and beguile Robespierre Greenaura, drummer and pansy brother of the infamous liberal dyke singer, Shay Greenaura. Say hello to the folks, RobO, you know the drill."

"Hello, world. I'm Rob Greenaura and I can take the Scorn." RobO flashed Chasten a wide self-deprecating grin and patted the thinning hair down on the top of his head.

Chasten shrugged his hoodie smooth over the back of his neck and smiled broadly. "Then let the games begin. Our first burning question, RobO, is—and we have done our research, so we do have some dirt—why is your sister quickly becoming a rich and famous musician with a cause, when you were the first one with star ambitions?"

"That's too easy, Chasten. I never had any star ambitions. I just liked crooning cover songs, and I was floored and amazed that my baby-sister wanted to play along."

"Aw, come on, man. Aren't you even a little jealous that the scrawny no-name drummer of your Frank Sinatra cover band achieved all of this success as a singer and a songwriter, while you were stuck tagging along?"

"Well the cover band was mostly for fun anyways. I never expected it to feed us long-term. Our dad died when I was ten and Shay was four years old, and our mom wasn't exactly reliable even before she died, too. So, I'd already been working as a busboy, and then as a bouncer for several clubs in DC, before I started trying to sing for more money. Shay had an after-school job, but she learned to play the drums so we could take home more of the band's pay."

"Got tired of ramen noodles?"

RobO chuckled. "Honestly, we got tired of living without power because we couldn't pay the utility bills. Even when Shay wasn't at work, she followed me to the gigs so she could have air conditioning and light for free for a while each night."

"So you took your underage baby sister along to clubs like The Bottom Line bar for her safety?"

"Ha! No, of course not. Have you met my sister? I took her along for my safety."

Chasten laughed boldly at the punchline in a deep rumble that was obviously playing it up for their listeners. "Point taken, RobO. So you taught your baby sister to play drums so you could keep her out of trouble and use her for slave wages?"

"Sort of. She actually taught herself to play drums by watching every night, I guess. I didn't have a clue until one night when our regular drummer got too pissing drunk to stand up and we were about to go on without any drums, she slipped in behind his kit and started playing."

"But how did she get from behind the drums to strumming a guitar and singing then? And how did you end up behind those drums?"

"We were waiting in the alley to go on at some scummy joint above a nice restaurant one night. Shay picked up Glen's guitar and sat on his amp fiddling around with it—just like she did just about every time we waited somewhere, but that night she started singing along. Some poem she'd been scribbling all over the back of envelopes and receipts. A more upscale club owner, Jane Karsen, walked out of the restaurant after dinner and heard Shay singing. She handed Shay her card and asked us to play an early evening gig at a coffee house she had just opened called the Daily Grind. Since the time slot allowed us to still play our regular gig that Friday, we went to the Daily Grind first. Shay and I played that gig with her singing and me playing the bass guitar. We had to borrow both guitars from Glen the first few weeks, but then found I found a three-piece jazz drum kit and an acoustic guitar on sale in some pawn shop. After that we played any gig we could get anyone to book with either of us singing lead."

"The masses just liked your sister best."

RobO rolled his eyes and shrugged. "No accounting for tastes, heh?"

"What about this Greenaura crap? Couldn't you guys make up a better stage name?"

"It's our name. Our father gave it to us. All I know is

that it means 'from the village of Greenaun,' which is in County Mayo, Ireland. Our father was of Irish descent, but his family had been here so long, and suffered so many separations, that I don't think he knew much more than that. At least, he never told me more than that."

"What about your mother?"

"She was part Italian and part Polish. She kept a list of family births and deaths in the front of her bible, but I don't think she ever knew where or how her own parents or brothers ended up. I think they gave up on her before we were even born. I don't remember any grandparents or uncles or aunts. None of the names on her list have led to anyone alive so far."

"You heard that, world. If you're related to these shady Greenaura musicians, please let us know. Maybe RobO will get sentimental and cut you in on the inheritance. Right?"

"Sure thing, Chasten, we'll split our whole stock of Irish whiskey and all our bail bonds with anyone who can show they're remotely related."

"Now don't be so damned generous, you bastard. Tell us how the hell you got from sleazy clubs in DC to Chicago in the first place."

"Well, it's really kind of a long story. Are you sure you want to hear it?"

Chasten smirked. "No, but I've gotta ask you to tell it anyway. How else am I going to get a balding, middle-aged drummer to fill out an hour long show? I'll interrupt you when I need to."

"Okay. You asked for it."

"Yes, I did."

"Our mom died just a few months after I turned eighteen, but Shay was still only twelve-years old. Child protective services gave me the choice of assuming guardianship for Shay, but they advised against it since they didn't feel I could take care of myself well enough yet. I opted to let them place Shay into the foster system for three years until I turned twenty-one and got a little more practice at raising myself."

"So you left your little sister hanging in the wind?"

"Yeah, but in my defense, I thought I was doing what was best for both of us. It wasn't until Shay and I were back together that I realized just how wrong I was."

"So what happened?"

"The foster family Shay was placed with over those three years essentially used her as a drug mule and beat her into secrecy."

"Whoa! Holy Cow!" Chasten's eyes grew wider. He leaned in toward RobO to listen.

"Yeah, I know. Unbelievable, right? I had my doubts, too, until Metro PD showed up on our doorstep one morning to question Shay. The foster parents had been busted for dealing at a little league baseball game. Based on their subsequent accusations against Shay, and the evidence they handed over in Shay's old school back-pack, the DA was pressing charges against Shay for possession with intent to distribute."

"So then what? As far as I know Shay Greenaura has no criminal record."

"No, she doesn't. But it scared the hell out of us since we knew it was her word against the foster parents' implications—and we didn't think that stood much of chance in convincing any judge. Lucky for us, the public defender worked out a deal. If Shay agreed to serve as a witness for the DA against the foster parents as needed, do 500 hours of community service, and serve two years of probation with active drug counseling, even though she swore she never used any, then the DA would not press charges."

"Okay, so how does that get you from Washington, D.C., to Chicago?"

"Well, Shay testified and the foster parents were convicted, but then they appealed and the conviction was overturned on a technicality, not too long after Shay finished her two years of probation with counseling. We were both afraid the foster parents would try to cause her some sort of misery in retribution. During the counseling, Shay saw something about a mission and shelter in Chicago called Second Start. I started poking around their web site and saw that they specialized in helping young adults get another start after drug-related misdemeanors. It seemed like our only real chance out, so we started saving for two one-way bus tickets to leave."

"And you gave up your cover band and your gigs to go?"

"I did give up the cover band. We couldn't take the other band members with us, and we didn't have any connections in Chicago to restart the band, or knowledge of the club scene there to arrange any gigs."

"But?"

"We kept our pawn-shop instruments. Shay and I played for money every chance we got on the way to Chicago, and all around the Second Start shelter once we got there. Many folks at the shelter helped us get paying gigs and promoted our work. Shay is a natural and it was easy for her star to rise once people could see her perform. She came out of her shell of fear and insecurity, too, and found a sense of belonging in the community."

"Aww. How rainbow-from-the-ass-ends-of-butterflies lovely is that?"

"Yep. A regular happy ending. For me, too. I met my wife Sylvia there. Syl had been arrested for possession of cocaine as a minor before escaping from her rich bitch parents in the suburbs to the Second Start shelter in downtown Chicago. The three of us just bonded, and when Syl got a job in the city's permit offices, she started networking with vendors who were willing to mentor us all on promoting our music. Everything worked out for the best."

"So you're not miffed about giving up your whole chance at fame and fortune to look after your sister?" Chasten's voice played the tonal registers of false incredulity.

Shaking his head, RobO gave a sheepish grin. "Nope.

I just want to keep my family safe. Shay and Syl experienced so many things because there wasn't anyone who cared to keep them safe."

"Safety is more important than fame and fortune, hey?"

"Yes."

"But you never get bummed out about it? I don't believe you."

RobO half nodded and played with the zipper on his green pleather jacket. "Well, sure, sometimes. Sometimes I feel I still can't really keep them safe. Sometimes I get tired of my brilliant little sister's talent for change, evolution, learning, personal growth. Whatever you want to call it. Getting caught up in all the hubbub associated with that talent can be overwhelming and tiring at times."

RobO shrugged out of his jacket and pushed up the shirtsleeve on his left forearm to reveal his tattoo. He held it up to show Chasten. "That's why I have this tattoo that says 'it is what it is' right where I can see it when I drum. I think everything, including change, power, and growth is good in moderation. Some things you still just have to accept and make the best of. I just have to accept that I can do more good behind the drums, supporting my sister and hopefully keeping my family safer, than I can pursuing my own fame and fortune as a singer. Sometimes what it is should be enough."

"Jeeze. Deep thoughts by RobO, folks."

"Yep. It is what it is. Don't you enjoy being a penny-ante shock DJ, Chasten Scorn?"

"Oh no, I'm not going to answer that. This isn't about me. In fact, it's time for me to ask you the question that matters most, RobO...what giveaway did you bring to appease our audience members?"

RobO smiled and reached behind him to pick up a hard-shell guitar case. "I've brought one of Shay's custom, green-pearl-sparkle, semi-hollow, body guitars." He unlatched the case and lifted the guitar out to show Chasten the sparkle beneath the studio lights.

"Well folks, I'm looking at it right now, and it is a thing of beauty even if you don't write lesbian-folk-pop songs. The first caller who can correctly name RobO's Frank Sinatra cover band wins."

†

Shay pushed open the steel exit door a crack and found a score of people crowding the alley behind the Maddux Theater in St. Paul. She quickly pulled the door shut again. The cold air fanned in behind her and washed over the entire sweaty band at her back.

"What's up?" RobO asked from behind her.

"They alley is lousy with media, fans, and," she sighed, "protesters." She looked at the ratty concrete floor and a dewdrop of sweat beaded down the edge of her nose to splash against the top of her boot.

"No other exit gets any better, I'm sure." RobO's voice

was calm and smooth.

"Let's just do it." Fallow flexed up and down on the tiptoes of his green Chuck Taylor's.

"I'll go in front." RobO nudged Shay away from the door.

Shay rubbed her palms over her face and pressed herself close to RobO's broad back.

†

The crowds parted around RobO letting him through. After twenty or so steps, he turned to smile at his sister and found that he could no longer see her. The crowd around him was looking behind him and shouting.

Hoots of "Shay, over here," and growls of "Jesus can still save you, sister" echoed around him. Smartphone cameras flashed. Bodies pushed past him.

The rest of the band was lost in the sea of people. Everyone and everything sparkled dewy with the night's humidity.

RobO spotted a small blond head bouncing above the writhing mass of humanity and turned to push his way back to Shay.

This alley, this venue, the security isn't built for this level of recognition. RobO used his arms in a breaststroke manner to swim through the crowd to rescue his baby sister. *I'll never keep her safe.*

Chapter Three

Attachment Disorders

In the paneled library of an old brownstone deep in the heart of Chicago, John Errington fell into a plush, leather, wingback chair, and rested his shaking hands on the Cherrywood fleet desk in front of him. Errington took deep breaths in and out with his face down, and then, with a strong exhale, looked up to where Weller waited along the wall beside the closed door. She faced the windows. Errington took comfort from her presence and from knowing that the tall, trim woman carried two FN 5.7's in reach and a strange knife in her hip pocket.

Errington massaged his head through the fine gray stubble on his temples and wondered about Weller's personal life. *She is a quiet woman. Attractive and athletic. Probably Midwestern.* She reminded him of his older sister—in appearance only. *Weller is cold, calm, and unreachable.* She was nothing like Errington's cheerful sister Mary. Then again, he wouldn't want to hire Mary to keep him alive during a mob trial. *Weller saved my life. Weller put her body in the way of a bullet with my name on it.* All before he could even blink and with no apparent regret on her part. Errington's hands took on a stronger tremble.

"Would you like a drink, Weller? I need one." Errington opened his bottom desk drawer and pulled out the good Scotch and two glasses. He poured himself four fingers and gestured to the empty glass.

"A splash. Thank you." Weller stepped forward to pick up the glass.

"To survival." Errington held up his glass.

"Yes, sir. Survival it is"

"Thank you, Weller. Thank you." Errington tipped back his glass and took a healthy gulp.

"You're welcome, sir."

He watched Weller. She held the glass close to her face and breathed in the sharp heather and peat smell of his favorite Scotch.

"How did you know, Weller? How do you know who to trust? Who to watch? Who to shoot?"

"He wasn't texting on his smart phone like most businessmen do on their way in and out of meetings. He was watching you from the moment we walked into the garage. It wasn't just common curiosity. He was focused on you and he was controlling his breathing...the way we are trained to do when we draw and shoot, so that we're accurate. Enough training and you don't even notice you notice these things."

"Are you ever scared?" Errington's hands began to steady themselves and the Scotch warmed his chest.

Weller nodded. "Yes, but not about things like this. I am scared by the things I can't control, or train to react to well." Weller sipped the Scotch.

A knock sounded at the door. She set the glass on his desk and turned toward the door with her dominant left hand near the small of her back. Errington knew one gun resided there in a leather paddle holster.

"Who is it?" asked Weller.

"Reyna Hinojosa, employee ID Mako. I'm here for Addison Weller, employee ID Seawolf."

Weller's arms relaxed. She opened the door just long enough to let a smaller Hispanic woman in a similar charcoal pantsuit enter.

"Hello, Addy."

"Welcome to Chicago, Reyna. Let me introduce you to Mr. Errington." Weller gave the woman a smile and then gestured toward Errington at his desk.

Reyna's dark brown eyes met his and she smiled at him without showing any teeth.

He noticed she was almost a foot shorter than Weller and decidedly more softly curved beneath her grey suit. "Hello, and no disrespect, Mrs. Hinojosa…"

"Please, sir, call me Reyna."

"Reyna, I know you must be capable to be part of Weller's team, but I don't see the point of switching my protection lead now."

"You trust Weller and she knows your routines." Reyna lifted her eyebrows and gave a slightly broader smile.

"Yes." Errington stared more closely at the woman.

"And she is a little taller, older, and more capable looking," Reyna continued.

Weller lowered her head, but Errington could still see the taller woman smiling at the carpet.

"Well…" he started to backtrack, suspecting his careful argument was somehow logically doomed already.

"It is okay to admit the facts, Mr. Errington. Weller is the best."

Errington blinked and pursed his lips, suppressing the words wanting to bubble out of him.

Weller cleared her throat. "And Reyna trained with me and taught me many of the things that make me good at protecting people. There is no one I trust more right now, not even myself, to continue to provide you the best protection."

"I don't understand. I'd just like you to stay too," Errington admitted.

"I'm sorry, sir. It just isn't in the best interests of either of us. Our experiences and the data show that after successfully defending someone's life, it is too hard not to become emotionally attached to that person. Emotional attachment causes a protection lead to lose their objectivity and situation awareness. Attachment might dull too many of those instincts that were trained into us."

Errington looked over at Reyna stationed beside his

office door where Weller was only minutes ago. He looked back at Weller. He couldn't refute her logic because he knew he felt more attached to the tall, stoic woman just from knowing she had saved his life.

He sighed. "All the same, I wish you could stay too. I do know you have a business to run, and probably other contracts that require your talent."

"Yes, sir, I do, but I have no doubt you will soon feel most secure with Reyna taking the lead. I have kept in contact with Reyna every week since we began your protection detail. She knows all your routines, each threat identified in our security assessment, and all our required and planned security responses for you. This is standard operating procedure for us. We always prepare three leads for any protection detail."

"So if my life is threatened two more times, I'm out of security leads you trust, or do you rotate back into the lead?"

"No, sir, you are not out of leads and I do not necessarily return to lead unless that is the best option determined by the primary protection team lead."

"Ha! Are you sure you didn't earn a law degree yourself?" Errington gave Weller a grin.

Weller smiled back at him and squeezed Reyna's forearm on her way out. Errington thought he saw a look of sympathy cross Reyna's face as she glanced after Weller. Then he was sure her eyes held a note of apology as their gazes met and the door closed behind Weller.

Chapter Four

Lead Balloon Boom

In the Chicago library's computer lab on a Saturday night near closing time, the fifteen people scattered around using the public computers could still feel a little of the cold November winds seeping in. At one terminal, a pair of gloved hands was working out a short message in upper case, bold, Times New Roman font, double spaced:

SHAY GREENAURA—I AM NEAR. I AM READY. YOU HAVE EVERYTHING TO FEAR STILL. I WILL DESTROY YOUR WORLD. HERE I COME...

†

Shay surveyed the crowd as the band exited Shank Hall. With the help of the Hall's security guards, they made their way toward their tour bus on Prospect Avenue. The thought of the quiet hum of the road and not much other noise as they left Milwaukee for Detroit sounded divine to her already. Fans pressed against them on all sides. Shay made eye contact, smiled, and tapped hands with many of them in passing, but did not stop to sign autographs or take gifts.

"Don't you still wish we had the time to stop and have a smoke with the one or two die-hard fans before we leave? Like we used to?" RobO marched tightly behind her right shoulder.

"I know. I do miss that." Shay smiled back at her bulky, looming older brother. "I bet you miss Syl, too, huh?" She kept stumbling forward.

"Yeah, this bit about having to leave my wife home while we travel kind of takes the fun out some, but not near as much as not having little Iva around."

"I know. I miss my girl. No one else smears soggy cheerios and sweet baby kisses on the great Shay Greenaura." Shay felt her shoulders slump.

She reached the bus and tugged the door open before stepping over a sheet of white paper on the floor just inside the door. Shay raced to grab her ringing smart phone off her bunk.

"Hello?" she answered in great anticipation knowing it was Syl, RobO's wife, calling so she could say goodnight to Iva. She lost focus on what Syl was actually saying when she noticed RobO had picked up the paper and, as he looked at it, his face turned deathly white.

"What? Wait, say again. What do you mean there was a bomb?" Although Shay spoke into the phone calmly, she felt like the bus was suddenly spinning like a top. "Is anybody hurt? How close were you and Iva?"

RobO looked up at her. She could see the hairs along his arms standing up.

"Sis?" he whispered.

She shook her head lightly and could feel the tears prickling her eyes. "I understand. We will reschedule Detroit, Syl. We'll be home as soon as we can get there. Here's RobO."

Shay passed the phone to RobO and he gave her the typed page. As Shay read the words of one of her songs rephrased into a threat, she felt dread sink like lead into the marrow of her bones.

†

RobO stared at the plastic sheeting and plywood used to seal the massive hole in the wall of his clapboard house. Debris filled the space where his living room used to be. Syl and Iva had been reading stories before bed when the car bomb went off outside in their front yard. He felt the tears start down his cheeks. He heard Shay coming in behind him and he turned to stop her.

"Don't, sis. You don't need to see this for anything."

"I want to see, RobO."

RobO sidestepped with a nod and let her in.

"Sweet Jesus." Shay covered her mouth with one hand and clutched her shirt to her chest with the other.

"It was close," RobO said.

"So close." Shay's eyes teared up.

"Mama, mama, I've got flowers," Iva cooed from outside in the yard.

RobO watched the sun, felt the cold November air, and listened to the sound stream through the gap in the plastic sheeting and plywood for several seconds. He tried to pull himself together before going back out to where Syl and Iva waited.

Shay dabbed at her eyes with the back of her hand and swallowed audibly. "We're all moving to our new church studio. The old nunnery's dormitory apartments are renovated enough now anyway. Okay?"

"All right. I will feel better if we're all together. Will the police detail come too?" RobO toed a shard of drywall near his foot.

"Yes, the police detail will come, too, at least until Beni gets back with help. He said something about hiring a real security service for the church studio and dormitory."

"And on travel?" RobO made a point of looking into his sister's blue eyes.

"We'll have to work that out. I want Syl and Iva protected." Shay's lips tightened into a thin, determined line.

"Me too." He bit his lower lip.

Chapter Five

Discarded Mail

Weller pushed open the outer door of a third-floor office suite in the Watergate building. She set her black duffel bag on the plush blue carpet and faced the camera on the inner door. She gave a small wave with both hands and turned in a slow circle. A buzzer sounded. Weller picked up her travel duffel and opened the inner door.

She saw Gina Wilson waiting inside the door and noticed her jade Jimmy Choo high heels sinking into the blue office carpet.

Gina pushed her purple Warby Parker glasses up a little higher on her thin straight nose.

"Welcome back, boss. You look like shit. Didn't you stop by your apartment on the way from the airport?"

"Thanks, Gina. No. I have stuff to do here first."

"What? Like stare at all the accounts I already settled? Or deprive yourself of sleep?"

"Yep. We got any milk in the fridge?"

"Well, in fact we do, but only because I took pity on your pathetic habits and threw out that disgusting milk-algae monster you left in there, and replaced it with a fresh carton when Reyna picked up her flight tickets."

"Oh, good. Thank you. You're a gem. I'm going to try out the comfort of my desk chair for a bit."

"Yeah, um, about that. You have a special visitor. A guy who knew our office location and came in asking for you by name. He said that Errington referred him and he knew you should be returning today."

Weller stopped her trek down the hall and turned back to Gina.

"Where is he? And what do you know already?"

"He is in the main conference room with a cup of coffee, watching out our window at the view. His name is Benito Goodson Jr. of Chicago. He holds a law degree and specializes in representing up-and-coming artists, and he does volunteer work with the largest Catholic diocese in Chicago. He says he is here to contract us for a very important job and that he is willing and able to pay a large sum of money to acquire the best protection detail for his client."

"Sounds simple enough. Did you start the file?"

"Yes, I made a file and put in as much info as we could gather on Mr. Goodson. I couldn't convince him to tell me about his client. He wants to speak to you first. He claims he only trusts us—you—because Errington said you saved the day."

Weller rubbed her face with both hands and smacked her cheeks a bit to bring back the color.

"Okay, Gina. Let me find out why the mysterious Mr. Goodson is so desperate, and why he is so willing to pay us a lot of good money. Then we will see if we can talk some sense into him about how this is supposed to all work and why."

"I knew you would. I'll get you a glass of milk."

Weller continued down the hall to drop her duffel in her office and straighten her suit.

†

Gina watched the boss go for a second and then shook her head before heading for the fridge. She wondered if Weller had slept more than one night yet at the apartment she bought after her wife died and she left the Diplomatic Security Service.

"I bet the bed doesn't even have sheets on it, and there isn't anything there except another alien algae-milk monster in the refrigerator, and lots of discarded mail on the counter," Gina muttered.

†

Weller eased into her office and dropped her duffle next to her empty coat rack. Her desk was devoid of everything except a picture frame, with a single black-and-white, five-by-seven-inch photo of her deceased wife, Elle.

Weller picked up the photo.

"Hi, hon. I'm home." Weller studied Elle's high cheekbones and her dark eyes a minute before tracing one fingertip over the edges of Elle's wide smile. Elle was holding her camera and the wind had caught and twisted the tip of her glossy dark hair. Weller remembered that day before they knew Elle was sick. They were at one of Elle's photo shoots in Central Park for a pro bono publicity spread she was doing to support the Homeless Youth Alliance's work. The sun was golden, the leaves were starting to turn colors, and the wind was playful and crisp. Elle had a twinkle in her eye and Weller thought they had all the luxury of time. Weller gave a sigh and set the photo back on the desk.

"I still miss you."

She let loose her French braid and wandered into the tiny executive bathroom attached to her office. Pulling a brush out of the stark steel medicine cabinet, she gave her hair a hundred brush strokes before twisting it into a bun and pinning it in place.

"Better," she told her reflection.

After slipping out of her suit jacket, she walked back to her desk and pulled off her shoulder harness with the heavy FN 5.7 and extra clip inside. She reached for the small of her back, pulled out the paddle holster with her second FN 5.7, and placed it on her desk next to its sister. Then she reached into the front, inner, hip pocket on her right side and pulled out her tactical, folding, karambit blade before unbuttoning her suit vest and sliding it off. She placed the vest on the coatrack then stripped off her fitted, white, oxford shirt and placed it with the vest. She padded back to her desk, drew open the bottom drawer, and selected a soft, black silk, V-neck that contrasted well with the charcoal gray of her suit. She added the tactical karambit and the paddle-holstered gun back to her suit pants before picking up her shoulder rig. Turning to the bookshelf behind her desk, she raised her hand and then tapped the book spine that served as her safe's facade so that it swung silently open. She keyed in the code and placed her shoulder rig with the other gun and clip inside, closed the safe door, and flipped the facade back into place.

A knock sounded at the door and Gina announced, "Milk delivery."

Weller pulled open the door and accepted the ice cold glass from Gina's outstretched hand. "Thank you."

"You bet, boss. I'll be in the video room watching the record while you're in with Goodson."

"Sounds good."

Weller downed the milk and set the empty glass on her desk before pulling her suit jacket back on and walking out of her office for the conference room.

†

Gina tipped the boss's door shut and noticed the stark office was still void of any personal detail of Weller's except for the picture of Elle facing the empty desk chair. On the floor next to the door, sitting next to the wall, was the small, black duffel full of Weller's dirty laundry from her last trip.

†

Weller eased open the heavy bullet-proof glass door of the conference room, using the time to observe Benito Goodson Jr. He was a short squat man in his fifties, with a bald spot, and thinning, dark-brown but graying hair. He was wearing a rumpled navy-blue suit and a white shirt with a vague coffee stain on the collar. His lavender tie looked like good quality but was tugged loose and rested a little sideways of center. He turned his face to Weller more fully, and she noted the dark circles under his eyes that spoke of too little sleep lately.

"Ms. Weller?" His voice was a soft tenor.

"Yes, Mr. Goodson, how can I help you?"

"Please, call me Beni."

Weller nodded and sat in a chair across from him at the long conference table.

Beni rolled his chair closer to the table and clasped his hands together on the table in front of him. Weller noticed his light brown eyes were a tad bloodshot—the vague red reminiscent of high blood pressure or severe allergies. His hands were soft and pale, the nails neat and clean, but his cuticles were ragged as if he chewed at them sometimes. She said nothing, waiting for him to break the silence and tell her more.

He cleared his throat and then tilted his head to his left side.

"I'm a lawyer by training, but I started managing gay artists and musicians several years back through a church charity group. One of my clients has achieved some unexpected and notable success over the last three years and this has brought up some unexpected challenges for me. Her success is starting to require management skills and resources I don't possess. She is not yet ready to accept my pleas of inadequacy and hire someone of more appropriate skills."

"I appreciate your distress, Beni, but how does this relate to your desire to consult with Vigiles Security Services? We are strictly in the business of providing security assessments and diplomatic protection details."

"Yes, Ms. Weller, I am in fact counting on that. My client's success has also recently inspired some, shall we say, less than desirable interest from an unknown and very threatening source. I was not sure how, or whom, to even ask about securing protection for my client until the police can identify and eliminate this threat. As I said, I am way beyond my limited managerial talents and outside of my family law education. I did, however, have the good fortune of graduating law school with John Errington. I remembered reading about the threats on John's life during the Lomguino crime family's trial last year. I called John for some advice and I got a glowing reference for you specifically. Can you provide my client protection services similar to those you provided for John?"

Weller only blinked back at him for a beat before asking, "Your client is an artist?"

"A musician." Beni touched one fingertip to the table top.

"We don't offer services for public performers, Mr. Goodson."

"Please, call me Beni."

Weller paused until he looked her in the eyes again. "Beni, we typically offer protection details for bureaucrats and executives who find themselves sudden targets due to their diplomatic or corporate responsibilities. We don't have the resources necessary to offer full security to a public performer."

"I understand, Ms. Weller. So you are saying that you will not provide any security services to my client because she is a musician? Or is it because she is a lesbian?"

Weller clenched her hands underneath the table. "I had no idea that your client is a lesbian and you know that I was unaware of that. I don't know her name."

"Yes, but you know I represent gay artists and musicians, and probably that I am gay myself. I reason that you also have no real legitimate reason to refuse to provide services to my client."

"Beni, I am just being honest. We are a small company of highly trained, former, diplomatic security-service agents. We offer a niche consulting service based on all of our experiences protecting ambassadors, foreign dignitaries, and such. While these folks might attend a few public events or give a very big public speech, they are not consistently traveling to monstrously large venues, announced several months in advance so that any threat has lots of planning opportunity. They are also not standing fully exposed on stages for hours at a time. There are not enough of us to staff and oversee every concert venue.

"We provided such great protection to John Errington because, for the limited duration of the trial, we could at least control his exposure to most threats. Most of the time, our roles are much more mundane and limited. We research the backgrounds of people our clients will have contact with before our clients meet these people. That is something that is hard to do with a musician who will have contact with hundreds of unknown and unexpected people. We pre-search and secure buildings and vehicles our client will be visiting or using—something we don't have enough staff to do expeditiously for a building as big as a concert venue. We plan routes and vary routines to ensure the safety of our client's schedules—which will be hard to do unless your musician is able to vary her schedule and her routine without advance notice."

Beni shook his head and then shrugged.

Weller continued. "We escort the client on their day-to-day activities—something I'm guessing this client would not want while performing on a stage?"

"Well, maybe if the escort posed as a stagehand?"

Weller raised one skeptical eyebrow at him.

Beni only gave her a hopeful smile.

"Mr. Goodman, we do basic security assessments of our client's office and domicile so that we can recommend and install multiple security systems, and train families and staff for basic emergencies. Usually our precautions, presence, and control are enough to protect our clients. John Errington was a rare exception, and I don't think our services would be sufficient to protect a public performer from the variety of threats such a person is likely to encounter."

"So you could do a security assessment for us?" Beni tapped his fingertip to the tabletop again and gave her a very big smile.

Weller sighed. "Yes, I can do that."

"And you could provide personal protection offstage?"

"Is your client willing to stay offstage until the threats to her life are neutralized?"

"No, my client is not willing to stay offstage, nor willing to change one single aspect of her daily habits that might deter her career."

"Then no, we cannot provide protection for your client."

"But my client doesn't want to protect her own life."

Weller felt her mouth become a taut line as she pressed her lips together.

Beni smiled amiably over at her.

"Okay, Beni, at this point we stop playing games and you tell me who your client is, and what specifically you want, or I escort you out of our office."

Beni laid both hands flat on the table in front of him. "My client is Shay Greenaura. A week ago someone set off a car bomb in front of her brother's residence in Chicago while Shay's daughter and sister-in-law were inside the house. The bomb was close enough to the house to kill two friends of the family who were sitting on the front porch, and close enough to lift the front wall and roof off the room where Shay's daughter was listening to her bedtime stories. At the same time in Milwaukee, someone left a note inside the band's RV."

Beni reached down to a leather portfolio resting on the floor beside him and pulled out a sheet of paper. "Here is a copy of the note." He laid it on the table.

Weller pulled the paper closer to her and scanned the contents.

"As you can see, the threat is to destroy her world. Shay understands that to mean harming her family. Specifically, her daughter. Another similar note arrived in the mail at the studio two days prior threatening Shay's daughter by name. With that note, there was a photo of Shay and Iva inside her brother's house in their pajamas." Beni smoothed his palm over his tie twice and cleared his throat. "And before you ask, the photo does appear to have been taken using a telephoto lens. The disturbing part is the photo is of wedding photographer quality."

Beni reached into his portfolio again and pulled out a copy of the photo before pushing it over to her.

Weller studied the photo, surprised that she vaguely recognized Shay Greenaura and that the photo did capture an intimate moment between Shay and her daughter.

"Shay wants protection for Iva and for her brother's wife, Sylvia. Truthfully, Ms. Weller, Shay is more afraid of failing her art than she is of being killed herself. She and her brother grew up very poor and in very difficult circumstances. Sometimes I think she would not have allowed herself to give birth to Iva if she had not already established enough of a career to ensure she could support a child. I don't think she would want to submit any child to the same circumstances she endured while growing up. But while Shay may be willing to sacrifice herself, her welfare very much still matters to me."

"As an investment?" Weller asked narrowing her eyes at him.

"No, Ms. Weller, as a friend and as someone who believes that what Shay Greenaura still has to give the world is something great and necessary. I also believe that Iva needs her mother for more than just financial security."

"So you want me to offer personal protection services to a client who does not want any protection herself?"

"I don't expect miracles, Ms. Weller, despite John Errington's assurances that you can deliver them. The Chicago police are offering at least a squad car to watch over the family's current residence in Chicago. Shay recently bought and renovated an abandoned church and convent in Pilsen. The whole family is now living in the convent's remodeled dormitories. Shay's studio and the office of her newly minted record label are in the convent's church. Syl and Iva will stay at the convent while the band is on the road. I expect you can provide the best security assessment of the convent and grounds at the very least, and that you can probably provide the best personal security services for the whole family and band in that location?" Beni eyed her over the table.

"Are the police working the bombing?" Weller asked.

"Yes, as well as the FBI to some degree. While I do trust them and Chicago's finest, we both know they have a whole city and all its visitors to protect and serve."

"And when the band goes on the road, what do you expect? I cannot protect someone who does not want to be protected."

Beni rubbed a hand over his jaw. "I know, Ms. Weller. I only ask that you be honest and upfront about your recommendations with the entire family and the band. Hopefully, Shay will learn to see reason on that front."

"I don't like the idea of taking a job that the client may not let us succeed at, Beni. As you know, failure can be very bad for business."

"Will you at least come see everything and do the security assessment? Will you make recommendations for defense systems and personal protection as you see fit? I'll make it worth your while."

Weller steepled her fingers and rested her chin on her thumbs with her lips on her forefingers. She mulled it over.

Beni pulled at his tie. "Shay has approved me to spend eighty thousand dollars for the assessment. I'll pay out another fifteen thousand dollars a week, above the cost of any equipment you deem necessary, for each week of personal protection offered until the bomber is collared."

"It would appear that celebrity protection is much more lucrative than our typical niche." Weller raised one eyebrow.

"Is it then?" Beni grinned.

"And where does the fifteen thousand dollars a week come from, Beni?"

"Why does that matter?" Beni's chest puffed up and he looked quickly to his left.

"I suspect you are paying some or all of those expenses, Mr. Goodson. That makes me skeptical about your client being able to see the value of cooperating with her personal protection team."

Beni bowed his head. "I will get out of your hair then, Ms. Weller. Thank you for your time."

Weller stood and offered her hand across the table. "We will at least provide the security assessment and protection during that assessment period, Mr. Goodson."

Beni's previously resigned face broke into a wide grin. "Oh, thank you."

"Thank you for your trust in this matter. If you leave a number where I can reach you, I will get back to you tomorrow afternoon with more details."

Chapter Six

Dream Class

Weller stood in the aisle of the plane's first-class section. As she stretched, she noted the plane's exits, the number and basic appearance of the visible flight crew, and what kinds of things people were stuffing in overhead bins. She identified the air marshal—a dreadlocked young man seated in the starboard side exit aisle. His long legs stretched in front of him. He had an oversized set of headphones around his neck and he was wearing a Chicago Bulls hoodie. He nodded and smiled at her when their eyes met. She smiled back and slid into her window seat, feeling a little naked with all of the service weapons locked in their metal travel cases and checked in the plane's hold.

The rest of Weller's chosen team, Drew Pinks, Reyna Hinojosa, and Jye Huong filed onto the plane. Drew had to lean forward with his six-foot-seven-inch frame in order to enter without whacking his head. He folded himself into the aisle seat next to Weller.

"Thanks for going first class this job, boss."

Weller grinned up at him. "You're welcome."

Reyna and Jye slid into their respective seats across the aisle from Drew.

Reyna passed one plain manila folder over to Jye, another one over to Drew, and Weller waited for them to peruse the client file and plan outline. When the flight attendant inquired, Reyna and Jye ordered club sodas with lime, Drew a double orange juice, and Weller a carton of milk.

After takeoff, Weller listened to the roar of the jets in companionable silence for a few minutes before looking at the other three. "Any questions?"

"Same assignments all week?" Reyna inquired.

"As far as I know now, yes," Weller answered.

Turbulence tossed the plane around. Drew stretched his left leg farther into the aisle and flexed his shiny black loafer back and forth a few times before stuffing it back under the seat in front of him. "Any chances we'll stay on for longer than a week?"

"Depends on what our assessment discovers. We may need to stay on until they can secure whatever services we recommend, or to help train the family, or until the defense systems we want are installed. So, Jye and Reyna will take the driving responsibilities for the foreseeable future. You will be the close protection lead for Iva and Sylvia Greenaura, Drew. I'll serve as the close protection lead for Robespierre and

Shay Greenaura until we have something better determined for the whole family. The rest of the band doesn't appear to be a target yet, but all the same, we'll treat them as secondary protection clients just like we would diplomatic staff. I want everyone focused on detecting any surveillance and explosive devices the entire time. Clear?"

All three of them nodded.

Jye raised his hand.

"Yes, sir?" Weller smiled at the tall, square-shouldered, former NCAA World Series catcher.

"So let me check my understanding. We're not equipped to handle this client. And even if we can't ensure anyone else who is equipped is in place in a few weeks, you're just going to pull us all out?" Jye gave Weller his skeptical face.

Reyna snorted. "Nope. Not a chance. Sorry, Weller, I know you too well to think you would walk away from anyone who still needs protection. So what's the bailout plan?"

Weller frowned. "I doubt you'll like it but I'll tell you anyway. If it comes down to it, I'll send you all home and do what I can to put the whole family under lockdown protection somewhere until you guys can capture the source of the threat."

Reyna nodded. "Actually, I can live with that. It's like we go to our attack mode a little early is all."

Weller shrugged. "Maybe. It's all hypothetical until we're on the ground and can assess what we have to work with and what is working against us. Meanwhile, we've got another hour or so in flight. I suggest we all get a little rest while we can."

Weller closed her eyes, quickly drifting into a familiar and uneasy dreamscape. Sunlight streamed through the hospice window. She stared down at the empty bed. The sheets were rumpled and smelled like Elle, antiseptic, and bleach. They weren't warm.

"I know this dream. Elle is dead and I get to sit in the empty bed and cry while they take her body to the crematorium," Weller told the room.

"Addy? Addy? Who on earth are you talking to?"

Addison Weller turned toward the door.

Elle Deere walked in and Addy froze in place. This was the Elle she had married, with dark-brown flashing eyes, thick silk hair, honey skin, and the high apple cheekbones of her Florida Seminole heritage, all glowing with mirth. This was not the gaunt and leukemia-withered Elle of Addy's usual hospice-induced nightmare-scapes.

"Hi, babe. You look great." Addy held out a hand and Elle took it.

"Hi, hon. Well, you know, it's a dream so I can pretty much look as fabulous as I want."

"Yeah, I guess so, but you look great to me. Does this mean you can kiss me however you want to?"

Elle giggled. "I suppose it does, but that probably isn't the best idea since you're on a plane and I'm sure you'd react to something that fabulous in a way that might be compromising."

Addy let Elle's southern drawl chase over her. She was going to enjoy the audial waves of loveliness while she could.

"I'm just glad I get a good dream and that I get to see you this time."

Elle tilted her head. "Oh, Addy, my love, I'm always with you."

"I know. The dreams just usually aren't good. I'm sorry."

"No need to apologize."

"I can never apologize enough, Elle. I failed you. I couldn't protect you from this. I couldn't save you. I couldn't control anything. I can't even control my own damn dreams."

"Addy, you can't believe that, baby."

"I have to believe that. It's true. It happened. You're gone."

"I know I can't argue you out of believing that right now, but you need to listen to me. We don't have much time and I have to warn you."

"About what, Elle?"

"You can't protect Shay Greenaura."

"I know, Elle. It's not a good situation. I won't be able to control anything this time either. Huh? It's just like Secretary Brayson. I'll make all these recommendations and not a damned one of them will be taken seriously or used to protect anyone until it's too late."

"No, Addy, it's not that. I mean it is that. You'll be

ignored and she'll be exposed. That isn't what I mean. Sometimes you have to give up control, take less precaution to protect someone—like you did me. You did save me, Addison Weller."

"But, Elle, I watched you suffer and then I watched you die. How is that saving you?"

"Wake up, Addy, you loved me. You let me love you...."

The room went black and then a wealth of sound rushed in.

An elbow nudged Addy in the ribs.

"Weller, wake up. We're about to land." Drew was putting his seat in the upright position.

"Right. Thanks." Weller rubbed her eyes, straightened in her seat, adjusted her shirt cuffs, and prepared for landing.

†

Weller rode shotgun while Jye steered their rented Chevy Tahoe around the outskirts of the old convent, circling the block.

"No fence around anything, and at least four entry drives that approach some part of the main buildings," Drew lamented from the back seat.

"And one police cruiser parked in front of one drive toward the church where Beni says the recording studio and offices are located," Reyna added.

"And lots of vegetation to hide in all around," Weller

finished the list.

"Is that car waiting to pick someone up at the bus stop or spying on our client?" Jye nodded toward a navy Nissan Altima with tinted windows parked near the corner.

"At least the grounds take up the whole block here," Weller observed.

"Yeah, gives a sniper at least an extra fifty yards to master in order to shoot our client from any one of those surrounding thousands of windows," Reyna said.

Weller shook her head. "All right, Jye, take us up to the church lot. Let's see if we can find Mr. Goodman and get some introductions and a tour squared away."

As they rolled down the drive toward the patrol car, a young officer stepped out to block the road. He walked across the front of the vehicle and motioned Jye to roll down the window. "Good afternoon, folks. This is private property. May I ask where you're headed?"

Jye started to answer, but Weller interrupted after glancing at the officer's name tag. "Hello, Officer Joyce. We're sorry to trespass. We didn't see any notices and we were curious about the old church. Would it be all right if we just drove by the front door before we turn around and head out? My friend here does a little woodworking and he's looking for some ideas for a door carving for our new parish hall."

Officer Joyce hooked both thumbs inside his duty belt and rocked back on his heels. "Okay. Drive safe."

Jye rolled up the window and eased forward.

"Oh, my," Reyna exploded.

"Not exactly trained for protection services are they?" Drew tweaked her.

"I forgot what it was like to be that green," Jye said.

"What, Jye, like two years ago?" Reyna teased.

"Ah now, Reyna, you know Jye got past his beat patrol days at least a year before they shipped him off to the cybercrimes division to be an uber-nerd," Drew answered.

"These grounds are huge." Jye tried to divert the conversation back to their security size-up.

They pulled into the church parking lot, and spotted a tour bus parked obviously along the eastern edge.

A couple of grizzled men in sweat suits emerged from the tour bus doors. One of the men pulled a pack of cigarettes out of his hoodie pocket and lit up a smoke. The other, in a skull cap, wandered around the back of the bus and tripped the undercarriage cargo doors open. The smoker peered at Weller as they exited their rental car.

Weller glanced around the parking lot. Several contractor vans were scattered around the edges, and parked next to a makeshift shop in the southeast corner was a welding truck. Two men were positioning a short, iron stair rail on top of their wooden workhorses. Weller wandered over toward the smoker in front of the tour bus.

The smoker dropped his butt and ground it out on the blacktop, giving Weller a good old-fashioned leer. "Can I help you?"

"Do you work here?" Weller inquired.

"Yes. I drive the band and I do some handiwork around the grounds."

"Ah, are you overseeing the remodeling?"

"No. Can I help you?"

"My name is Addy. We're here to see Shay."

"Everyone is."

"I'm supposed to check out the bus.

The smoker snorted. "Oh yeah? For what?"

"Interior design. More remodels."

"No shit? Who ordered that?"

"Beni."

"He hasn't spoken to me about it yet."

"Actually, we're supposed to meet him here in a few minutes. Do you think I could see inside the bus really quick? Just to get a head start?"

The smoker seemed to be taking his time looking over her tailored suit, white shirt, tidy hair, and black pearl earrings before finally looking into her eyes and nodding. "Okay, Ms. Addy, but you have to stay with me and don't mess with anything."

"Deal. Thanks. It's just Addy. My last name is Weller."

"I'm Duval." He wiped his hand clean on the chest of his hoodie and offered it.

Weller shook it.

"I'm Duval Sam. A lot of people call me Sam, but not because I like it. They just get confused about it since I have a last name for a first name and a first name for a last name, I guess." Duval turned and walked into the bus, waiting at the top of the steps for her to follow. He waited in the bus stairwell until she walked ahead of him. She could see the entirety of the bus in open view from the steps.

There were four captain's chair recliners in a greenish-orange pleather. A very old green afghan and battered blue-gray pillow lay in one of the chairs. Beyond the chairs, a kitchenette took up the middle-right side of the bus, and a table with dinette-style benches took up the left side. A simple cassette toilet in a boxed-off partition followed the kitchen. Split-level curtains in the same greenish-orange pleather as the captain's chairs hung along both sides of the aisle at the back of the bus. Weller thought the whole thing definitely needed a remodel.

She gestured to the pleather curtains. "May I look inside?"

Duval was hot on her heels. "Yes."

Behind the curtains, there were top and bottom bunks made of one-inch plywood in metal brackets with memory-foam pads, sleeping bags, and pillows on top. The underside of the top bunks bore an assortment of industry stickers advertising other bands, amplifiers, guitars, drumsticks, Greenpeace, Planned Parenthood, PFLAG, the Sierra Club, and snapshots of band members with family members taped in place.

Duval cleared his throat behind her. "Shay supports a lot of causes. Like me and Sonny."

Weller turned to Duval. His eyes were dark brown,

and the whites of his eyes were perfectly white. He looked a little too thin though, and he had some gnarly stubble barely visible against his ebony skin.

"How are you a cause?"

"Sonny, the other driver, and I are from the Open Door Mission downtown. Two years ago when Shay bought the bus, she came down to the mission to find drivers. She could have hired drivers anywhere, but she wanted to hire two from the rehabilitation program. Most of the people who work here are from one of the local missions or shelters. She takes care of us. You'll take care of her, right. She doesn't like high fashion. Keep it casual. Keep it retro or how you call it? Green?"

"I see. I will do my best, Duval. I might need your help some."

"I'll do what I can. Sonny will too."

Weller smiled at him and he smiled back.

"Thanks, Duval, and thanks for letting me look. I guess I'd better go up to the church and find Beni."

Duval walked out ahead of her and opened the bus door again.

Jye and Reyna were just outside talking to Sonny. Drew had his head poked into the undercarriage storage.

"Pretty buff multicultural team of designers," Duval said to her as they stepped back onto the parking lot.

"We try. See you, Duval."

"I bet so," Duval replied.

Chapter Seven

A Bad Bomb Target

Weller eyed the gap between the two church doors, and then reached out one hand to push the left door open with the simple flick of a wrist. She slid in through the gap and found a world of noise but no one directly in the line of sight. The church's interior was huge. Two-story tiers loomed over each side of the nave chancel areas. She could only see the nave ceiling by looking over the new layers of nine-foot-tall sheetrock cubbies filling it. In front of the first, blank, sheetrock wall facing the doors was an empty desk. She pushed the door open more so the rest of the team could enter with her.

Jye stopped to play with the door. "No deadbolt. No lock bar. No alarm sensors. One second to enter with a standard flathead screwdriver."

"If that," Reyna acknowledged.

"Where the hell is everybody?" Weller asked.

"Let's find out." Drew pulled open the wood panel door to the north galley.

They entered a long hallway with interior house doors at eight-foot intervals along the left-hand wall of the hall. Drew took point and Weller brought up the rear. The fourth door on the left sprang open and someone in a gorilla suit came barreling out growling with hands up. The gorilla tripped over its clunky paw shoes and Drew caught it in a bear hug, setting the costumed-being upright. The gorilla suit looked up at Drew and went mute. A woman with several DSLR cameras wrapped around her body took a quick turn out of the same doorway and plowed into the now stationary gorilla.

"What th…?" barked the woman. A Jesus imposter in a gas mask followed on her heels.

They stared at Drew who smiled down at them.

"Bad bar joke?" Drew asked the gawking strangers.

"Photoshoot for an album cover," the photographer answered.

Jesus lowered his gas mask and pointed at Drew. "Now, that is a convincing gorilla."

Drew laughed.

Weller growled from her vantage behind her team.

"We're looking for Benito Goodman. Do you know where we can find him?" Reyna asked the photographer.

"Never heard of him. But Shay may know." The photographer pointed down the hallway. "You can probably find her in one of the studios with the new talent."

"Thanks." Weller and the others filed past the photoshoot group.

"No problem. Nice coordinated costumes. You don't see bands in suits much these days." The photographer gestured to Weller's gray suit.

Weller nodded and walked on.

"How about we call ourselves the Gray Guards?" Jye quipped over his shoulder.

"The Gray Sharks," suggested Reyna.

"The Great Gray Gorillas," Drew added.

"Speak for yourself, Gargantuan. I'm more monkey or lemur-sized," Reyna smarted back to him.

"I guess we should all wear different color suits next gig," suggested Jye.

"Nah, everyone wants to looks as cool as the boss." Drew gestured with his thumb back at Weller's charcoal suit.

Weller smirked. "I'm your definition of cool? That settles it, you all are required to get a life when we get back home."

"Do you even own any other color suit?" Reyna asked.

Weller pointed down the hall. "Onward, Gorilla Monkey-fish squad."

Several painters in white coveralls passed them going in the opposite direction. They passed a door marked with a fire exit sign. It was propped open with a brick and two contractors and a woman in a parka were standing on the stoop smoking a few feet outside the door. It smelled like pot.

Reyna pointed to the top of the door.

Weller looked up.

The lead cable to the door alarm hung disconnected, a silver fray glinting above the cut through its black insulation. Weller poked her head out the door for a quick look and the three smokers took no notice. She looked beyond them and saw a small blond child on the sidewalk in a coat with one mitten pushing a tricycle toward the drive.

A thin blond woman in a long, camel-colored wool coat trailed behind the child offering encouragement. "Way to roll, Iva. Want to go all the way to that oak tree?" The woman pointed to a big tree near the drive.

The little girl looked back at the woman and started to say something, but then seemed to make eye contact with Weller.

Weller ducked her head back in and glanced at Reyna. "The door opens to a yard that fronts one of the drives."

"Not that we didn't know that any monkey can wander freely here," Reyna replied.

"It appears the kid is out there, too, with one adult."

"Sheesh," Jye seethed.

Drew shook his big head. "Damn."

"All right, let's find Beni and get this circus fixed up some." Weller pushed onward.

The farther they walked along the hall, the more complete the remodeling looked. Pale green paint accented some of the walls. Framed album covers, pictures of Shay with other musicians and some politicians hung in hand-crafted, reclaimed-wood frames in between and across from the doorways near the end of the hall. Funky, dark-green-plastic numbers labeled pale wooden doors. All were prime numbers and out of sequence.

Drew opened the blank door leading into the church's north transept.

Inside the transept, clusters of people were standing around a large soundboard and talking. Weller did not see Beni or anyone who looked like Shay. Discordant beats sounded out to the left and straight ahead of them. Weller approached the sweater-vested, headphone-adorned man at the soundboard and tapped him on the shoulder.

He stopped bouncing to the beat and slid the headphones back to rest on his neck. "Yeah?"

"I'm looking for Benito Goodman," Weller said.

The sweater-vested soundman shrugged. "Never heard of him."

"How about Shay Greenaura?" Weller asked.

The sweater vest smiled and then shrugged again. "Now Shay I know. Probably in one of the other studios?" He pointed to the door opposite the one they had entered. A hand knocked on the glass in front of them. Weller and the soundman both looked up to find a whiskered man in bad drag waving a ukulele and pointing to a tympani drum.

"Gotta get back to work, sugar." The soundman shrugged back into his headphones and turned toward his boards.

Weller walked toward the door and her team followed. The door led them into the ante-chamber of the main studio where, Weller supposed, the church chancel must have once been. A crowd of people pressed up near the glass partition and around the soundboards. High-quality speakers pumped music into the mixing room, overpowering Weller's ability to eavesdrop on anyone in the crowd in particular. The music sounded jaunty and syncopated like a Latin salsa to Weller. Two acoustic guitars, a violin, pan flutes, a conga, and a woman who called out in Portuguese.

The song ended. Weller watched the soundman flip the system over to a digital recording so the previously recorded tracks continued to play softly in the mixing room.

The singer bounced out of the recording room. She was a very tall, olive-skinned woman with arresting grey eyes. Weller noted the singer was a couple of inches taller than she was with a perfectly structured face, slightly upturned button nose, and full lips. She was casually well dressed and looked very familiar to Weller.

"Drew, close your mouth." Reyna elbowed the big man beside Weller.

"Sorry. I think that's one of those Victoria's Secret models," Drew replied.

"Yep. Page thirty-six, and likely 36DDs in a pink feathery negligee and sparkly angel wings." Jye sighed.

"Boys," Reyna huffed in warning.

"More watching the world and less catalogue surfing the next time you're on the late night guard duty, guys."

Weller seconded Reyna.

"Yes, boss," two voices chorused softly.

Weller pressed her back to the wall behind everyone and took her time surveying the room.

Reyna and Drew filled in the spaces closest to her.

Jye stayed closest to the door.

A cluster of well-wishers quickly surrounded the singer. Assorted onlookers occupied the thrift-store couches and refinished chairs scattered about the mixing room, but most were too deeply shadowed for Weller to see more than the top of heads or waving arms. The lights in the room were low, showcasing the recording area behind the glass. Black acoustic board covered the walls of both. Thick power cords trailed down from the soundboard and into several surge protectors installed in the floor below. The floor felt spongy and appeared to be some sort of bamboo parquet.

Weller noticed the rest of the musicians walk out of the recording room. The crowd around began clapping and continued until a shrill whistle sounded from a deep armchair closest to the sound engineer.

Silence ensued.

A blond head of ruffled curls appeared above the armchair back. "Great stuff, Simone. We just wanted to help you celebrate laying the first track, and let you know that we're all excited to be producing your record on our humble little home grown label." The blond stood and gestured with both arms wide to encompass the crowded studio as she stepped into full view.

Weller studied the petite figure in skinny jeans, bare feet, and a ratty, chocolate, oversized, men's shawl sweater. She looked about twelve years old and homeless, but she exuded enough charisma to convince everyone in the room she was the point of authority there.

"Fabulous, fabulous. Thank you, Shay. We're very glad to be here and we can't wait to do the duets with RobO," the tall exotic looking singer answered.

A bulky, strawberry-blond man, leaning against the wall near the soundboard, gave Simone a little wave and a great big grin.

"So model Simone is boffing our folksinging client?" Reyna whispered into Weller's ear.

Weller shrugged and heard her stomach rumble. She rubbed her empty belly.

"Okay, ladies and gents, there are snacks in the kitchen and beer will be here shortly. Take five and we'll come back for drinks and recording around two," Shay announced. She walked over to the strawberry-blond man who, Weller deduced, must be Shay's brother, RobO.

A slight man who looked like a bald baby bird joined RobO and Shay.

Jye nodded at the bald man. "The guitarist with the weird name?"

Drew nodded. "Yeah, looks like him."

Another woman with very short, dark, spiky hair in cargo pants, combat boots, and an ugly Christmas sweater sidled next to RobO.

Drew pointed her out with his chin. "That would be Jane Smith, the bass guitarist and violinist."

"Great, now we've got the whole band in one spot," Reyna said.

"Anyone see Beni?" Weller scanned the room.

"No, but it's pretty dim in here," Reyna answered.

"All right, let's go introduce ourselves." Weller started across the room toward Shay's clustered band.

†

Shay saw Jane elbow RobO and tilt her head toward two well-muscled men and two women in almost matching gray suits coming toward them.

RobO's eyes followed Jane's gaze.

"Who the hell are all the suits?" RobO asked.

Shay turned to look. She peered closer at the taller of the two women bearing down on her. The woman had a very square jaw, high cheekbones, large, expressive, coffee-colored eyes, prude posture, and a rolling, cocky-cop walk. The woman fitted her tailored suit like a fish in its own scales.

"Huh. I dunno. Maybe they're some modeling friends of Simone's?" Shay answered.

"Excuse me, dudes, I think you're lost. Can we help you with anything?" Fallow stepped in front of the biggest suited man, blocking his approach before Shay could stop him.

The large dark man looked down—a long way

down—at Shay's thin guitarist in his baggy chinos, frayed Henley, and wool Uttarasanga.

Fallow looked up at him.

Shay couldn't see Fallow's face, but knew from experience the guitarist was politely smiling.

The taller of the two suited women stepped around the large man and extended a hand toward Fallow.

"Hi, Mr. Kumas. We're an assessment team from Vigiles Security Services. I am the team lead, Addison Weller, and this is the rest of my team." Addison indicated each one in turn, starting with the large man. "Drew Pinks, Jye Huong, and Reyna Hinojosa."

"Um, a few questions?" Fallow stammered.

The tall Addison Weller smiled and nodded.

Fallow cleared his throat to begin but the door banged open and Beni rushed in, interrupting the moment.

Shay spotted Simone near the door and noticed her trailing Beni over toward them.

Shay greeted them both with a big smile. "Hello, Beni. Glad you're here to sort this out." She pointed a look at Beni and the man straightened his tie before smiling back.

Simone interrupted by sidling up close to Shay and Shay held up a hand signaling Beni to hold on while she addressed the model. "Ah, Simone, something you need, dear?"

"No, no. Everything is perfect. I just have much curiosity about your visitors in these suits." Simone threw one long arm over Shay's shoulders. She leaned a hip into

Shay and looked directly at Addison Weller with a toothy grin.

†

Weller kept her face blank, but while she looked at Simone draped over Shay her stomach clenched.

Simone met her eyes and gave a beguiling smile. "You are so tall. You are a model too. Yes?"

"No, ma'am, I am not," Weller replied.

"Ma'am? Please I am Simone. Simone Saez." Simone held out a hand.

Weller gave the woman's hand a brief grip. "Addison Weller, pleased to meet you." Weller resumed her blank waiting face as Simone continued to study her overtly. Weller suspected the model was waiting for one of them to admit they knew of her modeling fame at least. The team stayed silent.

Simone smiled a multi-watt grin at each of them in turn.

Weller stifled a small laugh. She watched Reyna's lips thin in response to the model's charms. Drew and Jye nodded and stared at the space just over Simone's shoulder, faces politely disinterested and waiting.

Simone shrugged and planted a dry kiss on Shay's cheek. "Again, I thank you and RobO for putting so much effort into making my little project a success. I look forward to great things with your record label."

"Nothing much has been done yet…," Shay looked abashed.

"No, no, this is not true. I have already had great fun and there appears to be more in store for me here. Even if the record never sells, I have accomplished a project I have dreamt about," Simone interrupted.

"Speaking of which, I know you don't want to worry about much promotion effort; but I have a list of our concerts for the spring quarter I'd like to give you. At least if we are in the same area, you can stop in and sing a few of the songs with RobO on stage, in between some of ours. It would give you a chance to promo the album and help us out with our multicultural reputation?" Shay gave a half shrug and a cock-eyed grin.

"Yes, I would very much like that. It sounds perfect. I will leave you to your business now." Simone released Shay and blew a kiss to RobO before retreating.

Weller made eye contact with Shay and then waited while the singer looked her up and down again.

"That's funny. Simone has never accused me of being a model." Shay's lips formed an obvious pout.

"That is because you're already a model. More of a model than Simone is," Weller answered.

"Huh?" Shay's face contorted.

Weller almost smiled. "You are a role model."

RobO laughed. "She's got you there...all those guys and girls screaming for you during the shows to come closer so they can get a better look at you, maybe figure out how you do it."

"Watching what you wear so they know what's cool," Fallow added.

"Copying what you do and what you say, because it might help them figure out how to be cooler," Beni added with a smile.

Shay shook her head slowly. "I never thought of it that way."

RobO patted his sister on the shoulder. "We noticed, sis."

"Shay, I think we should go somewhere a little more private and let Ms. Weller give you more specifics," Beni suggested.

RobO crooked his finger at Fallow and the two exchanged a few whispers before heading out of the studio. Jane flopped down on a couch near the soundboard.

"What specifics do I need?" Shay demanded.

"I'm sure Ms. Weller would like to tell you, but this is probably better discussed a little less publically," Beni persisted.

Shay directed a skeptical look at Beni. "Ten minutes, Beni. We've got records to make and work to do." Shay cut the main switch to the sound board and marched into the empty recording room.

Beni caught the door as it swung back and held it open for Weller.

Weller remained in place.

Beni waved his arm toward the door inviting them in.

"Please, Ms. Weller?"

Weller walked in. Drew, Jye, and Reyna followed her.

Shay was already perched on a wooden stool. Weller tried not to step on any of the instruments and cables scattered about as she walked over toward Shay and sat on the next nearest stool.

"You stick out like a sore thumb." Shay met her eyes. "Aren't you supposed to be subtle? Blend in?"

"I'm sorry, Ms. Greenaura, you seem to have us confused with spies," Weller answered.

"So you have to be this square?" Shay gestured a hand over Weller's suit.

"We prefer it," Weller replied.

"Great. Everyone will know I have my own goons. That ought to spook my fellow hippie collaborators right out of the park." Shay shook her head. "This won't do. You're going to have to try to be a little less conspicuous."

"We can try, but the clothing options that will successfully conceal our weapons are limited."

"You're armed?" Shay huffed.

Weller nodded.

"We don't believe in weapons around here. I can't have them around. It makes many of the people we work with too nervous, and I don't like the culture it exposes and encourages around my daughter."

"No one need see them unless we need them to save your life from an armed aggressor," Weller replied.

Silence stretched for a few beats. They both frowned

at the floor.

Shay broke the silence. "You don't look like a good bodyguard anyway."

"I'm not," Weller answered.

"Well, a bodyguard, one good bodyguard, is what I ordered and what Beni promised he would find for my daughter."

Weller looked down into Shay Greenaura's turbulent blue eyes and replied in a low voice, "We're four security experts who will provide your whole family with a personal protection detail for the price of one, ineffective, bodyguard."

"So the four of you will stalk around after my baby?" Shay demanded.

"No. One of us drives and plans the precautions for Iva, one of us guards Iva on the spot, one of us drives and plans precautions for you and the band, and one of us guards you on the spot."

Weller looked through the glass window. Fallow rolled a keg on a dolly into the outer room. RobO tapped the keg and started passing out green solo cups of beer. Fallow knocked on the studio door, popped in, and approached Weller with a cup of beer.

"Want a cold one?" he asked.

"No, thank you, Mr. Kumas," Weller answered.

"That is Fallow. Mr. Kumas was the abusive, jackass father, who beat the shit out of him and burned Fallow's scalp with an iron so he wouldn't have to pay for haircuts." Shay's voice lowered a register and she glared at Weller.

Weller nodded. "No thank you, Fallow. I'm more of a milk drinker."

Fallow grinned. "I've got soy milk in the kitchen."

"Never had it before, but it sounds interesting, if you don't mind sharing"

Fallow hurried off.

Weller heard Shay draw a deep breath and then sigh loudly. "Listen, folks, this whole thing, this sudden compulsion with protecting me, is Beni's idea. I wasn't the one who was attacked. It isn't me they're after and I've managed to take care of myself just fine. I can't quit doing the things I do with all the random people who want to approach me. This new label, this studio, the band, the songwriting collaborations, the touring, the music, is my art. It is my life, and I can't live my life in a protective bubble. I can't do the work I need to do surrounded by goons in suits watching everything I do. I need the freedom and openness that surround me to get this work done."

"There are times when everyone must take precautions though, and you are facing one. That isn't to say that you have to take all of these precautions from now on, and certainly not like someone just bombed your brother's house, all the time. But it matters to your family, to your daughter, that you are safe even when it doesn't matter to you," Weller said.

"It matters to me, but this is a step too far, right now, right here. I don't need this much precaution for me personally or my career. Our work can't bear any extra precautions right now. We're hot; but the next moment we might not be anymore. If we're going to break through as a record label, grow into more than a band, and do meaningful work, we have to be out there amongst as many random strangers as we can. We've got like four seconds to leverage all our hard-earned success to this point and keep the momentum growing." Shay's hands waved up and out emphasizing her points.

Beni shook his head. As soon as Shay stopped talking, he said, "I think Ms. Weller is right, Shay. You have to take more precautions right now. Don't you think it is important to be around for Iva? Surely you aren't willing to risk your life and not see your daughter grow up just to gain more exposure. You'll earn all that anyway. Even if the precautions set you back a little, you have *it*. You have that classic charisma and you're doing what you're meant to do and believe in. Precaution and a little more order for this bit aren't going to sink you."

"Beni, if it did, if it does, it won't matter if I'm alive. I'd be worthless to Iva, to RobO and Syl, to all the people who are depending on this right now," Shay argued.

Fallow came back into the room bearing a green solo cup of cold, vanilla soy milk. Weller took it with a very big smile that crinkled the edges of her eyes.

Fallow grinned back. "See if you like it."

Weller took a drink. The soy milk was cold, smooth, and vaguely vanilla in the back of her palette. "It's great, Fallow. Thank you," she pronounced.

"You're welcome." Fallow bounced back out of the room.

Weller's attention turned back to Shay.

"I'm sure this isn't the first or the last threat," Shay said. "Every time the band puts out another hit song, or I do another project that makes the press, I'm just going to get more of the nut-jobs after me. Hell, sometimes in Minnesota we even had busloads of Jehovah's Witnesses protesting the damn show, because we announced the name of our record label, 'Saving Graces,' and they didn't like a liberal lesbian and her hop-hippy lesbos borrowing Jesus' words for evil purposes.' I can't bow to that bullshit, even if one of them might know how to wire a bomb."

"I understand your concerns, Ms. Greenaura, and we're not here to sell you on a lifetime of protection. You want someone to do at least a basic security assessment this week?" Weller asked.

Shay nodded. "That we do need."

"And you want someone to at least provide full time protection for Iva and Syl for a while?" Weller prompted.

"Yes. Exactly," Shay agreed.

"We will do that. At least in the week it takes us to do the assessment, make our recommendations, and implement the ones that work for you—do you think you could consent to some basic protection, too? Give it a try, so to speak?" Weller held both hands open in front of her.

Shay's eyebrows twisted into a frown but she gave a slight nod. "All right, but I get to nix any precautions that interfere, or appear like they might interfere, with mine or the label's progress?"

"Within reason, yes, Ms. Greenaura," Weller answered, "but I reserve the right to protect myself and my team too. Fair enough?"

Shay smiled. "I'm willing to go along as long as we all understand each other. This is not going to alter my life. I can't afford that right now."

"Messed up priorities," Reyna mumbled from her position by the door.

Weller turned to look at Reyna, waiting to see if Reyna had a real question in mind. Reyna only smiled. "All good here, boss."

Beni rubbed his hands together, clapped, and smiled, "Well, that's better."

"One more thing," Shay said. "You all have to do a better job of blending in. You can select whatever clothing you want, but it has got to at least make you look like you're not waiting to off anyone around here and gearing up for an undertaking. We go by first names or nicknames around here, and I don't like multiple people falling all over me when I'm trying to work."

Weller granted Beni one stern glance.

Shay continued speaking, "The most important part is that my child will not be terrorized or otherwise derailed by this. I doubt she'll ask in specific terms, but she is a beauty with a lot of curiosity. You'll have to tell her you're part of the band, or RobO's friends, or something, anything. I don't want her to be scared or to think she has to depend on strangers to keep her safe. We care for her. You guys can be good shadows, right?"

Weller nodded. "We're used to being discreet."

"For diplomats and bureaucrats. Not for artists and peaceniks," stated Shay.

Reyna visibly bristled.

Jye bit his bottom lip.

Weller smirked. "We're fast learners."

"Good." Shay leveled a glare at her.

Silence reeled around the room for a few minutes.

"Then what do we call you while you're here?" Shay asked.

Weller stayed silent and so did her team.

"How about by your first names?" Shay prompted.

Drew stepped forward and offered his hand. "My name is Drew Pinks. You can call me Drew, or my nickname at home is 'Pinky'."

Shay looked up at the big black man whose hand swallowed her own and giggled. "You're called Pinky?"

"On account of my small, pinky-finger-like size in a crowd, and how nice I look in a pink polo." Drew stepped back with a smile.

"I am Jye Huong. I don't have a nickname, but I answer to anything if food is involved," Jye offered when Shay looked toward him.

"I am Reyna Hinojosa. Reyna is what everyone calls me anyway." Reyna looked intently at Shay.

"So Addison…," Shay started.

"Everyone calls her Weller," Reyna interrupted.

Weller glanced sideways at Reyna who was still looking directly at Shay.

"Isn't Addison your first name?" Shay asked, looking up at Weller.

Weller nodded.

Shay shook her head. "It's a last name for a first name and a stuffy one at that."

"Yes, but you can call me Addy," Weller said.

"That might work." Shay smiled.

Weller could see Reyna in her peripheral vision fidgeting.

"It will work." Weller turned her head to pin Reyna with a direct look before her friend could interrupt again.

RobO and Fallow entered the room when Shay waved to them through the window. "I think we have something worked out, guys. Where's Jane?"

"She went out to smoke," RobO answered.

"Do you guys have any questions for our temporary security service team?" Shay asked.

RobO scratched his chin.

"You were with the Secret Service?" Fallow asked Weller.

"No." Weller looked closer at his face. He was chewing his bottom lip and looking over each of the Vigiles team in turns.

"But you were federal agents?" Fallow asked.

"Some of us. Reyna and I were Diplomatic Security Service agents," Weller answered.

"Did you protect diplomats? Or does that mean you were the police force for consulates?" Fallow continued his questioning.

"We protected diplomats." Weller answered.

"Like who? Anybody you can name?" Fallow asked.

"Secretaries of State, ambassadors, visiting dignitaries. We worked in New York City, and in DC," Weller answered.

"Wait, like the Secretary of State, like our Secretary of State?" Shay asked.

"Yes." Weller confirmed.

"Like our late Secretary of State, Beatrice Brayson?" RobO asked.

"Yes." Weller confirmed.

"Wait a second. Wasn't Brayson the one who blew up?" Shay tilted her head to one side, making her blond curls tumbled with gravity.

"Yes." Weller stood up straight.

"Wasn't it a car bomber?" Fallow asked.

"Yes," Weller answered.

"While you were protecting her?" Shay stepped toward Weller.

"While Weller and I were part of the protection team. We were not on that shift lead." Reyna's voice was full of the tones of command.

"So it isn't your fault if it happens while you're sleeping?" Shay insisted.

"It is always the team's fault," Weller acknowledged.

"Weller, that isn't right and you…" Reyna started to defend them.

Shay interrupted, "It doesn't matter. At least one of you believes she should have done something different to protect Brayson. How do I know it is worth paying you to protect Iva from the same kind of threat? That you won't fuck it up again?" Shay looked directly into Weller's eyes.

Weller kept her face blank of all emotion and watched Shay's face heat up inches from her own. She thought Shay's lips were what old-timey authors probably would have deemed a bow mouth. They were cute, pink, pert, and prim in their apparent distaste.

"You would have to trust that we have learned from our mistakes and that we know what needs to be done now by everyone, including you, to protect yourself from that risk." Weller felt her stomach flipping like a fish.

Shay shook her head. "I don't trust you. I don't believe you can protect me without taking away too many of the freedoms I need to live and work. I'm not sure your services would protect me or Iva, even if we did everything you suggested. Maybe you're just pimping out services to undereducated private citizens because you fucked up too much for the government to keep you on?"

"We weren't fired…" Reyna blurted.

"Okay," Weller interrupted.

Reyna and Shay chorused, "What do you mean, 'okay'?"

"Okay. If you can't or won't trust us, Ms. Greenaura, then you're right, we can't protect you or Iva. And I'm not in the habit of accepting contracts for protection services I know we cannot successfully deliver. You need to find someone you do trust."

"Wait, you mean you're not taking the contract?" Beni pulled at his collar as he stepped into Weller's line of sight.

"Correct. We're going home. Thank you for the opportunity, and good luck." Weller stepped toward the door. Jye and Drew walked out the door immediately after her. Weller gestured for Reyna to go, but Reyna hesitated until Weller looked her in the eye. Once Reyna walked out the door, Weller glanced back at Shay.

Beni stood beside Shay smacking his hand against his forehead. Shay just snorted and gave a Weller an exaggerated wave goodbye.

Weller returned the wave with a small one of her own and wistful smile before closing the door gently.

†

RobO watched Shay flounce out of the recording area slapping the power main on the soundboard back into its "on" position before dropping into the armchair in the mixing room again.

Fallow sidled up next to RobO. "Shit, she's wound up. I've never seen her push anyone that far that fast. What is she testing?"

RobO shook his head and twisted the fiber nub poking out from the hem of his T-shirt. "I don't know. Maybe she was just pushing to see if they would break? Or maybe she just got over-emotional about it all again?"

"Yeah, well, she sucks at being a responsible bomb target," Fallow replied.

†

Weller, Reyna, Jye and Drew walked back through the first studio and returned down the hall along the church nave toward the front door.

"Weller. Weller, please wait. There's something I should have told you. I didn't know it was important in DC, but I realize it might be now." Beni called out from behind them. "It might matter to you,"

"What?" Weller turned to pin Beni with a glare. The rest of the team had continued walking past and ahead of her when she stopped.

Beni appeared to freeze in place.

"What, Beni? This better be good," Weller demanded.

"The car bombing at RobO's house. Just like what happened to Brayson, the bomber wasn't the driver. The driver of the car was a sixty-year-old retiree who volunteers for meals-on-wheels. She delivers dinner to an old man in the house across the street from RobO's place, every Friday night around that time. She always parks in front of RobO's though, because she approaches from that direction. RobO's front yard is only about eight feet from the street to the front porch there. The car blew from that side, while the owner was delivering dinner to the old man. The owner didn't know anything about who RobO, Syl, Iva, or Shay are."

"It was a professional hit? What does Chicago PD say about it?" Weller still pinned Beni with her eyes.

"They don't know or they won't tell us. Rumor is the case is being handed to the feds." Beni started to wring his hands.

"Guys, hold on," Weller called to the team over her shoulder.

"You want to take this?" Reyna marched back toward her.

"I do, but that doesn't mean Vigiles Security Services does. I still don't think there is much chance of actually protecting Shay, or maybe even Iva, well enough without Shay's cooperation," Weller answered.

"Weller, she can't admit it yet, but she knows. Shay knows she needs your help," Beni interjected.

"Do you want to take this because you think it's the same hitman as Brayson?" Reyna pressed.

"Maybe. Probably not."

"But *you*, you personally, have to be sure." Reyna fixed her with a gaze.

Weller rubbed her temple. "Yes."

"Then I'm in. There is absolutely zero chance you can protect anyone here and find out anything without risking harm to yourself without some backup," Reyna added.

"Okay." Weller smiled despite her misgivings.

"Me too," Jye added.

"Yup," Drew agreed.

"Now wait." Weller's challenged Jye and Drew. "You two have nothing personal in this and I can't say it's a good business move for my employees."

"Well, if you can't say it's a good business move, that means you also can't say it's a bad business move. And frankly, it's personal for me if it means that much to you and Reyna." Drew grinned.

"Ditto," Jye said.

Weller sighed and gave them each a small smile before looking back to Beni. "All right, Beni. Given Ms. Greenaura's reservations, we'll do our best."

"Oh, thank God." Beni beamed a full smile back at Weller.

"It has nothing to do with God, and this probably is not something you'll be thankful for in a few days." Weller put her hands in her pockets.

"One other thing." Beni glanced down and adjusted his tie.

Weller grimaced. "Another catch?"

Beni held up both hands. "I didn't know about it until today. That's why I was late. I got a call from one of the detectives in Violent Crimes. I thought it was about the car bomb, but Detective James was actually calling about something else entirely. He has been working a slew of violent rapes and murders. All of the victims are small, blond, blue-eyed women. He didn't really think much of it aside from thinking it was the perpetrator's type for some reason. What caught his attention was that the last victim survived. Detective James said the victim remembered her rapist calling her 'Shay' and telling her that he would 'fix her' and that she just needed to 'wait and watch and be afraid' until he came to 'destroy her world.' James says he was talking over the bomb forensics with the case lead and he saw the note and the pictures of Shay that we turned over. It was then that he realized the killer's type is probably his inspiration. He thinks this murdering rapist might really be after Shay."

"Shay doesn't know about any of this?" Weller prompted.

Beni shook his head.

"Why didn't Detective James call her?" Weller asked.

"I'm her lawyer and her manager. I don't want to do both jobs. I think she needs a damn manager, but that's neither here nor there. My point is, the police are supposed to call me first since I'm her legal counsel, and she has already been in for questioning and given her statements about the car bombing. I just haven't had time to tell her about it, and then I thought maybe I shouldn't tell her?"

"I think it is a problem and she needs to know about it. Forewarned is forearmed," Weller answered.

"It will freak her out," Beni protested.

"Maybe, but she needs to be alarmed. This place is

wide open. No one here has any clue what real security should be, why they need it, or how to get it."

Beni nodded. "I understand, Ms. Weller. Tell us what we should do and what we need to do to fix it all to keep ourselves safe. I'll do whatever I can to make it happen."

"You need to tell Shay everything you've told me."

"But you are head of security now, right?"

Weller took a deep breath and gave an intentionally aggrieved sigh. "At least for this week I am head of security. We can't protect Shay though if she doesn't know what is going on. She has to be interested in preserving her own safety as well as everyone else's."

Beni looked defeated. "Can't you tell her for me though?"

"I could, but she doesn't trust me. Remember? This has to come from someone she trusts. She needs to take the threat seriously or she won't cooperate with anything we recommend to make this place and the people in it any safer."

"All right, I'll talk to her." Beni pulled at his collar, and squared his shoulders. "She won't give you any more grief about protecting herself again."

"*Pffwwt.* Of course she will," snorted Reyna.

"What? You want it easy?" Drew smiled.

"Nah. It's never easy. That would be weird." Reyna shook her head.

"Yeah, that would be scary." Weller gave them the barest of grins.

Chapter Eight

Checks and Assurances

Duval Sam leaned against the wall in the hall across from the open doorway. He watched Reyna and Weller occupy the room closest to the convent's north exit that was just across from his own room. Their room held two utilitarian old metal twin-bed frames and mattresses leftover from the nuns. In contrast, a cheery copper-yellow color covered the walls. Bright blue down comforters, fluffy pillows, and multi-colored afghans adorned the beds.

Duval chewed his lower lip and watched them unpack for several minutes.

He watched Addy rest a black duffel on the bed and open it. She pulled out a few items and placed them on one of the refurbished oak bedside tables. The other woman, whose name was Reyna, did the same thing with her black duffel before picking up both bags and placing them in the closet together. She then removed her jacket and sat on the bed closest to the door.

Weller turned toward the doorway and looked at him. "Why did you say you were designers?" Duval fiddled with an empty cigarette pack in his pocket.

"We wanted to see how easy it would be for a crazy and inventive liar to work a way into the band's personal space."

"Oh." Duval looked at the ground and felt his cheeks darken. "I'm just an old ex-addict with a CDL."

"Don't sweat it, Mr. Sam. You at least asked questions. You challenged us and we can teach you the rest."

Duval looked up.

Weller smiled at him.

He nodded. "I'd like that. I'd like to help keep them all safe. They're special. They give so much."

"We will and you'll help do it," Weller affirmed.

Duval glanced at Reyna.

Reyna nodded. "We'll need all the help we can get."

Duval thought about it for a moment. "We'll all help. There isn't a body around here who would turn down that chance. I'll make sure of it."

"I know you will." Weller rested her hands in her lap and smiled up at him.

†

Shay looked through the Chicago radio station's glass window to where Addy stood outside on the sidewalk. Addy had her back to her and the DJ. Shay studied her new guardian and decided that Addy looked less obvious, but strangely no less intimidating. Today, she wore black engineer boots, fitted blue jeans, gray shawl sweater, and a white oxford layered over a waffle shirt. *She looks like a glamorously casual model.*

Weller had her earbuds with wires trailing to the smartphone in her jeans pocket. She was standing there as if she were stopping to carry on a conversation rather than watching the street. Shay wondered if she was listening to the show.

"Shay?" The DJ host of NPR's Breakout Music Now show interrupted her thoughts.

"Oh, yes, Meglyn. I'm sorry. I spaced out there for a second."

"No problem. We all know you have a lot on your mind. I said, 'I bet you didn't expect that movie soundtrack you produced as a little side project to get nominated for a Grammy and an Oscar. Did you?'"

Shay's focus shifted back to the green-eyed, red-haired, public-radio DJ across from her.

"Ah, no, I didn't. It was a lark. I made it just for the joy of making more music, of helping to tell a novel-length story on screen. The truth is that all of this attention is wonderful. It sort of authenticates that what we're doing is meaningful. That's what I want most. To be honest, the attention itself is a little overwhelming."

"What do you mean?"

"Attention and recognition gives us more power to do more good work with more and more people. At the same time, nothing really prepared us for how personal this kind of attention can be all of a sudden. Fans ask what we had for breakfast. People want you to sign their foreheads with sharpies. Larger record labels and corporate music labels offer to take us in and take us over—give us managers and publicists. I'm not ready. I'm not sure I'll ever be ready to give up our control. Right now, we decide what music to make, how to make it, how to tour it, how to promote it, and when we should do what. I haven't figured out yet how we stay small, home-grown, and value-driven, and still manage to capitalize on all this attention and recognition in the most positive way possible."

"That's a pretty altruistic and humble outlook."

"Thanks. I think it goes back to what drives our love of making and creating music. We've always known it is our best chance to feed ourselves, grow, help others, and change the world a little bit so that maybe one more person has a chance to feel valuable."

"We look forward to watching you figure it all out, and we will be excited to hear what happens with all of your upcoming projects. If their success is anything like this soundtrack project, you'll definitely be changing the world on a global scale. I think we're in good hands." Meglyn twirled her hand in the air signaling the show's impending finish.

"Thanks for your time and thanks to anyone and

everyone who bothers to listen to our stuff. We love making music for you, regardless of whether it earns any attention or recognition. It is just a joy to be out there performing." Shay looked out the window again. Addy slowly pulled her earbuds out and then turned around and looked directly at her.

Shay waved at Addy while the sound engineer closed the room's feed. Meglyn stepped up and offered Shay a hand. She shook it.

"Glad you could do it." Meglyn tilted her chin toward Addy, smiling. "Is that your new girlfriend?"

Shay looked back at Meglyn with her eyes wide, and gave her a giggle. "No, no, nothing like that. She's just a friend from a recent project."

"Seems those projects all go your way and even if this one doesn't, she is good looking." Meglyn's smile got wider.

"Thanks. See you around." Shay waved before wandering out to where Addy was waiting. Addy held open the door to the black SUV as soon as Jye pulled the beastly vehicle up to the curb in front of Shay.

"Did I sound okay?" Shay brushed by Addy into the back seat. She passed close enough to smell and feel the cold air clinging to Addy.

Addy nodded but kept her eyes on the street around the SUV as she climbed into the backseat beside Shay.

Jye pulled away from the curb, and Shay resisted an unexpected urge to grab Addy's hand and hold it. They drove home in silence.

Chapter Nine

Button Pushing

Syl and Iva stood on the back porch of the convent's main garden. Drew leaned against the brick behind them with his hands tucked in his jean pockets for warmth, basking in the weak but clear sunlight. He watched Reyna, Weller, and Duval walking from bush to bush, hedge to hedge, and tree to tree. As the three walked, he knew Weller was trying to put each visual obstacle between them.

Drew offered her thumbs up or thumbs down, indicating whether he could see her each time or not. Iva walked over to Drew and leaned against his leg. Her pudgy little hand mimicked his thumbs up or down to Weller for several rounds.

The door next to Drew squeaked open and Shay squeezed through. She looked over them all and then picked up Iva.

Iva wiggled a bit. "I want to stay, Momma."

"Aw come on, little tiger, Mommy has a break. Let's go play inside."

"Okay." Iva gave Shay back her own blue-eyed smile.

Drew waved at Weller and turned to follow them inside.

"Alone." Shay looked at Drew.

Drew balked.

"We'll stay inside. In the living area," Shay conceded.

Drew nodded, and settled back in place.

†

Shay pulled the door shut behind them, huffed a bit, and squeezed Iva.

Iva mimicked her Momma's huff.

"Hmm," Shay walked down the convent hall toward their newly finished suite. "That sounds pretty snotty now that you mention it." She grinned at Iva, tweaked the toddler's nose, and shook her head. "I don't know why they press my buttons."

"I don't know why buttons," parroted Iva.

†

The wind whipped around the brick foundations of the old convent dormitories, leaving Reyna and Weller chilled to the bone as they strolled along the exterior wall.

"This place has more holes than a pound of Swiss cheese in a sewer full of mice." Reyna pried open another window with an obviously broken lock.

"Well, let's at least take down the signs to the holes that scream, 'Hey, crazy murderers, use this path to go directly to your target in five minutes or less,'" Weller replied.

"Yeah, yeah. You got any public works contacts in Chi-town? We're gonna need something quick and easy to help limit access to some of these driveways."

"Yeah. I'll call in a favor with a road contractor and see if I can get them to order us the water-filled barriers wholesale and pronto."

"How'd the radio spot go?"

"I didn't see anything out of the ordinary there. No cars or people stuck near us or reappeared. In fact, no one seemed to notice us at all. I think the cold killed all curiosity." Weller rubbed her bare hands together for warmth.

"No, I meant, how did she sound?"

"Oh, good, I guess." Weller stared off into the distance.

"Good how? Like a good voice or like a good person and not a snotty unreasonable brat?"

Weller looked back at Reyna with wide eyes and raised eyebrows. "Gotta grudge?"

"No." Reyna laughed.

"You sure?"

"Okay, maybe. You can't say anyone who has ever paid us for protection services, rather than had us appointed to protect them, has been so averse to the basic premise of security."

Weller nodded. "Maybe she just has a different fear reaction. Like those little squids they sometimes use for Wahoo bait. You know? They squirt all over themselves with indignation because they're all shocked and scared and hoping to distract all attackers."

"Maybe. I think it just upset me that they're scared and they don't trust us, the experts, to make them any safer. You've spoiled me. I'm not used to being distrusted anymore."

"I think they're too scared to know how to trust, let alone who to trust."

"So you didn't answer my question. What kind of good?" Reyna noticed they were nearing their starting point. Soon they would head back in for warmth and dinner.

"Both. She was humble, honest, and credited others. And she had a really nice voice, smooth and smoky." Weller stared into the distance remembering and a little smile dawned over her face.

"That's an emotive answer for you."

Weller gave a very small shrug and didn't meet Reyna's eyes.

†

In an old furnace room in the basement of the convent dormitory, Drew looked on as RobO plugged a P90X DVD into an X-box.

"You work out to that?" Drew asked.

RobO looked down at his blooming pot belly and then up at Drew pointedly. "Sure, every day without fail for the last five years. That's why I have these abs of steel and thighs of iron."

Drew guffawed until his eyes teared up.

RobO laughed along.

"Aw, man, I'm sorry. I walked right into that one."

"No sweat. I just thought I should start trying something, you know? At least, when we're home and in this place there's plenty of room to try it without having to worry about the others poking fun at me. I'd just like to get back in shape and look something like I did then." RobO pointed up to a black-and-white press photo taped to the wall.

Drew stepped closer and peered at the grainy old clipping. In the picture, RobO looked about twenty years younger. Wrapped around an old school microphone, giving a good Bing Crosby purr, RobO looked skinny in a dark suit and tie with a mop of hair suavely combed back in a smooth wave.

"I know; I'll never get all that hair back."

"It doesn't matter. You don't need it. You guys have talent. I mean you can sing and play drums. I wish I could do that."

"Sort of. I mean I can play drums, but that's damn easy for most of Shay's songs. I don't think I could sing like that anymore. Shay just got more attention. She's a natural and she writes her own stuff. Once she took off, I just never had the time or the chance to do my thing. I mean, if you only get one, you wanna go with the one that's working."

"But you could go back to doing it again now, couldn't you?"

"I don't think so. I mean, it might be hard to even get noticed, and then if I did, it would be because I had to harp up my connection to Shay's band." RobO turned to the TV and pushed the play button on his X-box.

Drew retreated toward the door.

"Hey, you know you're welcome to work out with me if you want," RobO called over the din of the workout program.

Drew turned back toward him and looked sideways at the TV as the instructor began marching in place. "Yeah, sure, why not. Thanks." He stepped up next to RobO and started keeping pace with the marching man on TV.

Chapter Ten

Conspicuous is a Word

Weller and Duval walked toward the tour bus and a small cluster of cars in the church lot.

"I don't want anyone to be able to tell any of their cars are connected to Shay."

"Yeah, um about that." Duval gave Weller an exasperated face.

"What?"

Duval pointed to a lime green 1974 Chevy Nova with a bumper sticker that read: "Stay Green, Recycle."

"*Oof,*" Weller wheezed.

Duval grasped Weller's elbow and steered her to the other side of the bus and pointed to a matching lime-green, 2012 Toyota Prius, with the same bumper sticker and a vanity plate that read *RobOSyl.*

"Even better." Weller sighed.

"At least the bus is plain. They haven't gotten around

to having the same shop paint it yet." Duval smiled.

"Well, we'll just have to drive them around in our rental for now. What about Fallow and Jane?"

"The black Harley and the green Yamaha motorcycles parked up under the church eaves."

"All right. I want to put a gate with a lock and key up around that porch, under the eaves. Do you know anyone who does that sort of thing around here?"

"I do. I'll arrange to get it done."

"Thanks, and let's at least park these in the inner parking lot closer to the convent dormitories, out of plain sight, and put some car covers on them. No one gets in them until someone has done a basic bomb sweep. Same with the bus."

Duval nodded.

"Think we can get the gate crew to fence and gate that lot in by itself, too?" Weller pointed out the ideal edges of the fence border for securing the lot.

"I'll look into it. Sonny's brother is a welder. Maybe he could attach some wrought iron well enough to the brick walls of the convent to close the gap between the buildings and hang some sort of gate."

"That's a good start."

†

"Who plans the meals and gets all the groceries?" Weller asked.

"Syl does," Duval answered. "Usually on Saturdays, I take her to the stores to get everything for the week. We take turns cooking though. Usually in the same rotation if everyone is here. Syl has Sunday. I have Monday. Then Fallow, Jane, Sonny, RobO, and Shay."

Weller nodded. "How can we help?"

"If you all end up sticking around, Shay will probably want you to take a day, come to think of it...," Duval cast an evaluative glance at her.

Jye grinned. "I make a mean meatloaf."

With a confident smile, Weller met Duval's questioning look. "Yep. We can all cook. Taking a turn only seems fair since we're all big eaters, too. Has Syl had to increase the food stock with an extra trip with us around the last three days?"

"Yeah, she also took over the cooking rotation all three nights. She said it was easier right now with everything going on." Duval shrugged.

Frowning, Weller glanced off into the distance. "We like to be responsible guests. We'll give Beni and Shay our full assessment on Friday. I'll be sure to include us in the rotation when I make the recommendation to keep our current protection detail intact for the foreseeable future."

"I'm sure you've noticed Shay is vegan."

Weller nodded.

"I can make a killer soy meatloaf too," Jye offered.

"She's also all for using only the certified organics too, but Syl can find most everything these days in that vein anyway."

"We'll keep that in mind. Thanks for the hints, Duval."

"No problem."

†

A thickset workman in a Carhart coat and beanie cap used a backhoe to hold a ten-foot by ten-foot section of wrought iron fence in place, while a welder mated it to a steel beam set into the corner of the brick convent dormitory. The welder finished the seam and moved down the fence to mate the next steel beam already posted in the ground.

Weller stood watching next to Sonny and Duval. "Once those three sections are in, they can set up that gate over the drive into the lot, and put in the gate opener and keypad."

"You think that will work?" Sonny asked.

"I do. It should help to keep visitors from strolling up to the bus and our cars as easily as they could before. We should change the code once a week."

"Okay." Sonny rubbed his chin with one work-gloved hand.

"The light on the corner of the building lights up most of the lot, but it wouldn't hurt to get another put on the other corner by the gate. Know an electrician who could get it done before Friday?" Weller asked

"I don't, but I'm sure Mike will." Sonny tilted his head

toward the backhoe operator.

"Thanks. Now I think it's time I teach Duval how to inspect all these vehicles." Weller gestured toward Shay's Nova and ushered Duval ahead of her.

†

In the yard, Syl, Reyna, and Drew all paused. Iva stopped mid-walk and pointed to her mother's car.

"Did they lose a ball?" Iva asked as Weller, Duval, and Sonny bent over and walked around the car peering underneath.

A motor revved up and peeled out on the street nearby. Reyna turned to look, but she saw nothing except the taillights of a dark pickup truck in the distance.

Reyna replied to Iva. "No, little one, they just want to see what the underside of all those cars look like. Addy likes cars a whole lot."

"Oh. I like to look at the underside of Mama and Fallow's skateboards." Iva scampered toward the parking lot.

Reyna reached out and picked up the child, swinging her up onto her shoulders in one graceful motion. "Whoa, little one, we can look but you gotta stay safe with us while that big backhoe is working over there."

Syl gaped openly at Reyna. Iva giggled.

Shay popped her head out of the door on the Church studio's south porch. "Hey. Hey, Iva."

Iva's little hands fluttered on top of Reyna's head,

"*Ooo*, Momma is outside. Let's go see her."

"Okay," Reyna agreed, and marched that way with Iva emitting giggles with each bounce.

Shay frowned at Reyna briefly before smiling up at her daughter.

Chapter Eleven

Playing with Dolls and Doubts

"Give me liberty or give me death." Shay put her hands on her thin hips.

"Really? That's what you're gonna go with?" Weller asked.

"Iberdy or death. May I have a cheese stick please?" Iva tugged on Weller's pants.

Weller directed a questioning look at Shay.

"Soy sticks are in the butter drawer behind you." Shay nodded at the two-door commercial refrigerator behind Weller in the convent's galley kitchen.

"Sure, kiddo." Weller smiled down at Iva.

Iva gave a hop and a clap and followed Weller to the fridge.

Weller opened the fridge, selected a soy cheese stick, and offered it to Iva. "This one?"

"Yes, please."

"Want me to open it for you or would you like to open it?"

"Me," squealed the perpetually happy child.

Weller used her thumbnail to separate the plastic wrap's edges to make it easier for Iva before handing over the cheese stick.

Iva managed to open it just fine and took a bite. She turned her big, round, blue eyes up to Weller. "Mmmmm. Thank you, Addy."

"You're welcome, Iva."

"You want one too?"

"No, thank you." Weller eyed the white, incredibly uniform, stub in Iva's hand with skepticism.

"Tastes like string cheese," Shay insisted.

"I bet." Weller eyed Iva's mother.

Shay was still waiting with her hands on her hips. "I want some alone time with my daughter."

"Not a problem." Weller drew herself up to leave the kitchen, but Shay stood between her and the exit.

Her blue eyes bored into Weller. "You mean it's not a problem if we want to be alone inside and at home."

Weller cocked her head. "Of course."

"She wants to go to the American Girl store in my car, and I want to take her and have some time with just the two of us doing what she wants to do."

Weller sucked in a deeper breath and rolled her head to each side, stretching her neck. "Without anyone else along?"

"Without anyone else. Just a mother and daughter going to a doll store."

"I would rather two of us ride along."

"What? Do you get off on stalking shoppers?" Shay seethed in a hiss of air between her teeth.

Weller watched Shay actually stamp her green Toms shoes on the avocado-colored tile floor. Weller held in a laugh.

"I mean it, Addy. I just don't get you. What motivates you? Why do you try to control what's around us every waking moment?"

Weller repressed a smirk. "It's my duty. I'm paid to protect people. You are paying me to protect Iva…to really protect Iva from any significant harm. I also need to protect you."

"I don't want us to be anyone's paid duty. That isn't really protection...it's...it's...it's...oh. I don't know what it is. It just doesn't feel right." Shay clenched her fists at her sides.

Iva turned in slow lazy circles in front of her mother nibbling on her cheese stick.

Weller, reaching a hand behind her head, rubbed the back of her neck and pulled her ponytail tighter. A lock of hair escaped in the process and fell over her forehead.

Shay watched Addy's dark hair, mesmerized by its luster in the kitchen fluorescents. She almost reached out to brush it away, but Addy turned abruptly and strode back over to the fridge.

She pulled out the vanilla soy milk, picked up a glass from the drying rack, and poured herself a few ounces. She held the carton up to Shay and raised her eyebrows.

"Um. No. Thanks, I'm good," Shay replied to the unspoken offer.

"Would you like some, Iva?"

Iva shook her head. "I'm good."

Addy smiled. "Yes, you are."

Shay wanted to stay aggravated with Addy, but the two of them were too cute together. She smiled despite herself. "So you're a convert?"

Addy put the soy milk back into the fridge and tossed her a dry look. "I wouldn't go that far."

"But soy milk isn't half bad?"

"No, it is good, but it isn't milk." Addy raised the glass and tipped a cheers before taking a healthy swallow.

Inspiration hit Shay and she felt it flash across her face before she could suppress it.

"What?" Addy asked.

"That's exactly it, Addy. It isn't that this protection stuff is bad, but it isn't comfortable. It isn't that you, Reyna, Jye, and Drew are bad to have around, but you're not exactly family—yet you're all up in our family grill."

Shay watched Addy pucker her lips and tuck in her chin, giving her a look of goofy disbelief. "We're not so bad to have around, heh?" She wiggled her brows at Iva.

Iva giggled and Shay gave a belly laugh, too. "Okay, okay, most of you aren't bad to have around. I think Reyna has a little grudge against me. Huh?"

Addy held up her finger and thumb about a half-inch apart. "Maybe. A little. You're not as graciously accepting of our security efforts as most diplomats."

"Oh? I never would have guessed."

They laughed together.

"But seriously," Shay said.

Addy frowned. "I know. I see your point. I'm sorry." She held up her soy milk glass, "Much like I make do by enjoying this soy milk here for all it is worth while I'm without a cow, I'm asking you to try to make do with us as surrogate family until this threat is past. I want to see you and Iva live happily ever after when we ride out of here."

"Can I just have some normal time with Iva? We're on the road and working so often. This is the one time of the year that I've left open for us to be at home for a while. Time to focus on Iva alone is the one thing I most want. It's the one thing that keeps me going."

Addy said nothing.

"Please? Just give us an hour in a pretty tame store in the middle of a Thursday before the holiday shopping season?" Shay batted her eyelashes and put a touch of song into her request.

"What about crowds? You'll be a target the whole time. What if someone recognizes you, Shay?"

"I'm a lesbian folk singer for crying out loud, not some pop diva and not some important politician. No one will recognize me and there should be just enough of a crowd today to ensure that no crazies ever have a chance to corner us alone long enough to do us any real harm."

"You're the lead singer of a band with three top forty alternative hits this year, and the producer of a soundtrack that won a Grammy and an Oscar. Not to mention that you have this whole, very noticeable, lime-green theme going on that tips off most folks. And, according to Fallow, a large portion of your 'Greenfanas' are enamored enough to follow you from show to show over hundreds of miles. Odds are you'll be noticed in your home town these days. And a few seconds of total exposure might be just enough to tempt the bomber."

Shay granted Addy a purposeful glare. She pointed at Iva's ears and shook her head.

Shifting back on her heels, Addy made a contrite face. "I'm sorry."

Shay heaved a sigh. "What about if you ride along?"

"That helps, but I don't recommend it."

"But you won't stop me…"

"Shay, I can't stop you. This isn't a prison sentence. It's an effort to keep you alive long enough to see that Iva grows up and to let Iva get to know her mother."

"I get it. That's why we're taking you. You'd better hurry if you're coming with." Shay picked up Iva and bolted out of the kitchen.

"Damn, hell-fire stupidity, punk-ass behavior."

Shay heard Addy hissing as her heavy footsteps trailed them hurriedly down the hall.

†

Weller was relieved to find that Shay was at least right about being recognized within the store. Keeping herself separate enough to see every approach to the pair of blonds, Weller watched them roam the aisles, telling each other stories and pointing out details for a good uninterrupted ten minutes. Weller was not surprised to see the young, bubbly, dark-haired sales associate approach with a toothy smile. What surprised her was when the woman addressed her rather than Shay with a bright smile.

"Is there anything I can help you with? Are you looking for something for a particular age group?"

Weller looked back at Shay and Iva.

Shay met her glance, but remained silent.

"No, no thank you. I'm just with them." Weller gestured to where Shay and Iva were perched twenty feet away in the mock, 1940s era, kitchen display which featured the Emily doll.

The sales associate—her name tag said, "Lisa"—looked over to Shay for confirmation only to have Shay stare back at her with a blank look.

"Really?" Weller challenged Shay.

Shay broke into a grin and looked up at Weller through her long, delicate, golden eyelashes. Weller felt her stomach do a tight flip before Shay turned her gaze to favor Lisa with a smile. "Yeah, she's with us."

"Wif us." Iva ran over to Weller and pulled her by the hand over to join them in Emily's world.

Lisa followed. "Well then," she clapped her hands together lightly in front of her chest, "is there anything I can do to help all of you?"

"We are okay for now, but thank you for offering," Shay answered.

Weller watched Lisa studying Shay's face a little more closely when the collar of Shay's navy peacoat settled to reveal more of her upturned jaw.

Lisa cocked her head to one side and looked like she was about to say something more, but then she turned back toward the register area with a departing smile.

Weller let out a relieved breath and perched on the step to the kitchen display with her back to the wall.

Iva darted from packaged doll to packaged doll along the aisle, proclaiming additions to her list of promising features with each step down the line. "This one is a baby. This one has hair. This one has a blue dress. Oh, this one has blue jeans and peace shirt like you, Momma."

"Yes, she does, Iva." Shay's indulgent smile appeared to slip as she looked from Iva to the boxes of dolls.

"Which one do you like, Mama? Can I have them all? Can we get them now?"

"Whoa, little one." Shay looked bewildered. "Addy?"

"Yeah?"

"I'm not sure what to do."

"About?"

"This. All of these dolls."

"They're expensive," Weller observed.

"Yeah. I mean I have the money. We do have the money, now, but…."

"You're not sure you should treat her like that."

"No. I know I shouldn't, but she gets so little from me. I'm such a horrible mother. I've no clue how to do this. I've never seen anyone do it right."

"She doesn't want stuff, Shay. She wants you. Your time and attention. Remember when you were three-years old? What would have convinced you that your mother loved you more than anything in this situation?"

"But I have to keep her safe, too. It's not just about time and attention, is it?" Shay's brow furrowed and she twisted her hands.

"I have a feeling there is more to this great internal debate of yours than just the price of dolls in Chicago," Weller said.

Shay's blue eyes watered.

Weller lifted her hand, tempted to touch her, but then stuffed it in her pocket. "I'm no expert on parenting, Shay. No one ever is if you ask me, but I think that sometimes the only way to keep your kid safe is to love her well. If you don't, she'll just keep getting into harm's way, trying to get someone to pay attention to her and love her well enough."

Shay leveled an intense gaze at Weller before deadpanning, "Wow."

"What?" Weller cocked her head to one side.

"I had you pegged for an emotional midget."

"Ah, thanks. Happy to inspire confidence."

"I'm woman enough to admit when I'm wrong." Shay smiled.

"Yes, you are wrong. Wrong about my emotional maturity and about your ability to parent well. So maybe you didn't have a good example of what you should do, but you definitely know what you wished your parents would have done, could have done for you."

"Point taken. I'm sorry for pre-judging you, Addy."

"No worries."

"And thank you. You've given me a lot to think about."

"You're welcome. Oh, and I think it's dwarf."

"Dwarf?"

"Yeah, I think you meant I'm an emotional dwarf. I think 'midget' might be considered socially insensitive terminology these days."

In between barks of laughter, Shay replied, "You're probably right. Maybe emotionally handicapped is better?"

Smiling, Weller admitted under her breath, "Definitely more accurate." A sharp pang of missing Elle nipped at her heart. She watched Shay kneel down to Iva's level.

"Baby, why don't you think about it and I'll help you write Santa a note letting him know which doll you would like the most?"

Iva's small pink tongue twisted against her lips. "You

will help me write?"

"Absolutely. We can do it before your bedtime story tonight."

"Yes." Iva turned back to the dolls and swiveled her head from one desirable set to the next, as if memorizing each one's merits.

After a few minutes more of reflection, Iva walked over to Weller. She leaned her head against the side of Weller's leg and rubbed at her eyes.

"I think your mini-me is crashing." Weller gave the child a smile and a gentle back rub.

"Crashing?" Iva's big blue eyes stared up at her inquiringly.

"You look a little tired."

"Hmm." The child leaned more heavily against her leg and Weller looked to Shay.

"My mini-me?" Shay inquired softly.

"You have to admit she is like a miniature version of you."

"Hmm. You mean sassy and troublesome?"

Weller heard herself answering more earnestly than she intended, "No. A dreamy-eyed mess."

Swallowing visibly, Shay gave a soft grin. "Ah, yes. My sweet mess."

"Yep." Weller reached out to ruffle a hand through Iva's bouncy blond mane.

"Sweet mess, sweetness, sweet mess," agreed Iva.

"Shall we go, love?" Weller asked the child.

"Okay." Iva wandered into Shay's waiting arms.

They exited the store together with Shay carrying Iva a half step in front and to the right of Weller.

Iva rested her head on Shay's shoulder and struggled to keep her eyes open. Her lashes fluttered like butterflies.

Weller resisted the urge to wrap an arm around the two of them. She suspected her body heat would be welcome by both against the biting winds blowing off the lake.

They reached the corner and waited for the crosswalk to light up.

Weller surveyed the area. No one was paying them any undue attention. Several cars stopped at the light beside them.

They started across when the crosswalk sign lit up. As they neared the curb, Weller looked up to her right at a black Ford F150 idling loudly near the curb. She could taste the exhaust spilling out into the cold air and her stomach gave a prescient lurch sending the "something-seems-off" tingles creeping down her shoulders toward the palms of her hands.

Shuffle-stepping into the crosswalk gave Weller a few more seconds to take a closer look at the truck's driver. She could discern little about him in his puffy black winter jacket, his black wool cap pulled low, and black sunglasses aside from the fact that he preferred black. He seemed to be looking only at the light though, paying them no particular attention.

Weller looked down toward truck's front license plate. She stepped up on the curb. The plate holder was empty.

Shay and Iva were stepping into the parking lot a few steps ahead of her. Weller had no other choice but to continue on keeping them within the shelter of her quick reach.

As they were passing through a second row of cars, still three rows back from Shay's car, Weller heard an engine rev and tires squeal.

Shay, still carrying Iva, was nearly three steps ahead of Weller as they passed between two cars.

Weller felt and saw the truck enter the parking lot on the lane in front of Shay at a high speed. Taking several large steps forward, she rolled Shay and Iva into her arms as using all of her body weight to move all three of them backward into the sheltering side of a parked Chevy Trailblazer.

The move knocked the air out of Shay and she let out an audible, "*umpf.*"

Iva's eyes snapped open.

The black truck whizzed by the back end of the maroon Trailblazer rushing over the place where they would have stepped. It was going so fast that the breeze off it passing smacked Weller's face with hot exhaust fumes and shook the Trailblazer.

The truck made the turn at the end of the row with tires screaming and left a wealth of rubber on the blacktop.

Weller stayed holding Shay and Iva in place between her own body and the body of the Trailblazer.

Shay's eyes were wide.

Weller could feel her shiver and barked, “Stay.”

Shay nodded and tightened her arms around Iva who was tearing up

Weller dashed between parked cars trying to catch up with the tailgate of the truck. It fishtailed and then righted itself back out onto the street before speeding away. She couldn’t run fast enough to make out any of the back license plate numbers before coming to a thudding stop at the end of the parking lot pavement.

“Shit.” She chopped both hands through the air in frustration and watched the truck fade away before jogging back to Iva and Shay.

Weller found Shay holding Iva very tightly, swaying back and forth while still tucked in next to the Trailblazer where she had left them.

Shay’s voice was low and full of trembling treble. “It’s okay, sweet baby. It’s okay. We’re all right.” Her blue eyes were very large and luminescent above her very white cheeks.

Iva’s face, tucked against Shay’s neck, made it impossible for Weller to see her expression.

Weller, fearing shock would render them both too vulnerable, calmed her breathing and put on a light smile. “Hey, beautiful ladies, do you know why bananas have to put on sunscreen before they go to the beach?”

Almost simultaneously, Shay and Iva looked up toward her with the same deer-in-the-headlights expression.

Weller consciously put her hands in her pockets, gave them a great big smile, and rocked back and forth on her heels as if she had no worries in the world. "No guesses?"

Mother and daughter shook their heads dully in unison.

"Ah, so they don't peel." Weller held up both hands like a vaudeville comedian punctuating the ta-da moment.

Iva smiled a little.

"What do you call cheese that's not yours?" Weller continued.

Iva wrinkled her little nose, thinking.

"Nacho Cheese," cheered Weller, sending Iva into a good laugh.

"Nacho Cheese. Nacho Cheese," Iva parroted.

Shay's face gained a little more color again and there was a smile on the edge of her lips.

"Knock, knock," Weller chorused.

"Who's there?" Shay played along.

"Lettuce," Weller deadpanned.

Shay's nose wrinkled as she tried to figure out where the joke was going. "Lettuce who?"

"Lettuce get in the car, it's freezing out here." Weller wrapped her arms around herself and did a little tap dance.

"Let's go home and play some more, Momma," Iva seconded.

"Okay, baby, let's go." Shay hugged her little girl and mouthed out above Iva's golden head, "That was close."

"Yes. Yes, it was." Weller put an arm around her two blond charges and walked them to their car. Shay walked so close to her that Weller could feel the roll in Shay's hip bone knocking against her leg with each step.

Chapter Twelve

One Part Paranoia

Shay shifted the shiny green Nova down and let it idle as they paused at the stoplight. She noticed Addy's focus was on the side mirror. Addy craned her neck to peer over her left shoulder so intensely that Shay became worried enough to peer over her own shoulder to the back seat. Iva, in her car seat, was already asleep and drooling against the wing of her headrest. Seeing nothing there of concern, Shay looked back up at the stoplight and waited for it to change. The light turned green and Shay rolled through the intersection. Addy placed her left hand lightly on Shay's right shoulder.

Addy spoke softly. "Shay, I want you to turn right at the third intersection and then drive down Wacker, take a left on Clark, then a right on Adams, and another left onto Desplaines Street. There is a fire station on Desplaines near the interstate. I want you to pull into the fire station's parking lot."

Shay's body gave an involuntary shiver. "The truck?" she asked.

"No. We're okay. It's probably nothing, but there is a little silver Mercedes that is doing a good job of distantly staying near us. I just like taking precautions. You know my grandpa always says the recipe for making it to tomorrow is one-part paranoia, two parts precaution, and a good dose of luck." Addy's voice stayed soft and level, making Shay's body relax a bit in its rich alto timbre.

Shay chuckled slightly at the corny recipe.

"Do you know anyone who drives a little silver Mercedes?" Addy asked.

"I'm not sure. I think Beni's husband drives something silver, but I thought it was a Lexus."

"Would Beni have him follow you for any reason?"

"No. Marcus is an accountant and his idea of helping protect or watch anyone generally involves doing their taxes for them, or finding them a double discount at the high-end department stores."

Addy patted her shoulder again. "Probably nothing anyway. Maybe someone is just headed the same direction we are. Given our earlier experience, I'd like to wait it out at the station a few minutes."

Shay pursed her lips and hoped it was true.

As they traveled down Adams Street and Shay signaled her turn onto Desplaines Street, Addy's fingertips again came to rest on her shoulder. Shay shifted the Nova down and stopped to wait at the turn. She glanced up at

Addy.

Addy's brown eyes met hers and Shay watched them go from coffee-colored dark concentration to a mesmerizing honey brown.

"Do you see the station over there?" Addy's fingers lifted off Shay's shoulder and gestured toward the station sign on their right a few blocks up Desplaines.

Shay nodded. "Is the Mercedes still there?" She made the turn and drove on to the last stoplight before the station.

"It is a little over a block back and is signaling to turn right."

Shay relaxed a little more. The light changed and she rolled through it coasted the short distance into the station's lot. She parked right in front of the station's walkup entrance. After taking a very long and deep shaky breath, and blowing it out slowly, she looked to Addy for further instruction.

Addy gave her a sincere smile that crinkled the edges of her dark eyes and Shay couldn't help but smile back despite her uncertainty.

"You did great. We'll wait here ten minutes or so. Maybe they'll drive by to check us out and I can get a better look at a license plate," Addy said.

Shay nodded before turning around in her seat to check on Iva. Her baby was sound asleep, head lolling a little in her car seat, and her sweet little eyelashes looked golden and delicate against her pale soft cheeks. Shay felt her love for her "mini-me" welling in her chest and taking over her whole being. The thought of someone hurting Iva flushed her face again and made her heartbeat flutter.

"We're all safe. I will do everything humanly possible to keep us safe. We'll get back home," Addy reassured.

Minutes passed in silence and the Mercedes did not reappear.

Shay turned forward again and gripped the steering wheel. Her knuckles showed white.

"I would like to drive us the rest of the way home."

Shay nodded and then swallowed before crying, "This was stupid. I'm an ass."

Addy grasped her right hand from the steering wheel and squeezed it. "Yes, but you're learning."

A bitter laugh escaped Shay and she looked at their linked hands. She realized that putting them in this situation was stupid of her, but Addy still made her feel safe.

"It takes a little time to go from that 'everything-should-still-be-normal' denial mindset to the 'oh-shit-someone-is-trying-to-kill-me' acceptance posture that allows you to defend yourself."

Shay bowed her head. "Sure the hell does. This sucks. I don't want to live like this, Addy, and I really don't want Iva to have to live like this. The threat to Iva scares the holy crap out of me." Just the act of saying it froze Shay's core from the inside out and sent a clenching shiver up her spine to bunch all the muscles in her neck.

Addy let go of her hand. Shay felt a tear spill down the side of her nose and she rubbed it away with a swipe of her forearm.

Addy placed her hand on the top center of Shay's back. Her hand was warm across Shay's spine and it restored Shay's grounding a little. The tension in her neck eased and she felt the budding heat of anger replacing her fear and denial. "How could anyone want to hurt us? Why? It doesn't make any sense."

Addy's hand gave a soothing little rub on her back. "It never really does."

For a brief second—the tiniest fraction of a moment when she looked at Addy—Shay saw a flicker of something very open and vulnerable cross Addy's face. It retreated into steady calm before Shay could interpret the look.

Shay unbuckled her seat belt. "Ready to trade?"

"Sure." Addy unbuckled, pushed open her door, and folded her taller form out of the Nova.

Shay bounced out of the seat and walked around to Addy's side before Addy even finished stepping back from the door. Addy stood in place and cast a wide gaze around the whole area, before looking at Shay. "Still no Mercedes."

"Good." Shay sighed.

Addy grinned and then gently gestured Shay into the open passenger seat.

Shay sat inside, buckled her seatbelt with a loud clap, and looked up at Addy still standing in the open door. "What?"

Addy nodded at the sleeping Iva and lifted two eyebrows at Shay.

"Oh, once she's out she can sleep through an

industrial air horn." Shay smiled. "Just like her momma."

Addy returned the smile and closed the door.

Shay waited with her hands clasped. Addy walked to the other side of the Nova and cast a long look around before folding herself into the driver's seat. Shay watched Addy take her time adjusting the seat, the mirrors, studying the gears, and finding the emergency brake.

Addy started the car up again, took a deep breath, and closed her eyes for a second.

Curiosity got the better of her and Shay asked, "What are you doing?"

Eyes opening slowly, Addy looked at her. "I'm just feeling and listening to everything, learning to wear the seat and the steering wheel and the dimensions of the car like a second skin."

"Should I stay quiet and leave you two alone?"

"Nah, we're intimately acquainted now—she's sort of an easy gal."

Shay felt her face blush to the root of her hair. She played it off with a snort and a laugh. "Well, she is supposed to be fast and fuel efficient."

Addy steered the Nova smoothly through the congested city streets and the quickly fading winter afternoon. With the heater on and the tension of having to be in control passing, Shay found her own eyelids growing heavy as they pulled onto I-94.

Weller noticed that Shay was finally relaxed enough

to close her eyes. She refocused on the freeway and the traffic around them. A red G35 glided ahead of them and the only glint of silver or black that Weller saw in the rearview came from vehicles that were obviously not either a Mercedes or a murderous Ford Pickup.

An eighteen-wheeler hauling a bulldozer pulled onto the interstate next to Weller and hung in the far right lane. Weller saw the first sign for the exit to I-55 and started slowing to fall in behind the large truck. A quick glance in the rearview mirrors revealed a startling flash of silver speeding up in the distance. Weller peered harder at the growing shape in the rearview mirror, trying to discern if it was the right size and style to be their strange Mercedes tail.

A sudden bang sounded ahead of them, followed by large rubber chunks of shredded tire turned road gator smacking into the Nova's front bumper. Weller knew that the eighteen-wheeler had blown a tire. Instinctually she slowed down and tensed.

The truck driver struggled to keep the rig straight, but the entire left front wheel appeared blown. Air brakes squealed, and the Peterbilt 389's naked tire rim threw sparks as it bit into the roadway. The truck was slowing down, but the heavy bulldozer sitting on its trailer fishtailed right unexpectedly and the canted angle of the rig pushed the top-heavy load over sideways.

Time slowed for Weller.

The bulldozer snapped its chains and came tumbling off the Peterbilt's flatbed trailer and over into their lane.

Shay screamed and flung her left arm back toward Iva.

Iva matched her mother's scream with a startled wail.

Weller flinched before downshifting the Nova and shoving her foot wholeheartedly into the car's antiquated emergency foot-brake. She managed to steer the car's resulting one-hundred-eighty-degree skid behind the flailed truck into a stop against the concrete retaining wall.

The Nova came to a rest at the ready, but facing traffic. Ten feet behind them, the truck lay spread across three lanes of traffic like a log jam, and the bulldozer rested across a lane and a half three feet in front and to the right of them. They were trapped in the Nova on both sides, but undented. Cars bolted, jagged, and squealed all around them trying to stop and accommodate all of the sudden obstacles. A minivan taxi managed to stop in just enough time to avoid plowing into the overturned bulldozer before a blue Ford Focus smacked into it from behind.

Weller's gaze raced around the interstate looking for the Silver Mercedes, but spotted nothing. The Peterbilt driver's side door faced the ground, but the driver popped the passenger side door facing skyward and pulled himself out.

"Holy motherfucking super shit," Shay shrilled. Weller knew then that she must be okay.

Weller checked the rearview for Iva and found the child wide-eyed and crying but seemingly unharmed. After letting go of the steering wheel and pulling out her phone to dial 911, she noticed a small tremor in her left hand. As the call went through, Weller watched Shay unbuckling her seat belt, apparently intending on crawling her way back to Iva. She placed a firm hand on Shay's thigh and held her in her seat. The emergency operator came on and Weller reported the scene concisely before the operator confirmed someone had already called it in. After closing the call, Weller turned her attention back to Shay.

"Shay?" She noticed that the small woman had both arms wrapped around her head like she could shelter or at least hide herself from the fallout. Weller stretched across Shay to grab her released seat belt and clicked it back into place.

Shay grabbed onto Weller's arm. Her eyes were panicked.

"We're okay. We're all okay," Weller articulated with authority for both Shay and Iva.

"We're okay?" Iva hiccupped.

"Yes, kiddo. We're A-Okay," Weller answered Iva.

Shay's grip on Weller's arm slackened a little.

"But we're all gonna stay in our seats with our seatbelts on until things calm down out there." Weller eyed them both.

Shay nodded and put both of her hands in her lap before giving Weller a pleading look.

Weller gave her a thin smile. "Tell us a story, Shay. What was your favorite toy ever?"

Shay took a deep rattling breath and let it go slowly.

She dabbed her eyes dry on her sleeves and turned her head to give Iva a smile.

Weller started texting Reyna as Shay's story bubbled on and the sirens of all the first responders loomed closer outside the Nova.

Chapter Thirteen

Right as Might for a Rainy Night

He prodded the blond-haired whore in her bottom lip with his boot knife and watched to be sure the wound oozed and didn't well up. Her blue eyes stared dim and lifeless in the cold. "I guess playtime is over, huh, bitch?"

He gave a satisfied sigh and dragged the small woman's limp body behind a dumpster. Looking around the dark deserted alley on Chicago's South Side, he gave the night a broad grin. He didn't bother to cover her with anything or to wipe his semen or fingerprints off the body. He knew there was no need.

He whispered gleefully, "It's not like those cop shows on TV. Those bastards can't do anything to find me without a matching comparison sample of my prints and DNA and I'll never give them a reason to collect that. I'll inflict misery on you stupid, life-stealing cunts."

His feelings of immense power surged up, warm all

the way from the base of his spine to the crown of his head. He raised his arms in triumph and looked to the heavens. "Vengeance feels good, doesn't it, Mitch? I promise I'm getting closer to Shay Greenaura. Practice makes perfect."

†

Dawn was breaking outside the window of the small, makeshift, kitchen lab. Hands encased in purple latex gloves paused above a shiny pair of cast cutters and a dozen castor beans on a polycarbonate tray. A sheet of paper on the table beside the tray advised the median lethal ingested dose of ricin was roughly one milligram per kilo.

The echoes of Mitch Dane's guitar wailed in the dying chorus of his grunge cover of Eddie Rabbit's "I Love a Rainy Night" from a tape playing in an old boombox set in the window sill. A softly accented voice above the gloved hands chortled. "Just in case my first chase doesn't work out as planned."

Chapter Fourteen

Post-Dozer Doldrums

Sitting by the soundboard, Shay strummed her favorite black Martin acoustic guitar. She picked a pattern mindlessly, gazing at RobO on the other side of the glass, warming up his voice inside the sound booth.

Weller waited silently, leaning against the doorframe, looking full of words Shay didn't think she would say unless bluntly asked. Shay tried. "We're just waiting on Simone to show so we can lay down the vocals to a Plena song she has in mind. What are you thinking about?"

In the full minute before Addy answered, Shay hummed an interweaving melody to the tune she picked and strummed from the Martin.

"There are no words yet?" Addy asked.

Shay shook her head slightly. "Almost, but not yet."

"You might not need them. The music conveys a vulnerability that speaks volumes."

Shay's eyes drifted toward the doorway, where Weller leaned like a lanky lioness. Searching Addy's eyes, she found a hint of something very deep lying just beneath their dark surfaces. There were tired blue smudges under Addy's eyes this morning and Shay wondered at that.

Addy smiled slightly and the warmth in her eyes stunned the words dead on the tip of Shay's tongue. Shay set her guitar aside.

Addy didn't budge a muscle.

Shay started talking at a soft ramble. "Addy, so much happened yesterday and I'm so..." She tried to work her words into a thank you, but footsteps and voices rang down the hall.

Addy shifted to face the door and Shay's words trailed off. She realized her thanks and her questions would have to wait for later.

Jye appeared with Simone. Simone let go of Jye's arm and poured herself onto Weller's arm.

Jye's face was blank as Shay watched him slip out the door and back into the hall.

"It is good to have so many other tall people around." Simone's startling smoke-colored eyes twinkled. She leaned in enough to greet Addy with an uninvited kiss on both cheeks.

Shay watched the Brazilian model's plush lips make sound and steady contact with both of Addy's prominent cheekbones. She felt the resounding kisses to her guard's cheeks like a mild slap. She shook her head to clear it and wondered why the hell she was suddenly fixated on anyone else's greeting habits. Although she knew Simone kissed just about everyone hello, a little voice wiggling in her head protested that Simone seemed sincerer kissing Addy than she did in most of her usual greetings.

Addy mumbled a polite but markedly more formal greeting in return to Simone. "Hello, Ms. Saez."

Simone squeezed Addy's stiffened forearm. "When I called last night, Syl told me about your close call yesterday. I am so glad you are all unharmed."

Weller's mind flashed back to the bulldozer tumbling toward them and her stomach clenched.

Simone sashayed across the room and leaned down over Shay with one hand on each of Shay's shoulders. She delivered sound kisses to the smaller, trapped woman's forehead. "I can't believe you went through that. It sounds very scary." Simone briefly placed a well-manicured hand on Shay's pale cheek. "Did I mention I am so very glad you are okay?"

Shay smiled. "Thank you. It was very, very scary."

RobO popped out of the inner studio. "Hi, Simone."

Simone's hand fell from Shay's face and she stood.

"Hello, hello." She wrapped RobO in a brief boisterous hug.

RobO beamed.

"I hear that tall, luscious creature," Simone tossed a predatory and appreciative glance back at Weller, "saved

Shay and Iva from becoming road burns yesterday."

RobO looked over at Weller, too, and smiled very broadly. "Yes, she did. Everyone came home in one piece and without a scratch in the Nova's paint job."

"Hmmm. Such a big bad butch stud." Simone hummed. Something in the woman's eyes told Weller the comment was sardonic.

"It wasn't like that. I mean it seemed like a real threat. Like someone was trying to kill us. Or at least target us for a really bad day." Shay frowned.

Simone looked pointedly at Shay "You think that someone wants to target you?" Weller noticed disdain flash over the model's face in a microsecond.

Shay shrugged and shook her head.

"So you want the reputation that comes with having your own security?" Simone asked with a big smile.

"No. Never. I don't know that I need it, but I don't want anything to happen to Iva. I've never really had anything to worry about before the bomb, but right now I don't want to take chances." Shay rubbed her palms back and forth over her knees.

Simone turned back to Weller and gave her a long once over. It reminded Weller of a high-school homecoming queen appraising her after a particularly catty voting period.

Simone's hips led the way as she stepped very close to Weller and placed a hand on her folded arms. Leaning over, she mock whispered, "Exactly what are you guarding here? Your chance to get into a celebrity's panties?" Simone blew a light and suggestive breath into Weller's ear to punctuate her question. She drew back and continued in full voice. "So you actually reduce the chance of anything bad happening to our Greenauras?"

Weller watched Shay's face play host to a range of emotions. She worried about if Simone's prattle would diminish Shay's recent acceptance of her need for protection. Weller did not look at Simone or bother to reply.

Simone shrugged and turned to Shay. "I'm sure you have nothing more to really worry about. You know you are bound to encounter some crackpot fans, but we cannot let that change us. Heh? Not that having a brutishly brusque *despota* around isn't any fun."

Shay reddened a bit. "It isn't like that…"

"Ah, no? No, worries, my dear. I am only teasing you. You are so adorable when you flame up." Simone grasped Shay's chin and placed a quick kiss on the stammering singer's lips.

Something clicked, a question started to percolate up from Weller's tightened stomach and into her forebrain. She reached out, clapped a meaningful hand on Simone's shoulder, and forced the model to turn and face her.

Simone's eyes flashed anger for the briefest second before she mimed a wide-eyed whimper of surprise.

"What the hell, Addy?" Shay stood.

Weller slowly shook her head. "Nothing. Nothing. I'm sorry." She knew her glare at Simone wouldn't convince anyone she meant that apology.

Simone's gaze back at Weller was hot and her lips curved into a smile that Weller quickly classified as predatory and hungry.

RobO cleared his throat. "Let's go warm up a little. Okay, Simone?"

Simone granted Weller a "kiss-my-ass" grin and promptly turned on her heel to follow RobO into the sound room.

Weller's shoulders fell. She took in the angry glare emanating her way from Shay before she stepped backward and walked out of the room. She shut the door softly on Shay's glare and took up staring blankly down the hall over Jye's shoulder.

"What is it, boss?" Jye placed a hand on her elbow.

Weller bit her lip. "What kind of car did Simone arrive in?"

"She was driven here. Black Lincoln Town Car. The standard airport shuttle rental variety." Jye looked expectantly at her.

Weller continued to brood in silence.

†

RobO was happily burbling ideas at Shay as he sat on a metal stool at the galley kitchen's island block. He ran his hands repeatedly through his thinning blond hair and rubbed his stubbly chin while his skulking sister opened and slammed closed random kitchen cabinets. He wasn't sure what had gone wrong in the studio, but he knew it was nothing to do with the quality of his and Simone's playback. He thought they had nailed it this time.

Shay fumed though, so he fidgeted. He recognized Shay's mood as a jealous anger, but damned if he could figure out if Shay was jealous and angry with him, Weller, or Simone. The air between the guard and the model in the studio definitely crackled and he wished Fallow was around to wager odds on whether a mattress smack down or a catfight was more likely between the two women. He saw Weller and Jye looking blank and oblivious near the doorway beside him.

Shay finally settled into pouring herself a glass of the vanilla soy milk and made an effort to smile.

RobO accepted her half-hearted attempt at encouragement. "What do you think about adding a bit of vibrato to my voice in the last chorus of the second song?" He waited. She stared out the small kitchen window and contemplated his question.

Weller said, "I'm going to go see Detective James. I should be back before Beni gets here for the assessment briefing. Jye, you've got point alone on Shay and RobO until then."

"Got it like Gorilla glue, El Jefe," Jye replied.

Weller gave RobO a brief smile as she walked out but didn't glance toward his sister.

Several minutes later, Shay pulled her gaze back into the kitchen and frowned. "Where the fuck did Addy go?" she barked.

RobO grimaced and shot Jye an apologetic look.

Jye gave him a quick conciliatory wink.

"On an errand." RobO retreated out the door leaving his frustrated sister to herself.

Shay looked up at Jye, thinking to ask the tall square-shouldered guard directly what Weller planned, but convinced herself that it would be a waste of time. He would just give some calm, reasonable answer that totally made sense and yet scared the hell out of her. She loved and hated having Addy's constant shadow at hand.

Chapter Fifteen

Blue-Blooded Counsel and Enlightenment

Inside the gray and white, square, glassed building that Chicago's District Five detectives called home on 111th street, Weller stared out a conference room window at the concrete prairies of Chicago's South Side.

Detective James cleared his throat. "Agent Weller?"

Weller turned around to face Detective James and found him to be an attractive man of average height with thinning salt-and-pepper hair and brown eyes. He looked a bit tired but seemed in good spirits. He smiled.

"Actually, I'm not an agent anymore. I've gone into the private sector. Please just call me Addy." Weller shook his hand.

"Beni mentioned you were heading the personal protection team he hired and that you had DSS experience. I wasn't sure if you were retired, moonlighting, or what."

The detective left his postulations hanging open and

Weller recognized the casual approach to interrogation. "Neither. I decided to leave on my own volition."

"Hmm. And, give up that federal pension, huh? This private sector work must be very lucrative."

"It has its perks." Weller tried not to think of how great Shay looked playing her guitar.

"Well anyway, you have new information?" Detective James pulled out a battered office chair and sat at the conference table.

"Yesterday, while we were out, a black Ford F150 came very close to tagging Shay and Iva near Navy Pier. It could have been accidental, but it didn't feel that way. It felt like a taunt. The driver was male, but I couldn't get any descriptive features or a license plate number."

"You were out alone with them?" James gave her a look of disbelief.

Weller swallowed. "Yes. Against all advice, my client insisted on it that way, or threatened to leave with no security. Short of violating her personal freedoms by duct taping her to a chair in her home, there is only so far I can go in forcing her to follow my recommended precautions."

"I see." James nodded and the wrinkles at the corners of his mouth momentarily grew deeper.

"Also, did you see anything about that eighteen-wheeler turnover on I-94 yesterday?" Weller asked.

"I heard about it on the traffic report. Lost a bulldozer on the freeway and blocked traffic for hours."

"Yeah. The bulldozer missed smacking our car by a

few feet. Again, it could be an accident."

"But it doesn't feel that way?" James concluded.

"No, it doesn't. The eighteen-wheeler was in good shape, the driver was driving reasonably, and the tires didn't look shoddy. The left front wheel blew as if on cue, sending him over and into our lane and putting the weight of the load all leaning toward us in just the right space to flatten us at expected speeds."

James seemed to be searching her face.

Weller looked back at him, polite and collected, but serious. "We have completed an overall security assessment and made some modifications to the grounds of the Greenaura's property. I have also prepared a list of recommended precautions for Shay Greenaura. None of this is directly related to your work on the investigative side and I wouldn't want to interfere with the investigation in any way. I'd still like to leave you a copy of the recommendations and changes we've made. There is some chance this knowledge will prove useful to you later. I believe there will be further attempts at drawing Shay out, and maybe more attempts to hurt her, her family, or band members. From what Beni has told me, I'm guessing you believe there will be future threats too." She handed James a green folder.

James, pulling it in front of him, laid his hands on top of its closed face. "Yes. I do think things will escalate until we catch the perp. You will be there to guard the Greenauras. Right?"

"I don't know. Shay Greenaura would only agree to

contract through to today initially. Of course, one of my recommendations is to keep our services or acquire equivalent protection services from another qualified vendor of their choice." Weller took a seat across from him at the table.

"I'm sure you will be chosen."

The image of Shay's furrowed brow and the displeased curl of her lips as Weller last saw her came to mind. "I hope so, but I wouldn't make that assumption. Regardless, I will keep you informed about what happens and what precautions I know they choose to implement."

"Why?" James asked.

Weller smiled knowing he didn't really need it explained. He just wanted to hear her motivations and intentions articulated. "I want my client protected until her life returns to normal, and I know her life can't really return to normal until we somehow eliminate the source of the threat. Preferably by arresting and prosecuting him in short order. Some of the precautions taken in the meantime might cause him to alter his behavior and make it more difficult for you to obtain information or evidence. Hopefully, if you are at least aware of what we are doing, you know what you might expect and what you might want to look for in any given situation related to the Greenauras."

"I appreciate it. Are you this detailed with every client?" James asked.

"Yes."

"You strike me as someone who doesn't accept failure

very well, Addy."

"No, I don't. Too many failures are completely preventable with a little effort and education."

James' eyes went a little glossy for a moment and the thumb of his right hand tapped out a few measures on the top of the green folder where it still rested closed on the table. After several minutes, James eyes refocused and he looked directly at Weller.

"I don't think the car bombing and my rape-murder cases are related. I think there are two threats, but I can't say anyone else here does. I'd like to think I'm wrong and that the perp just decided to terrorize Shay by threatening her family. That way he could get off on destroying her life and having that kind of power and control over her. Sort of prolong his high so to speak. What if I'm right though? If these are two distinct threats, then I think that Shay Greenaura needs a hell of a lot more protection and luck than she would if it were just the one threat source. I advise you to find a way to get the Greenauras to honor your recommendations. Educate them for me. Otherwise, I don't know. We've got a big case load, and whatever I can manage to work enough overtime to find probably won't be soon enough to protect them from one threat let alone two. I think you have to educate them on what they need, and why they need it, or someone will get hurt."

"Any further advice?" Weller asked.

"Try keeping her away from crowds. Most of the rape-murder victims were found after large gatherings or concerts, and the car bomb went off during one of her concerts. Either the crowds get him off or they just provide him with the right opportunity."

"Thanks. I'll try, but I doubt she'll give up many, if any, of her performances and events. It's her job, but it also seems to be her obsession."

James nodded. "So really, Addy, how's the private sector treating you? I can't say I'm not tempted, but once in blue always in blue. You know? I'm not sure I could give up the family that comes with this shield."

Weller gave a half shrug. "It's fine. The good, the bad, and the ugly, they follow you everywhere—the way you classify them just shifts around."

"Better pay though?" James rose to escort her back to the front door.

Weller met his gaze, shrugged again, gave a small smile, and then a discreet nod as she passed by him.

James laughed. "I'll see you around, Addy. Stay warm."

"Yeah, you too."

†

"What's with Weller?" Beni asked as they all waited for her to return.

Syl sat beside him on the overstuffed sofa and folded her thin hands in her lap.

Reyna shrugged. "Her wife died."

"Her wife? Weller's gay?" Beni's eyes went wide.

"Yeah." Reyna shrugged again.

"Are you?" Beni asked.

"Me? No. I love my teddy bear of a husband."

"You're married?" Syl spoke so quietly that it was difficult to tell it was a question.

"Yeah. Fifteen years. Weller introduced us at a bar in Annapolis. Jerome is a sub mechanic," Reyna replied.

"You're Navy?" Beni asked.

"I'm an Annapolis graduate. Weller and I were in the same class and we both became Navy security specialists for our whole stints. Then we went civilian with the Diplomatic Security Service after our five years of required active duty after school."

"And you left the Diplomatic Security Service because Brayson was killed?" Beni asked.

"Sort of. Weller's wife had leukemia, so she took FMLA for six weeks. She was Brayson's security lead when she went out on leave. When she came back, after Elle died, Weller was still on Brayson's team, but there was a new lead. The new lead took fewer precautions and Weller's objections didn't change his mind before disaster took advantage of the lightened security."

Beni scratched behind his left ear. "What happened?"

Reyna frowned and shifted her weight from her left foot to her right. "Brayson had a meeting with a consulate in a brownstone in New York City. Weller would have never let the meeting happen in the front room of the old house, but the new lead, Cainen, saw no harm in it since Brayson's location and the meeting weren't publicized. A car slammed into the brownstone and then blew up. The driver was someone who went by that address on the way to work every day. He turned in front of the brownstone and a small explosive device took out his brakes and power steering just in time to run into the house. A second explosive device was remotely triggered once the car was in the house. Weller and I were with Brayson's car in back."

"They blamed you?" Beni guessed.

"No, Weller felt responsible. The service blamed a crazy homegrown terrorist organization and ruled it a one-time event directed specifically at Brayson because of her prior talks with the Israeli consulate. Cainen moved to the Secret Service and the vice president's protection team. Weller insisted it was a professional hit, but no one agreed and wouldn't take any of the extra precautions or keep the investigation open like she suggested."

"Weller felt responsible?" Beni voiced his empathy.

"We were, in a way. But, the service wouldn't listen to us about how to fix it, so Weller left and started Vigiles Security Services. I followed. We hired some disgruntled tech gurus from the last NSA layoffs to run the DC office and handle the information systems and background investigations. We hired Drew and two others from the Pennsylvania State Troopers office, off the governor's security team when he didn't win reelection two years ago. Then we got Jye and another crack-shot youth from the

Metropolitan police department when the new mayor appointed a new chief last year. Seems there are a lot of disgruntled and disenchanted security experts of all varieties out there. People who really want to protect and serve at a superior level. Weller listens to all of us. Lets us design our own tools, uses our talents, and makes sure we have meaningful work. We all call her the Boss, or El Jefe." Reyna offered Beni a smile.

"El Jefe and behind her back we call her the mama bear. It's good to be one of the mama bear's cubs and very bad to fuck with any of the mama bear's cubs," Drew interjected as he entered the room again.

"She doesn't like to make mistakes, does she?" Beni asked.

"Actually, I think she is okay with making a mistake once, but she isn't any good at cutting herself any slack in getting that mistake fixed forever more," Reyna answered.

"We all make mistakes. Some aren't our fault, some can't be controlled anyway, and some just can't be fixed," Beni said.

"Tell that to Shay. Ain't no way Weller is going to cut herself slack on anything, even if a client is completely forgiving." Drew huffed a short breath out his broad nose.

"Shay knows. Shay's made those kinds of mistakes." Syl rolled her eyes.

"What do you mean?" Reyna asked.

"Iva's father," Beni intoned lowly.

"Mitch 'The Doodle' Dane," Syl said, with a wry

smile.

"The Doodle? Aside from the goofy name, what about him was a mistake?" Reyna asked.

"He is a guitar doodling nutball. A gifted musician with serious issues." Beni gestured his finger in a circular motion at his temple. "A loose screw."

"A loose cannon," Syl added.

"Is he violent?" Reyna asked.

"Sure, when he is drunk. Just like RobO and Shay's daddy." Syl finished her statement with a puff of air before clearing her bangs away from her eyes.

"But wait, I thought Shay has always been a lesbian." Reyna tilted her head to one side. "Right?"

Beni raised one hand and waggled it in the classic so-so gesture. "She is usually attracted to tall, dark, cynical, and virulent women of questionable character."

"Like Simone?" Drew asked.

"Well, yeah, but I don't think there is anything going on there," Beni answered.

"Not yet. But how does Mitch fit?" Reyna rubbed a thumb over her chin.

"Mitch is sort of the barely masculine version of that type. Long brown wavy hair, rail thin, interesting scars, smart, charming, a talented guitarist, and totally unpredictable. I guess she thought it would be different if it were a guy. She wanted stability. RobO did too. They had enough chaos as kids," Syl explained.

"So this Mitch, he holds a grudge? Enough to kill his

own kid?" Reyna inquired.

Syl looked nervous and said, "I hope not."

"Probably," admitted Beni, "but Mitch isn't the car bomb type. That would require too much planning. He is more likely to slap someone to death in the heat of the moment."

Chapter Sixteen

The Security Assessment Meeting

Shay thought over everything Beni had told her in the last hour. "Addy was married to a woman?"

Smiling his usual benevolent smile, Beni's dark eyes twinkled. "Yes, but I fail to see how that is relevant."

"Really? I bet you do, you old shyster lawyer. But, I'll tell you anyway. I've made an ass of myself assuming Addy and her team couldn't possibly approve of my sexual orientation."

"I wouldn't exactly say that you've made an ass out of yourself, my dear. At least not because of that assumption."

"Hmm. I won't ask what assumptions have made me an ass."

"Yes. That is irrelevant for this meeting."

"So your point, right now, is that you think I should retain Vigiles Security Services for as long as possible in whatever capacity they recommend? Carte blanche, assuming they name a price we can afford?"

"I would if it were me."

"That's your advice as a lawyer, as our manager, or as a friend?" Shay sat in an old wooden library chair at the trestle table with peeling paint they had salvaged from the convent dining hall.

"All of the above, Shay. What are you unsure about? I'll make a list like a good lawyer and we'll make Weller clarify all the details."

"You trust them? You trust her?"

"I do. Do you?"

"I just don't know why they bother. I don't understand why she really does this. I'm not some important diplomat and the fate of the nation doesn't depend on anything I will ever accomplish. I don't want to be some egotistical, rock-star snob who thinks she needs a staff full of paid devotion." Shay bounced her left leg up and down and chewed on her fingernails.

"First off, they are probably motivated to do this by many things, in addition to the pay. Second, the threat to your life is very real right now. Third, what motivates you? Is their motivation important so long as they can be trusted to do their best to protect you and your family?"

"Fair enough, I guess." Shay watched the door for Addy's return. She knew that Addy had to be somewhere in the building and that she and Reyna had probably already discussed the assessment results with Drew and Jye.

"While I know you don't like the reminder I also

think you have to be more realistic about this, Shay. You are reaching a point in your career where you have to depend on some real, trained, and paid staff if you want to have the time and energy to pursue more projects, to reach more audiences, and all that jazz." Beni lifted both hands up and out in a "don't-you-see" gesture and his eyes bugged out a bit.

Shay sulked, but didn't bother to refute the point this time. "But do they really have to intimidate Simone or any of the other artists and engineers around here?"

Beni scribbled the word "intimidation" with a question mark on his legal pad and signaled Shay to continue.

Shay debated what else she really needed to know, but the rest of her questions seemed either too emotional, irrelevant, or at least too obvious.

Beni raised his eyebrows.

Shay shrugged.

"Any requests?" Beni prompted.

At that moment, Addy silently walked into the room carrying a tablet computer.

Beni smiled. "Hello."

Shay made silent eye contact and noticed that Addy was wearing her charcoal suit and pristine white oxford again. Her long dark hair was neatly French-braided and her eyes were like black coffee, offering Shay a rueful smile.

Shay shoved one hand through her own unruly curls and mirrored Weller's smile.

"Hi," Weller offered a general greeting.

"Hi," Shay replied.

Silence stretched a little bit and then Beni cleared his throat, "Um. I could be in China for all you two seem to notice. Am I needed here?"

Addy's voice was warm and inclusive. "Good evening, Mr. Goodman. Thank you for being here." Her eyes never left Shay's.

"Hello," Beni bellowed.

His sudden boisterousness caught Shay off guard.

Addy's gaze did turn to him then. "I apologize if I am late. I thought we were meeting at seven?"

"You're right. I came by early to take care of some other business for the band," Beni confirmed.

"Ah. Well, I'm ready if you both are?" Addy looked to Shay.

"Shoot...actually, no don't shoot. Keep the gun in its little nest inside that suit, but go ahead and tell us what you've found." Shay slid her glance briefly sideways and focused on not blushing outright.

Beni loosened his trademark lavender tie and clasped his hands on the table in front of him before leaning back to listen.

"Reyna will bring in two hard copies of our security assessment report when we're done here. I will leave those in your possession," Addy looked at Beni, "and we will also leave an outline of our security procedures and training materials with Duval for future reference."

"You've trained Duval?" Beni asked.

"Some, yes, and Sonny, on the basic security procedures for monitoring the property and what to look for in terms of security maintenance. In summary, our assessment found that initially anyone could access anywhere on the property in a matter of minutes without creating any alarm, leaving a very high risk level for everyone who lives here and all visitors. It is similar to a public bus station. We have implemented several precautions over the week that significantly reduce risk levels for Syl and Iva in particular, but also for the rest of the band in the dormitory and living spaces. We have put in place some protections that at least minimize the risk of surprise within the church. We have several recommendations that will reduce the overall risk level for everyone here to something more comparable to a professional office building."

Shay was startled. "Like an office building?"

"She just means the same kind of risk an average Joe would face going to work in a standard office," Beni interjected.

Shay puffed a stream of air upwards at a curl falling into her sight line and settled back.

"As for the precautions we have already implemented." Addy tapped the tablet and paused to consult a few screens. "There is the fenced in dormitory parking lot, locks for every window, dead bolts and lock bars for every external door to the dormitory, and one-way push bar locks on all the fire doors in the church. We installed water and concrete barriers that force all traffic to flow in through the front of the church or up the drive to your gated lot. In addition, there is a cellular alarm system for the dormitory and the basic, wireless, outdoor video monitoring system with the monitor in the kitchen."

Addy looked up at Shay. "Any questions about any of that stuff?"

"The video system records?" Beni inquired.

"No, it is just a monitoring system. We have arranged for a more complex video security with recording and remote connectivity to be installed if you approve. We do recommend using both systems."

"What other recommendations do you have?" Shay looked into Addy's dark eyes. She wanted to reach across the table and grab Addy's hands, to see if she could rattle this professional persona. She wasn't entirely sure that wouldn't get her own hands reflexively stabbed.

"All of these are pending your approval and I can review each one by cost with options." Addy again tapped the tablet. "We have also arranged to have the entire property fenced in and automatic gate openers installed for each drive entrance. We do recommend that you keep all but the two we have open now completely locked to the public for the time being."

Shay's chest felt a little hollowed out and her head felt heavy with the information. She nodded when Addy glanced up at her.

"If both the fence and the advanced video system are

approved, then we also recommend installing two cameras at each gate and in the church parking lot. We also recommend hiring a basic business security service to provide at least one security guard for the church every day the studios are open. Ideally, we would install another monitoring station and security guard for the video system somewhere in the church. We recommend hiring a full-time receptionist for the studio, but I'm guessing you are headed that way anyway?"

Shay nodded again. "And, eventually, we will hire a studio manager who can keep the place running for other artists even when we're out touring."

"Good." Addy continued, "The remaining two recommendations are a little costlier…"

"We will entertain them all for now," Beni assured her.

Addy looked at Beni for a long moment and Shay could visibly read the plea for assistance in her expression before she plunged on. "Since things are still under a fair amount of renovation, it would be a good time to think about adding a safe room to the church and another to the dormitory. We can help you design them to get as much safety function out of them as you care to budget. We minimally recommend a room with enough structural reinforcement to serve as a tornado shelter, some steel plating to resist common firearm calibers, and an internally locking, solid-core door, with reinforced hinges and strike plates, to resist tire iron battering and the like."

Addy paused for a breath and then filled the silence in

a hurry. “And, finally, we recommend you retain personal protection services, with us or another comparable vendor, for the family, and potentially expandable to the band, at least until the bomber has been arrested. From that point, we recommend hiring a small but permanent staff of security guards from a local service to travel with the band and help manage crowd control and other typical security tasks. I don’t believe you’ll need to continue such intense close protection permanently, but I do believe it is worthwhile to do so right now and we would like to fulfill that role.”

Beni looked at Shay. Shay let the room go quiet for several moments. She studied Addy.

Addy turned off the tablet, sat up straight, and placed her hands in her lap.

“You don’t talk up your services much, and you haven’t made any supportive arguments mentioning your past successes. Like say, I dunno, saving our lives twice already? Don’t you want to throw those in?” Shay placed both hands face down on the table in front of her, taking up some of the space between herself and Addy as if she could close this renewed gap of formality.

Addy cleared her throat and then, somewhat hoarsely, offered, “Talk is cheap, and what is past is past. I’m here to explain what we want to do to help protect you from this point on.”

“And I’m ready to accept your recommendations and your protection.” Shay watched Addy’s face register surprise at such an easy consent. “Just as soon as you are ready to accept my gratitude for saving my daughter's life, not once, but twice, personally, in one day," Shay finished.

Addy met her eyes. "It wasn't…"

"Damn it, Addy, no! This is not the deal. We either both gracefully accept this now or we both fitfully and rudely decline now. I offer you my gratitude and if you accept then I accept your protection." Shay smacked her hand down on the trestle table's top.

"I gracefully accept your gratitude, Shay Greenaura. You are welcome." A wry smile raised one corner of Addy's lips. She leaned back in her chair and crossed her arms.

"Well, if that isn't something. Thank holy heaven and motherfucking *yeehaw*. The mighty Addison Weller might be human after all." Shay threw both hands up in the air like a born-again Christian at a southern revival.

"I thought you said graceful acceptance," Weller deadpanned.

Shay grinned like a mad woman and cocked a mock glare at Weller. "Who said this wasn't graceful? Right, Beni?"

Beni laughed. "The most graceful negotiation I've participated in today anyway."

Chapter Seventeen

Thanksgiving

"Arctic ninja space monkeys fly from the butt of a universal turtle." Shay spoke from the cold iron bench beside the church studio's external fire door.

"Excuse me?" Weller turned toward Shay, suspecting seizures.

"Oh, sorry, just thinking up some completely ridiculous names for a parody album a friend wants to do." Shay blushed.

"Might be a bit long." Weller gazed at the yard around them again.

"Yeah, you're right. But it beats blank stupidity. I've got to suggest something." Shay nibbled a sharp edge off her thumbnail.

Weller sat down on the bench next to Shay.

"Whoa, Madame Weller. Not that I'm complaining since your body heat does add warmth to this cold bench, but are you professionally allowed to sit so close?"

Weller smirked. "Sure. I can even verbally interact with you long enough to criticize your album name choices."

"Hmm. There is that." Shay scooted closer to Weller until they were hip to hip on the bench. "So how about just Arctic Ninja Space Monkeys?"

Weller did enjoy the increased warmth of Shay near her, and the smell of her patchouli and mint shampoo. "I don't know. I kind of like the title Blank Stupidity."

Shay sat up straighter and smacked a hand down on Weller's knee. "Oh, wow, hey, that might be something. What about 'Blank Stupidity Knows no Whores'?"

Weller tensed up and glanced down at Shay's hand still on her knee. "Uh, okay."

Shay turned to Weller. "Great. Thanks. I can play with that idea." She gave Weller a warm peck on the cheek before standing and bolting for the studio door.

Weller's lips gave a small twitch and she placed a hand on her cheek giving it a little rub. She noticed she was alone on the bench and cast one more look around before getting up to follow Shay into the studios.

†

"I'm gonna go over to the church and get some songwriting time in." Shay pushed back from the dining table.

RobO cleared his throat and fixed Shay with a fatherly

glare.

Shay pantomimed the surly shrug of a teenager whose parent reminded her to take out the trash.

RobO tilted his head toward Syl.

"Thank you for dinner, Syl. I really liked the eggplant pecan curry," Shay offered.

Syl's thin face and mild brown eyes looked up at Shay in surprise. "You did?"

"For sure. It was great. Thanks for making extra for us," Fallow announced from the end of the table.

"Yeah, I would never have suspected eggplant could taste that good," Drew seconded the praise.

Syl's focus seemed to remain on Shay so she gave her a smile. "Really, Syl, that one is a keeper."

Syl smiled too and confessed, "It came out of that Molly Katzen cookbook I found at the Salvation Army."

"You're very sweet to look for recipes to feed me. Thank you, Syl. You're the best," Shay encouraged her spindly, less-than-confident sister-in-law.

Syl took on a healthy glow. "You're welcome. I like taking care of you guys."

Jane stood, picked up the empty serving platter, and started stacking up finished plates. "We can't say we don't like being taken care of either, Syl. I'll help with the dishes."

Shay looked to RobO again.

RobO winked and gestured with his head toward the door. "Go play songbird."

Shay paused in the hall until Addy joined her.

They crossed the yard to the church side by side in the cold dark night.

Shay paused for a second and tossed her head back to peer at the sky. “I can’t help but try to spot a star luminescing through our city glare.”

Silent, Addy paused beside her.

Shay listened to the city sounds traveling from great distances all around them in the cold air. “Not that we don’t all have much better lives now, but sometimes I miss the simplicity we had in the early days.”

Weller noticed Shay’s pale delicate neck, extended in the darkness, and the fine flutter of her lashes against the cold. With Shay’s face tilted up, Weller found herself admiring the singer’s impish nose and heart-shaped chin.

Shay’s eyes closed and the singing voice that emanated from her small body didn’t seem feasible to Weller. Shay’s voice carried the words in a rich raspy contralto, “I would defy all, all but you. You see through to what is most true. All I can say is stay, stay with me. Stay with me though I defy it, though I deny it. You, I need to walk with me.”

Shay’s articulation of the tune was so different, so much more like a lament, that it took Weller until the last line to recognize the cheery old gospel song.

Shay’s eyes fluttered open and she seemed to realize Weller still waited nearby. “Sorry.”

“No worries.” Weller swallowed. “That was beautiful.”

"Let's go inside and I can try this stuff out inside, where you'll be warm." Shay continued walking toward the studio.

Weller quickened her step and held the door open as she reached it a step ahead of Shay.

They walked down the hall toward one of the smaller studios together. "I'm going to need to go out on my own for ten days, starting Tuesday. At least, I was supposed to do so, to do several promotional and charity gigs for a solo blues project I started months ago." Shay glanced at Weller.

"Okay. Will you use the bus?" Weller was glad Shay at least tried to consult her for her thoughts on security ahead of time now.

Shay's eyes seemed to search her face for something further, but Weller was careful to show nothing but courteous expectancy.

"Yes, and we'll need to cover a lot of miles, so I planned on taking both Duval and Sonny to drive." Shay pushed through the soundproofed second door into the studio.

"Then we should talk through a few things so we can prepare some precautions before we split the protection team."

Shay sighed. "Fine, like what?"

"I'm not sure yet. Tell me about you and RobO."

"What, you don't have a file? You don't know everything about me and everyone around here?" Shay perched on the edge of a concert stool.

"I have files of facts that tell me nothing about what you all think or why," Weller clarified.

"They're my only family and I'm theirs."

"RobO raised you?" Weller pulled up a stool and perched nearly shoulder-to-shoulder with Shay.

Shay stared off silently into the distance for a while. "Sort of. He was barely eighteen when our mother died and he could have been my legal guardian. He didn't really have a place to live, or clothes, or food, or any way to take care of himself, let alone an undersized awkward twelve-year-old. I went into a foster home. RobO visited. My foster parents weren't very suitable but they managed to fool the social worker during reviews. They used me as a drug runner. It wasn't as bad as it sounds, not at first. I didn't know what I had or that it would get anyone in trouble. But, one night, I came back with the same package I'd left with and no cash. The dealer didn't want it. My foster father lost his shit and beat the crap out of me. He was in the process of raping me the second time when his wife came home and they got into a fight. The neighbors eventually called the police, but when the cops showed up my foster parents decided to unify. The officers didn't believe a word I said, just like my CPS case manager never believed it. After three years in their house, RobO was able to get me out. He had saved enough from working two jobs waiting tables during the day and singing in different bars at night to rent an efficiency and feed us ramen."

Weller said nothing, waiting to see if there was more

that Shay would want to add. Shay looked up, Weller could see her holding back small tears as the edges of her nose and ears pinkened. Weller pulled out a white handkerchief and held it out to her.

Shay waved it off and used the cuffs of her sweater to dab at her eyes. “Not your usual class of client, huh?”

“Yeah, you’re unique, in more ways than one, but that doesn’t change anything. You have a legitimate need right now for the kind of security services we can and will provide.” Weller stuffed the handkerchief back into her pocket.

“I have a legitimate need to not feel so emotionally exposed. What about you, Addy? Dish a little dirt, huh? Who raised you?”

“I had a pretty boring and normal childhood. My parents raised me. For most of my childhood, we lived in the same house in Dallas that they still live in today. My mom was a charge nurse and my dad was an electrical engineer. I have two brothers, one older and one younger. We’re all two years apart. They both grew up to be doctors. A podiatrist and a pediatrician. About the darkest secret we’ve got is my mom’s dad. He worked for the CIA in the Philippines for twenty years and nobody knows exactly what he did there. By the time I knew him he was a fishing guide in South Texas and taught an occasional martial arts class. He taught me Eskrima style fighting and how to fish, and strangely enough, is still one of my best friends.”

Shay gave Weller a look of mild disbelief.

"What?" Weller smiled.

Her voice laced with laconic sarcasm, Shay cajoled, "No show dog? No white picket fence?"

"Hmm. No, no dog, so no fence. But I am the black sheep of the family," Weller offered.

"Oh yeah?" Shay perked up.

"Yeah, I'm the only one in what my parents call a 'violent and dangerous' occupation and the only one of their children who doesn't live within a twenty-mile radius of them." Weller shrugged.

"Shit. Never mind, Polly Perfect. I wasn't looking for reasons to suspect you're flawless." Shay patted the top of Weller's thigh twice.

Curiosity creased Weller's brow. "Perfect?"

"Logical, prepared, decisive, reasonable, independent...from near birth. Oh, and of course surrounded by other immaculate over-achievers who couldn't mime a shameful moment if their lives depended on it." Shay picked up her Martin acoustic guitar and started tuning it with a slightly sad smile.

†

"Why are you still here? Why are you still the protection lead, Weller? You saved their lives, even if it wasn't an assassination attempt. We both know in our little bumbling bellies it was, but even if it wasn't, by your own policies you should have relinquished the lead and traded out. So why haven't you?" Reyna ruffled around inside her duffel bag in the closet of their shared room.

Weller sat on the edge of her bed, shrugged, and then inspected the condition of her fingernails. "I don't trust this contract or this situation. I don't want to leave anyone else responsible for a mess I created in the first place."

"So you don't think you're too attached to Shay after saving her life, and you don't think you're too involved in this because of the potential Brayson connection?" Reyna stood in front of Weller.

Weller stared at Reyna's black boots in front of her and said nothing.

"You're too close to this Weller. You've talked more with Shay every day than you have with me, your own best friend, on any given day since Elle died."

Placing her hands in her lap, Weller looked up. "I'm still here and I'm staying in lead."

Reyna frowned and her brown eyes softened. "Weller, I'm telling you, Shay has some issues."

"I know, Reyna. We'll look into Mitch Dane."

"Of course, we will. But, it's more than that. This woman…"

Weller cut her off, "Reyna, I don't care."

"But…"

Weller leveled a heated glare at Reyna. "I. Don't. Care."

Reyna took a step back and put her hands on her hips. "You don't care?" Her voice rose an octave at the end of her question, pinging a shrill note of disbelief. “Great. That’s some thanks I get for trying to be the voice of reason here.”

The room seemed suddenly impossibly small to Weller. She shook her head. “I can’t care. You know that.”

“I know you believe you can turn off your emotions, but mark my words, Weller, I don’t believe anyone can do that. I think you’re lying to yourself. We have to care to protect.” Reyna stalked out with a huff.

Chapter Eighteen

Down and Dirty Blues

Tossing the information Reyna had sent her earlier about Mitch Dane out of her head, Weller reviewed the situation at hand one more time. She knew Duval and Sonny were standing at opposing ends of the bus, scanning the area just like she had taught them. She was sure that Jye still stood at the back door of the Welter Water Club and Speakeasy. The bouncers were still busy admitting, or in some cases rejecting, folks who knocked on the door in the back of the twenty-four-hour Welter Diner. This night was by invitation only even if you knew the right Speakeasy knock. A Saint Paul police officer stood against the wall at the dead end of the bar watching over everything. He wore his hair high and tight, and even though his belly bulged over his duty belt, he had a military bearing.

According to the fire department's permit on the wall, the place had a capacity of two hundred people. Weller estimated they were nearing that maximum. She looked toward the stage.

She watched as Shay adjusted her microphone and plugged in a sparkly, pearl-white semi-hollow body, electric guitar that reminded Weller of Elvis. The Speakeasy's stage stood only a foot above the ground, but the closest table was at least four feet away from the edge of the stage. Weller felt fine about her chances of quickly neutralizing anyone who braved that gap to reach Shay. The crowd murmured and glasses clinked and jingled, some of them shining effervescent under the shifting lights as Weller scanned the room one more time.

The sound system crackled just before Shay began "Good evening, everybody. I'm Shay Greenaura. Thanks for joining me at the Welter Water Club and thanks to the Club's owner, Skye O'Neal, for hosting me and offering up fifty percent of tonight's profits to support the Future of Music Coalition."

The small crowd gave a healthy roar. Weller took a deep breath and let it go slowly. She tensed and relaxed every muscle from her neck to her calves, listening to her body for any prescient or intuitive echoes of danger. Nothing tingled.

Shay strummed a soft A-minor chord one string at a time and then cleared her throat. "I'm pleased to present an experimental new musical project tonight, just a girl and her guitar playing some down and dirty blues."

A series of encouragements and whistles echoed around the room, and before they fell silent, Shay's guitar was crying out an earnest litany of syncopated slide notes. Her voice bloomed from a low keen to a hot wail and an unexpected flock of goosebumps rose up and flew over Weller's shoulders at the sounds. In a glance, their eyes met. Shay gave a breathy growl and a grin and a warm thrill sailed south from Weller's belly button.

†

Tired but still buzzing with post-show energy, Shay paused outside the bus's toilet and watched the night highway pass by outside. She shifted her gaze toward the front of the bus and noticed Addy sitting in the captain's chair closest to the bus door. Toddling her way up the aisle of the moving bus, she flopped into the chair next to Addy and swiveled it to face her.

Addy took no visible notice and kept staring out toward the empty highway.

Shay pulled her knees up and settled her afghan tighter around her shoulders. She wiggled deeper into the seat and rested her arms on her knees and her chin on her arms.

Addy still stared absently out of the front window and Shay took the opportunity to study her profile in the dim light. A smooth wide forehead, high cheekbones, and sharp jaw did give her the angular good looks of a model. A paper-thin white scar underscored a quarter-inch on her fine left eyebrow giving her a look of calm cunning. Her perfectly proportioned nose was mostly model strait, but had a slight hitch near the bridge where a break had likely mended. It lent her a little mystery without marring her classic beauty any in Shay's eyes. Shay sighed. Her security lead was undeniably attractive, but also annoyingly concrete and staid compared to the tall, dark, artsy, and effusive types that normally heated her libido. "So, Addy, what did you think of the show?"

"The crowd was very enthusiastic. I'd say your talents were very well received."

The off-hand compliment hung in thinly heated bus air for several pregnant seconds before Shay realized why it stung. Addy hadn't even glanced at her.

"I mean, what was your opinion of the music?" For some reason, Shay wanted an all-out endorsement from the woman. When their eyes had met on occasion during the show, she could have sworn that she, her music at least, was having some very visceral effect on Addy. She thought those glances had marked the threads of understanding and affection twining tighter between them.

"First of all, as a security expert, I'm not really qualified to have a meaningful opinion."

"Sure, you are. Everyone is entitled to an opinion. It's my job as an artist to find the useful kernel of intelligence within it."

"Second, I would say I was too distracted with doing my job well to really give the music a fair assessment." Addy's face stayed bland, dull, and distant.

Shay heard herself ask in a small voice, "Are you

disappointed in me?"

Addy looked at her then, brown eyes darker than Belgian chocolate in the dimness, and raised both eyebrows. "How so?"

"About Mitch, I mean. You think that I'm the cliché rocker who slept around and that I just ended up pregnant."

"It's not for me to say. Who am I to judge your life?" Weller's voice was low and level.

"Don't you like me enough to care?" Shay was hoping to spark more emotional light in Addy's expression.

"No, the opposite. I like you too much to judge your personal choices. I don't see what you saw in him or why you'd go that route to get Iva—but there is probably more to the story than I know. Most importantly, it isn't any of my business." There was still no obvious emotion in her tone of voice.

Shay heaved a long sigh and tried again. "No, you have the whole story. I was a big ol' slut. I got Iva by accident and I was scared I couldn't give her a good home by myself. I used Mitch. I forced him into being a dad, and when I didn't like the results, I dumped his ass and had Beni get him out of Iva's life."

"It doesn't matter. I'm still not going to judge you."

Shay felt her anger spark and fire the apples of her cheeks. "Why the hell not?"

"That kind of righteousness is ugly and counterproductive. I have done things even I don't like and there are certainly things about me that people don't like.

None of that matters. It's none of my business what other people think of me and it's none of your business what other people think of you."

"Addy, don't be an idiot. I'm an entertainer. My business is what people think of me." Shay resisted the urge to add *and I want it to be my business what you think of me.*

"Is it? Or is your business just that people think of you, that they notice your music, and what it is about?" Addy's dark eyes danced in the dimness and the lines of her mouth appeared determined to argue it further.

"That's isn't my point, Addy. Your business is to give advice on security isn't it? Don't you make decisions about what is safe and how to protect someone?"

"Yes."

"So at some point you have to make judgments." Shay poked the air with one finger.

Addy simply nodded. "Yes." Her face was stern and she crossed her arms.

Shay argued, "So it is my business, my concern, that you think well of me. At least, that you think well enough of me that you feel motivated to protect me."

"That is exactly why I don't make judgments about your life. I can't be that attached or I might not be objective enough to make the right decision to keep you safe."

"Must you stand off like this from everyone?" Shay asked.

"It's my job." Addy answered.

"So what? You don't just do this because it's a job.

What motivates you to protect me besides the paycheck?"

"I've learned not to question my motives too deeply. Those motives are never as pure and well-intended as I'll convince myself they are later. I serve others because it is all that fully satisfies me."

"So you're satisfied to take a bullet for me." Shay narrowed her eyes and challenged Addy. She noticed Addy nearly rolled her eyes. "Or maybe I should be asking, would you take a bullet for me?"

Addy only frowned until lines pronounced firm tracks beside both corners of her mouth. "Yes, I would take a bullet for you."

"Why?" Shay asked and rubbed her own face with both hands. Her eyes felt gritty and even wrapped in the afghan she felt chilled.

"Because if we get to that point, where there is a bullet coming for you, I didn't do my job right. I didn't protect you the way I am trained to. The way you have paid me to. The way I promised myself I would. At that point, it is my responsibility to fix it and taking the bullet is the only chance I have to make it right and to keep you safe." The words were almost what Shay hoped to hear, but Addy's tone was still only matter-of-fact.

"So you would take a bullet for anyone you promised to protect?" Shay watched Addy's mouth.

Addy's lips stayed thin and tightly committed to their down-turn. "Yes, that is what you buy with me. That commitment is my worth."

"So it has nothing to do with me. I'm nothing special." Shay stated and waited.

Addy was silent.

"I'm not special in any way to you? Not more or less worth protecting than anyone else with a checkbook that can back your contract?" Shay heard a shrill edge creep into her tone.

Addy shook her head. "Shay, that isn't the point. I don't take contracts that don't make sense."

"Ah, so you do judge something."

"Of course, at some point we all have to make decisions. But, I don't have to make a decision about the appropriateness of your past. That is different. Only you can judge that."

In the cold, the heat of her anger made the shiver that passed down her spine feel sharp. "I'm worth more than my past, Addy. I haven't made all the right choices, but I do work hard. I'm worth caring about."

"I know. That's why I don't judge your past." Addy's voice went hoarse and a flicker of something Shay couldn't interpret passed in her eyes.

"That doesn't mean you care. You wouldn't take a bullet for me if I hadn't paid you to, would you?" Shay stood up and threw the afghan off.

Addy visibly swallowed but gave no further answer.

Shay marched off toward the back of the bus, but the soft dull words of Addy's late reply followed her. "Yes. I would take a bullet for you even if you hadn't paid us to protect you."

Shay stopped beside her bunk and admired the carpet as anger, hope, and fatigue warred in her head over the suddenly deafening hum of their wheels on the road. She turned to the bunk and pulled back the curtain, knowing she needed rest.

She glanced toward the front of the bus. As before, Addy sat watching the road. Shay resisted the urge to run back up front and crawl into her lap. She shook her head to clear it, climbed into the bunk, and curled into the fetal position instead.

Chapter Nineteen

Yuletide Gala Going

Looking at the date marker on her steel dress watch, Weller noted it was only five days before Christmas. She didn't mind so much for herself, but she had a moment's regret for scheduling a job that would keep the rest of her team away from home for the holidays. Small drifts of snow graced the edges of the blacktop road into Humboldt Park as Duval drove them toward Chicago's Institute of Puerto Rican Arts and Culture for a benefit gala. Based in the park's recently renovated stables, the Alps-themed Institute looked more like a turn-of-the-century mansion to Weller than a former home to horses. Warmly glowing windows reminded Weller of storybook winter lodges.

Duval pulled to a stop near the front doors.

Weller opened the passenger door, hopped out into the cold, her breath making steam, and then opened the back door for RobO, Shay, and Jye. A few short steps, with Weller's right hand hovering over the small of Shay's back, brought them inside.

Helping Shay out of her woolen camel trench coat at the coat check, Weller caught her first glance at the musician's dress. The broad V-neck of the forest green and gold tunic dress highlighted Shay's delicate collarbones, and the little bit of toned leg showing between the dress' hem and her boots was definitely distracting. Weller deliberately turned her head back toward the guys to watch them giving up their own coats.

RobO smoothed the lapels of his black tuxedo and then adjusted the edges of his festive black, red, and green tartan tie.

"You look great," Shay told him.

"Back at ya, kid." RobO smiled.

"Are you ready?" Shay asked.

RobO rubbed his freshly shaved cheek and gave a rueful chuckle. "Sure, why not?" He held his arm out for Shay.

Shay tucked her hand under and around RobO's arm and they strolled into the main gallery with Jye hustling slightly ahead of them and Weller trailing closely behind.

A handsome man in a double-breasted tuxedo with a ruby bolo tie that Weller recognized from her preparations as Miguel Avillo, the Institute's event manager, quickly greeted them. "Shay. RobO. Welcome and thank you so much. I can't believe your studio is providing the music totally free—and what music. I have already seen Simone and the band has already done the setup and sound check. I must tell you that no entertainment I have worked with for these charity galas has ever come totally free and on time, much less early." The corner of Miguel's eyes crinkled when he smiled and his hands moved about like eager magpies.

Shay let go of RobO's arm to give Miguel a small hug. "We are so very glad to do this. RobO and Simone were looking for more chances to practice material for their Latin American music project in front of live audiences, and we really believe in the Center for Changing Lives' model of helping this community. You know I'm all about grassroots-driven social services. I certainly couldn't have changed my own life without this kind of help and support."

Miguel cocked his head and narrowed his eyes and mock-whispered back to her, "I don't know about that, Shay. I think you would have found your own way sooner or later. I am glad that our city's fine community services made it a little easier, and perhaps have brought you into your current glory a little sooner."

Shay bobbed her head and Weller watched her blush.

RobO smiled down at his sister and squeezed her hand.

"But enough seriousness," Miguel said, "why did you not tell me that you are a vegan? Lucky for you, one of your friends saw fit to let that information out or there would not have been much for you to eat! The chef was able to change your mole chicken and chili enchilada dinner into a fava bean soup. He has modified your polenta and spinach salad to accommodate you, although I am supposed to warn you that your dessert will be simply the cranberry cumin sorbet. You will miss out on the dark chocolate plantains and sopapillas that go along. Of course, I will eat everything and tell you how divine it really is so that you can live vicariously through me." He bowed his head briefly and ended his speech with, "I am selfless like this."

A furrow appeared between Shay's eyebrows, but she still smiled sweetly. "Oh, I do appreciate it, Miguel. Thank you for going out of the way to make me anything at all. I usually just eat what I can and try not be a pest."

RobO said, "And that is why she is still a waif—even though we in fact do make enough money to actually eat these days—while the rest of us are expanding." He rubbed his belly for emphasis.

Miguel said, "No worries, my friends. We are glad you are here tonight. I must make the rounds again before the doors really open. We will seat everyone for dinner by seven. We will do the announcements and awards during dinner and then we will invite everyone back here to the main gallery for the music and dancing. I have created some green rooms for you all in the classrooms just beyond the coat check where you came inside. You will find Simone in the first one and the rest of the band in another around the corner. There is an empty room in between if you need it for anything else, my friends." Miguel gazed directly at Weller and Jye before pausing for an expectant beat.

Shay looked at a loss for a second and then started to offer an explanation, "These are our friends…"

Weller stepped forward and offered her hand directly to Miguel. "I am Addy Weller and this is my associate, Jye Huong. We are prospective investors in Shay's new recording label and we were visiting the studio when we heard about tonight's event. I hope you don't mind. I know we are not expected for dinner, but I still hope you will accept our sudden appearance and our ad-hoc donation to the Center's fund. It is such a rare opportunity for us to see one of the label's acts in action at a smaller community event, and to be able to give something ourselves to the community."

"Mr. Huong and Ms. Weller, I am charmed and pleased to meet you. Welcome. I sincerely hope you enjoy your visit." Miguel turned Weller's hand over in his and gave her the lightest of kisses on her middle knuckle.

Weller gave him a broad smile in return. Miguel nodded once before striding off to take care of his business.

Weller found RobO and Shay looking at her with their mouths slightly agape. "What?" she asked.

The siblings shrugged and shook their heads in unison. Shay said, "You're just so smooth...I mean, who knew?"

"And a good liar." RobO gave her a wide grin.

"Well, I do live in DC and I have spent a lifetime observing some of the best and worst diplomats."

"But you're really making a donation?" Shay inquired.

"Yes. One of the perks of being the boss. I can choose

our charitable contributions at will."

"Thank you," Shay replied.

Weller basked in the sudden hints of light dancing in Shay's blue eyes and for the briefest of moments, the room narrowed to contain the two of them alone.

Shay licked her lips. "Thank you for protecting us tonight, for being discreet about it, and for helping a cause we care about."

"You're very welcome," Weller rasped through the dryness tripping up her vocal chords.

"Shall we go find Simone and the band now?" RobO asked.

†

The door to the first classroom was shut, but they could all hear Simone's mezzo-soprano voice loitering through warm-up exercises behind it. A cacophony of laughter and glasses clinking flowed from one of the classrooms around the corner.

"Jye and I will go hang with the band. You girls might want privacy for girly conversations and it sounds like the band has beer," RobO suggested.

"Okay. I'll probably be just a minute. I don't want to interrupt her routine, but I should see if she needs anything." Shay watched as RobO and Jye headed further down the hall. She looked at the closed door before glancing back at Weller.

Weller reached out to open it for her, but Shay's grip

on her wrist stopped her. "Let's just knock first."

Weller nodded and dropped her hand to her side. The skin at her wrist was warm from Shay's brief grasp.

Shay let loose a long exhale and knocked firmly on the door three times.

Simone cracked open the door and poked her head out, offering Shay a large welcoming smile. "I am glad that you are here. I waited to dress until I got here, but now I could use a bit of help." Simone pulled Shay inside the room by the wrist.

Weller stepped up ready to ease in after Shay, but Simone pushed the door mostly closed behind Shay. It left only her smoldering gray eyes and artfully disheveled hair visible to Weller. "If you don't mind, it is a little private."

"I'm not looking at you." Weller put a palm on the door.

Simone turned her head and spoke to Shay in a singsong tone. "Surely you are safe alone with me at least until I am zipped into my dress?"

Shay's face appeared over Simone's arm barring the opening and she gave Weller a pleading look.

Weller bit her lip and nodded before turning to face the hall. The door shut. Weller felt the muscles in her stomach tighten and the stress tic just to the outside of her eyebrow scar start to twitch.

†

Shay felt like an utterly drab wallflower after taking one look at Simone's perfectly tantalizing hair and makeup. The model held her designer dress against her—revealing the upper and inner curves of her caramel-colored breasts. The Givenchy label showed on the inside lining of the green silk dress near the base of the zipper. Shay supposed such dresses were probably part of Simone's modeling job perks, but the price tag and tailoring were more than she would ever consider dropping on something to wear. Her own dress for the Grammy's had come from a warehouse of used bridesmaid dresses near Hoboken, New Jersey.

Simone batted her lashes. "Zip me up?"

Shay put on her big girl britches and tentatively touched the smooth fabric, tugging the one-strap-worn-over-the-shoulder aspect of it a little higher up Simone's well-muscled shoulder. She suddenly felt very sorry for RobO having to shine on stage next to Simone. The pale green of the dress accented Simone's complexion and smoky green-gray eyes. The asymmetrical hem revealed nearly all of one very long leg. Shay used one hand to smooth the fabric along the fine zipper's edges and the other to tug the zipper up carefully. She clasped the top clip, locking the edges of the fabric together unseen next to Simone's soft warm skin.

Simone did a slow demonstrative twirl and purred, "Thank you."

Her green-gray eyes bore into Shay's with an intensity that felt sensually virile, or at least left Shay feeling febrile and in need of human touch.

"And hello…" Simone whispered, stepping closer to Shay. Simone clasped Shay's shoulders and planted a steamy lingering kiss on each of her temples.

Shay swallowed deeply and tried to interpret the sudden heady flirtation for the pre-show adrenaline she knew it must be. She suspected Simone was omni-sexual and any warm body would do right now, but she couldn't see that as a reason to deflect Simone's physical advances. After all, she knew that it helped level the edges before a show sometimes and she reasoned that it would be ridiculous to reject affection from a beautiful woman.

Simone spun them both around slowly, pressed herself against Shay, and pinned Shay to the wall of the impromptu green room. She delivered a string of eager kisses down Shay's neck and collar bones.

Shay leaned into Simone, meeting the press of her body with more pressure. A slow level growl left Simone and tickled the nape of Shay's neck.

Simone pressed a long strong thigh closer in between Shay's legs. Caught against the wall like that, Shay suddenly felt too pinned.

She tried to relax into the advances again. Closing her eyes, she kissed Simone back with as much sincerity as she could muster, thinking that maybe she needed this too. It had been too long since she indulged herself like this after the fall-out and stress over Mitch. She wound her hands into the dark hair cascading down Simone's back and thought of pressing herself closer to Addy's long lithe form.

"Shit." Shay startled, realizing she was picturing Addy. She opened her eyes.

Simone's languid eyes were more gray than green looking back at her. She gave Shay a cursory assessment before inquiring in a honeyed voice, "Something wrong?"

Shay felt her face heat and stammered, "No. God, no. I just...it...now...I mean I don't think it's such a good idea." Shay straightened creating a fraction of space between the most overheated parts of her body and Simone's insistence.

Simone relinquished her hold on Shay and stepped back slowly, offering her a big lazy smile. "Oh, I understand. No problem, my dear. I can wait until a better time when we have less business to take care of."

Shay breathed relief. "Wow. Thank you for understanding."

Simone winked. "I can wait until you've gotten over your one-sided fascination with the protective goon, too."

Shay felt her eyes go wide and she shook her head back and forth dramatically, but she couldn't manage to voice any denial.

Simone gave a full-bellied chuckle. "No, no need to be embarrassed. I am tempted myself. Addison Weller is very tempting just not very reachable." Simone shrugged with an empathetic pout. "No reasons we cannot tempt each other instead, in time, I think." Simone took another step back and blew Shay a kiss over the open palm of one hand before opening the door to gesture Addy inside the room.

As Addy walked in, Shay watched Simone give a cat-who-got-the-cream smile before sashaying past Addy to go mingle with the charity's guests and contributors. She leaned back against the wall and fanned her face frantically to help dissipate the blush she felt still burning her skin.

"Everything okay?" Addy asked.

"Yes," Shay heard herself snap.

Weller's eyebrows rose inquisitively.

Shay sighed and tried again, "Everything is fine. Let's go find the guys. I need a cold beer."

As she headed for the door, Addy stopped her with the touch of one broad warm hand to her shoulder.

Shay froze in place.

Addy's hand lifted from her shoulder and brushed a stray curl out of Shay's eyes for her. Addy's warm brown eyes held only reassurance.

Shay's mouth went dry. She placed one hand on the soft lapel of Addy's fine wool jacket. Addy leaned in a bit, her eyes seemingly on Shay's lips. She could feel her heart thrumming like a bass drum down to the base of her soles.

Addy placed her hand over Shay's and for the briefest of seconds she could see Addy's expression contort before all expression closed off again. Addy swiveled toward the door, tucking Shay's hand on her arm as RobO had done earlier. "Let's go."

Shay found she could not reply. She was still reeling with the idea that they might have almost just kissed.

Addy's voice cracked beside her. "We'll go find the guitarists—they always know where to get good hooch.

Right?"

Chapter Twenty

Hurl

Suddenly awake for no reason, Shay rolled out of her warm bed to a spike of queasy discomfort. She swiped at the sweat beading her brow and made a nauseated run for the bathroom. Sinking to the honeycomb tile floor in front of the toilet, she clutched the graciously cold porcelain with both hands and threw up everything she had eaten at the gala. Thirty seconds later, she heaved again, and again, and again. The pain in her stomach and the rawness in her throat brought tears to her eyes. Chalking it up to a simple case of food poisoning, she didn't worry until her whole body began to shake and she started to hyperventilate. Stabbing pain rippled from her upper abdominal ribs to her back muscles and her vision narrowed. She placed her forehead on the cool rim of the toilet and tried to steady her breathing.

†

The alarm on Weller's smart phone chimed twice before she forced herself out of bed to do the rounds. She pulled her charcoal shawl-collar sweater on over her black tank top and sweat pants, but decided to go barefoot in hopes that the cold seeping up her legs from the wooden floor would shock her more awake and alert.

Reyna rolled over in her bunk and opened her eyes.

"Just the predawn round." Weller tucked her paddle-holstered FN 5.7 into the back of her sweat pants.

"Okay. Have fun," Reyna mumbled, closed her eyes again, and curled further under her duvet.

Weller smiled and padded quietly out of the room.

She was surprised to see a patch of light painting the floor of the hall to the family's bedrooms so she stalked closer to listen for clues. She could make out two female voices, but neither voice wore tones of panic. Leaving her weapon snoozing in its holster, she entered the hall.

Syl was standing just outside the family's bathroom holding Iva's hand.

"What's going on, ladies?" Weller gave them a smile.

Syl looked up eagerly at Weller. "Oh, good, you're here. Shay is sick. I keep telling her that we need to take her to the hospital, but she won't listen."

Something prickled the hair at the back of Weller's neck.

Iva sleepily reached her free hand toward Weller. "Addy, Momma is ick."

"Yes, little bit, she is sick, but we'll take care of her."

Weller squeezed Iva's hand.

"We will." Syl bent down to gather Iva up into her arms. "I think you and I should go back to bed for now."

"Then I can help? When I wake up?" Iva asked.

Syl looked to Weller.

"Yes. You two can help in the morning. I will take care of things until then. Good night, Syl. Good night, Iva. Sweet dreams."

"Good night." Iva placed her head on Syl's shoulder. Syl carried the child to her bedroom farther down the hall.

Weller stepped into the bathroom and found Shay on her side, curled around the toilet, with a red bath towel mostly pulled over her legs and hips. Her eyes were bloodshot and unfocused.

"The hospital might not be a bad idea," Weller suggested.

"No. I think it's just a really nasty bout of food poisoning. Anyway, I don't have anything left to throw up anymore." Shay's eyes almost focused as she looked up at Weller.

"The hospital can give you fluids to help you feel better."

Shay shook her head. "I should start getting better now. I just need rest."

"All right. Let's get you back in bed then." Weller held out her hand.

Shay pushed the red towel aside, revealing an oversized green "Chicks dig Recyclers" T-shirt. and tattered blue-green-tartan flannel boxers.

"No wonder you're cold," Weller observed.

"Didn't expect to be nestled with the tile so long." Shay remained on the black-and-white honeycomb tile floor, and her blue eyes looked very big and dark against her pale drawn face. Her blond hair was a tousled mess, but she had apparently managed to keep vomit out of her hair. Weller took that has a good sign.

Shay lifted her head from the floor and pushed herself up onto her right elbow, but seemed unable to make any further progress getting up on her own.

Weller stepped forward in the bathroom, crouched down like a catcher beside Shay, and placed an arm around Shay's back.

"Thank you," Shay said with her eyes downcast.

"No problem." Weller smoothed a ruffle of blond curls off Shay's forehead with her free hand. "Can you get up?"

Shay nodded. "Eventually. I think so."

Weller slipped her other arm under Shay's knees and stood up carefully bringing Shay off the ground into her arms. She was just small enough that Weller could manage the lift. "Is this okay?"

"Okay." Shay closed her eyes. Her face took on a green tinge.

Weller maneuvered them out of the bathroom, across the hall, and into Shay's bedroom. She placed Shay on the bed, arranged the covers over her, and then stood straight until she heard a satisfying crack in her back.

Shay struggled to stay awake, but her eyelids felt so very sandy and heavy. Weller was saying something to her, so she forced herself to focus. Weller seemed to expect some sort of answer so she sighed out one cracked word, "Thirsty."

She thought that was enough to convince Weller to leave the room, so she let her eyes drift shut and soft blackness descended.

†

"We've tried hydrating her all day. She seems to be less and less conscious every ten minutes. We're going to the ER," Weller announced.

"Shay agreed to go?" RobO looked surprised.

"Yes," Weller confirmed.

"Something is really wrong." RobO twisted his hands. His eyes went wide and wild like those of a panicked horse.

Weller squeezed his shoulder. "She is definitely not well, and I think we should take her in to see what they can do to keep it from getting any worse. We're down to brass tacks now, even if she hadn't agreed to go."

Syl appeared in the doorway with Iva on her hip.

"Which hospital?" RobO chewed on his lip.

"Stroger," Weller answered.

"She would want to go to Rush." Syl insisted. "Her primary care doctor has privileges there."

Weller shook her head. "We're going to Stroger."

Syl frowned. "Why?"

"One, I know from past experience Stroger will work with us on her security. Two, it is just better to security to do differently than expected."

"Okay." RobO nodded absently, "I'll get some shoes and come with you. I've got her power of attorney and such."

"We want to go too. Please," Syl said.

Weller nodded, knowing it was far faster and easier to go with an entourage than it would be to try to convince the worried family that the wait would be long and uncomfortable. "Okay, but we'll take two cars. Drew and Reyna will drive you and Iva, Syl. Jye and I will take RobO and Shay."

Chapter Twenty-one

Waiting Room Winks

"Catch forty winks, Weller. I've got this right now," Reyna directed.

Weller blinked.

"Seriously, you know you want us to take this in shifts and I can't sleep for shit in hospitals. We both know you can sleep anywhere—at least enough to juice back up. Yeah?" Reyna prompted her further.

"Yeah." Weller rubbed her face with both hands. "I'll be in the waiting room."

"Okay." Reyna leaned back against the hall wall.

Weller found the one waiting room without a TV. She settled in the back corner on a faux wooden bench with a nappy brocade seat. A fake Benjamin Ficus plant sat next to it. She forced herself to shut down by focusing on breathing slowly, listening to each breath as it folded in and then out into the chilly air-conditioned room. She tensed and released each muscle from the top of her scalp down to her fingertips, then down to her feet. Sleep swallowed her whole.

"Addy? Addy, love?" Elle's voice called from somewhere near.

The dreamscape swam into focus. They cuddled in an oversized plastic Adirondack chair in the rooftop garden above their apartment, watching the sunset glow behind the New York City lights. Addy tested the veracity of the dream, hoping to keep it from skidding off into an abandoned hospices scene, by squeezing Elle closer in her arms. Elle felt so solid and hummed her appreciation as she squeezed Addy back.

"Hi." Addy's heard her own voice, giddy over the feel of Elle in her arms again.

Elle gave her a quizzical look and answered, "Hi, back. Where did you just go, space cadet?"

Addy shrugged. "Everywhere. Nowhere. I miss you."

"You're holding me," Elle pointed out. "You can't miss something you have in your hands, silly." She kissed the tip of Addy's nose.

"I'm worried," Addy admitted openly. She was still pretty sure this was a dream.

Elle tilted her head and looked into Addy's eyes.

Addy knew the look was a question so she tried to explain. "I can't find peace anymore. Everything is a threat. I can't...I don't know. I don't think I'm really living anymore. I'm just surviving, Elle."

Her dusky-skinned half-Seminole wife looked tanned still, but noticeably paled. "I know, honey. I'm not sure how to help. Why are you just surviving?"

"I don't have you. I don't have you to share it all with anymore. I know I always carry your love, my love for you, and our memories—but it isn't enough." The sadness weighed heavily through Addy's shoulders.

"I know it hurts." Elle's deep golden-brown eyes sent empathy back at Addy.

"What do I do now?"

"You have to love, Addy. You need to find a way to let go and just love like you do me."

Addy could feel the tears welling in her eyes. "How? I don't remember how." Her voice cracked on the last word and she swallowed back the lump of grief growing in her throat.

"You know those days we fished out on the docks in San Antonio Bay?" Elle asked.

Addy nodded.

"Do you remember those silver fish? You know the ones your *cePoca* called 'the elusive and nearly mythical silver king'?" Elle continued.

"Tarpon." Addy supplied the fish's name and almost smiled at her wife.

"Yeah. Tarpon. You know how I caught that massive one after angling it in for hours?" Elle asked.

"Yeah." Addy did smile then. She remembered the South Texas sun warm on their skins, sea salt soft in the air, and the childishly wide grins of her wife and grandfather.

"And then, after all of that work to get it in, do you remember how you and your ce*Poca* were afraid to tell me I had to cut it loose and let it go?" Elle asked.

Addy felt her eyes starting to tear up at the lovely sound of Elle's Seminole name for her grandfather. "Yes, we were afraid to tell you. You'd worked so hard, and no one, I mean no one, ever catches those monsters around there anymore. It was killing us." Addy traced her hand over the jaw of Elle's smiling face. "But you didn't mind a bit."

"No, I didn't mind. That moment, with you and *cePoca*, wrestling that beautiful strong fish back into the water, was perfect. Watching the sunlight sparkle off his silver scales as he got his wind back and swam out toward the Gulf was every bit as wonderful as catching him in the first place."

Addy thought about it and basked in the love in Elle's eyes looking back at her.

The sounds of people talking grew louder around Addy. She sighed and gulped in a big breath of the twilight on the rooftop and Elle, knowing it would fade fast soon. "I love you," Addy told Elle.

"I know, babe. I will always know. Love each moment you're in. Love sharing it with the people you're with. Just like the day we caught and released that silver king. I'm you. I'm in your head and your heart and I blossom new each time you love anyone or anything."

"Weller?" Syl's thin hand carefully touched the sleeping guard's forearm.

Weller's eyes blinked rapidly and she sat up. "Hi, Syl. Any news?"

"Not really. They say Shay isn't as shocky, but something isn't right with her kidneys and she is still unconscious."

†

The attending physician, Dr. Merell, looked like the kind of guy who could drink cold coffee that's been sitting in the pot for five days and then come up looking ready for action. He spoke directly to RobO in the corridor outside the ICU for several minutes. Weller studied RobO's face carefully the whole time, watching it go from near panic to a frowning acceptance. Dr. Merell rolled his hands through the air a few times, emphasizing some point, and then gave RobO a square pat on the right shoulder before walking away.

RobO shuffled back to where the rest of them were waiting. "Apparently all the throwing up and such has given her a severe electrolyte imbalance, and they are worried her kidneys aren't functioning right. They're going to put her on dialysis and see how it goes from there, but the doc thinks it will take several days in the ICU before we know more. He did say that she was otherwise strong, young, and healthy. That means she has very good odds of pulling through just fine with the right sustaining care."

In the silence, Iva raised her bleary head off Reyna's shoulder. "Can I sleep with Momma?"

Weller walked over and Reyna passed the child into her arms.

Iva wrapped two chubby arms firmly around Weller's neck. "Will you take me?"

"Not tonight, love," Weller answered. "Momma feels pretty sick still, and she wants you to get good sleep tonight. Will you take Auntie Syl, Uncle RobO, Drew, and Reyna home with you and help them go to bed?"

Iva's earnest blue eyes tracked to her deflated aunt and uncle and then back to Weller. She patted Weller's back and then wiggled toward the floor. "I will, Addy. Will you watch over Momma for me while we sleep, and give her my Boo Bunny if she gets scared?"

Weller nodded solemnly.

Iva turned back to Reyna, collected the Boo Bunny from her, and offered it to Weller.

Weller accepted the Boo Bunny and cradled him in the crook of her arm like a baby. "Yes, I will, Iva."

Iva took Syl by the hand and led her toward the elevators. Drew followed them, but RobO hung back a few steps with Reyna.

Weller looked up at him.

His eyebrows drew together and he looked tired and smaller than usual. "Shay had a physical eight months ago to get a life insurance policy. I mentioned it to the doctor, because he said it was really weird for food poisoning to lead to such a severe kidney problem unless a patient has some kind of pre-existing issue or precursor for it. I've got a copy of the blood work from the insurance physical in a file at home, but I'm pretty sure she would have said something if she thought she had any sort of kidney issues."

Reyna placed a hand on his forearm. "You're probably right. Let's find the lab results from her last blood work and bring them in for the doctor to double-check."

RobO nodded and then walked out with Reyna.

Chapter Twenty-two

Since We're Here Anyway

Shay woke to find Addy reclined in the hospital room's one chair, long legs stretched out before her, and heavy shadows darkening her eyes.

"Addy, go home. Let Jye sit in if someone still has to," Shay pleaded from her bed.

"Jye is watching the hall and the nurse's station."

"Do I really need two guards watching over me while I'm in bed with hospital security all around? And you look like absolute hell," Shay said, trying to reason with her.

"Thanks, you look swell too." Addy gave her a lopsided grin.

"Aren't you glad that I'm out of the ICU and a little more with it now?"

"Yes, those were a very long and scary seven days." Addy's brown eyes were very dark with sincerity.

"I know. I missed Christmas." Shay pouted at having

missed the chance to see Iva's face full of wonder at the finery of their first Christmas in their new home.

"We can have it again here. At least you didn't miss New Year's Eve. Iva is pretty excited about the noise-makers and glitter."

"Yeah, woohoo, I get to ring in the New Year on intermittent dialysis." Shay twirled one forefinger in a circle.

Addy grinned. "Yeah, but you get to do it in your own private hospital room, and you're awake to do it."

"My point exactly. So I can help look after myself while you go get some real rest in a real bed."

Addy's eyes drifted away and, for a moment, Shay swore she could see an old hurt paling Addy's face.

"I'm not taking any more chances until you've won your way back out of here." Addy waved an arm around indicating the austere hospital room with its Pepto Bismal pink walls.

Her phrasing piqued Shay's curiosity. "What are you willing to take a chance on? I mean, what would you ever bet on blindly?"

"Blind bets are for suckers." Addy rubbed at her eyes. "I'm not betting on anything I'm not fully informed about." Silence stretched for a few seconds before Addy pulled herself up out of the chair and approached Shay's bedside. Her hands gripped the bed railing and her knuckles turned a little white.

Shay stretched a finger up to brush Weller's left hand. "What is it? What is it that is really eating you?"

"Why do you take a risk with Simone? I mean, why do you spend the extra time supporting and promoting her album? Do you really think she needs the support as a musician for the project to be successful, or are you betting she cares, I mean really cares, about you or RobO?"

Shay sucked in her bottom lip and thought about it. "Addy, I'm not really sure why. I just know you can't ever win more than you're willing to bet. I'm willing to bet everything I have, my life, for a chance to make our world a little better. A little more filled with music and laughter—a little freer to love and be loved in—and to support my family and the other artists I believe are trying to make the same kind of difference. The one thing RobO and I needed and could never find when we were kids was unconditional love. I think a whole lot of people can't find that. I think a whole lot of people don't even realize it is the one and only thing we all need, and that everyone wants it, but no one is willing to risk giving it away for free without any guarantees of getting it back. But, I think I have to give away a whole lot of it for free before I have a chance at getting it…a chance of deserving it. I'll pay for that chance with my life if I need to."

"But, Shay, you don't need to. You don't need to bleed to save the world. You don't have to die from the exhaustion of trying to give everyone else a chance to be heard or to be loved."

Shay snorted. "I don't? Are you sure? Because that's not what my whole life story indicates. It doesn't matter how wonderful we are, or how much we accomplish, or even how much we give to others…it's never been enough to get anyone I know really loved and understood."

"Shay, love isn't earned. We don't get what we deserve." Weller stared blindly forward.

"Why not?" Shay demanded.

"Love is built. I mean it is grown, and the more you share it, the bigger it gets." Addy released the bedrail and gestured a spiral growing upwards with her hands.

Shay smiled at the sight of the typically stoic woman acting so animated. "But how do you build it if not by earning it, through a thousand little social exchanges that please or help your loved ones?"

"Semantics, Ms. Greenaura, semantics. I think it is all about being willing to discover everything with someone, sharing the discoveries, building shared moments together. Good and bad moments. Moments where you don't give or get anything, you just are, and you just are together." Addy's brown eyes seemed to warm into golden tones.

"Wow. Who are you and what did you do with Addison Weller?" Shay sniffled to hide the tears prickling her eyes. She knew she wanted that in fact, she just didn't think it existed for her. She watched a blush spread across Addy's cheeks. "You must have been a fantastic wife."

Addy showed surprise. "Reyna told you?"

"Yeah, she mentioned it to RobO, Beni, and Syl, when they asked about you. I'm sorry, Addy. Is it a secret?" Shay suddenly worried Addy's distance and stoicism would slam back into place.

"Oh." Weller stared at the window. "No, it isn't a secret."

"I'm sorry, Addy. We shouldn't have been asking about your personal life, should we?" Shay guessed.

"No, it's okay, Shay. You're supposed to be curious. It could save your life."

"Oh." Shay waited.

Addy took a deep breath and rested her hands on the bedrail again. "Elle was a great wife. I learned about love because she let me discover it with her."

"What was Elle like?" Shay asked.

Weller swallowed and licked her lips. "Why do you want to know that? I mean, no one ever asks what Elle was like, only about what happened, or how I'm doing since."

"I don't know. I'm just curious, I guess. Someone you love and respect so much, well, she must be very special. I wish I could have met her." Shay picked at the edges of her hospital blanket.

"Elle was a force of nature. She took in the whole world and made it better for everyone. She had that gift of being able to make anyone feel valuable, and it showed through her art."

"She was an artist?"

"A photographer. She had an eye, a unique perspective. She could take the ugliest, meanest parts of New York City, and turn them into these frozen moments of tragic beauty. She did a lot of work with homeless shelters. She did a whole exhibit showing that there were beautiful moments in everyone's day. She would work at the shelters and talk to everyone there, have each person show her the one thing they saw that day that was most beautiful. Some of the pictures were just of the people showing her something. They'd have this amazing expression of trust and hope all over their faces, and the light would be spilling across them like holy water."

Shay startled. She knew some work like that. "Did she take a photo of a homeless veteran pointing up at the sunlight streaming through an American flag hung from a fire escape between two buildings?"

Addy tilted her head, "Yes." She smiled.

"Your wife was Elle Deere?" Shay asked.

"Yeah." Addy fixed Shay with a look of wonder. "You follow photography?"

"I'm an art junkie. Audio, visual, performance. It doesn't matter. I live for art. But honestly, I saw that photo at a charity event we played for Wounded Warriors, and I asked who the photographer was because I wanted to see more of her work." Shay remembered.

"Ah. Well, Elle was exactly like that. Brave enough to look for beauty in everyone and everything. It was contagious. It showed me that truth has many faces and it gave me a definition of love."

"I like your definition of love. Mind if I steal it for a song?" Shay asked.

"Why not? You own the conversation rights as much as I do." Addy reached out and tousled the curls at the top of

Shay's head.

Shay gave Addy a mock glare.

"What?" Addy's blank face of innocence quickly broke into a broad smile.

Shay shook her head, grinned, and weakly smacked Addy in the abs with the back of her hand.

Addy mimed a surprised "O" face.

"Thanks, Addy."

"My pleasure. Thanks for asking about Elle. It felt good to talk about who she was and the good she did."

†

Reyna entered the room to find Weller and Shay watching a National Geographic documentary about the Giant Crystal Cave. Weller looked up at Reyna immediately and smiled a hello.

"A place as beautiful as it is deadly…" Reyna mimicked the documentary and Shay looked up too.

"You've seen it?" Shay asked. She looked more like Iva's sister than her mother, bundled in the oversized VIP hospital bed.

"My husband, Jerome, is a technical cave diver. If it's about anything underwater and in the dark I've seen it," Reyna answered.

Shay still appeared pale and shaky, even though more alert. Reyna took a deep breath. "I have some things to tell you gals. Do you feel up to talking about your security,

Shay?"

"Sure. What's up?" Shay replied.

Weller cocked her head, grabbed the remote, and turned off the TV.

Reyna walked closer to Shay's bedside and cleared her throat. "First, Shay, I want you to know that you can tell me to stop talking at any time you want. While it is good for you to know and be involved with every aspect of your own security, it isn't an absolute necessity all the time. There is no shame in crying 'uncle' and telling me you're too tired, overwhelmed, confused, or preoccupied to hear or think about something right now. Okay?" Reyna made her voice level and calm, just as she knew Weller would want it.

Reyna's disclaimer was a normal part of their operating standards when dealing with emotionally overtaxed clients. It was very familiar to Weller since she and Reyna had both said it before to a dozen clients after an attack of one kind or another. But, this time, it gave Weller a strange chill along her spine and made her stomach clench.

Then it occurred to Weller, the disclaimer meant there had been an attack. Reyna was here, saying these things, because there was a real and probable threat. Weller also realized, for the first time in her career, she wanted to wrap her entire body around her client like a protective cocoon. She shook her head trying to dislodge the thought.

Reyna looked to Weller and hesitated. "Weller?"

"I'm ready. Go ahead." Weller pressed closer to the

side of Shay's bed, closing their circle tighter and enabling her to watch the door over Reyna's shoulder. She felt the weight of the FN 5.7 in its paddle holster concealed at the small of her back like a safety anchor.

"After RobO gave the blood work from your last lab report to your ICU physician, the physician advised RobO that this was probably more than food poisoning. So I started doing some investigating myself. Syl called some friends at the city health department and they couldn't find any history or indicators of salmonella or poor food preparation tactics for the venue or the caterer. I called in a favor with a friend at the CDC, and she had one of the staff microbiologists along with a health analyst from their quarantine center at the airport meet me and Miguel yesterday. They found bits of ricin powder in the kitchen. The FBI is working to source it, but they refuse to call you an intended target until they know more…" Reyna's briefing petered out slowly.

Weller stood up straighter and Reyna met her eyes. "But so far, you're the only one at any recent time in this entire city showing any symptoms that indicate exposure to it. Apparently, there isn't even a way to be sure that ricin is what led to you getting sick. The CDC folks say there isn't any chance of detecting it in your bloodstream anymore."

Weller looked at Shay.

Shay's face looked shocked. "Do you think someone tried to poison me to death by making it look like food poisoning?"

Weller's mind raced around trying to fit different

pieces and possibilities together, but it didn't really make much sense. *Poison? Why poison?*

Reyna cleared her throat again.

Weller took Shay's hand and held it lightly. "Shay, we will never know for sure, but I doubt the poisoner fully intended to poison you to death. Ricin is easy to make, but it isn't a very efficient way to kill anyone through ingestion. Usually poisoners mail you a letter full of the dust and hope you inhale enough of it to kill you. That is more effective. Sometimes they inject someone with the concentrated form of it. That works pretty expediently, too. But, the planning and coordination required to get it into your food somehow, and just your food, that indicates a lot of skill and intelligence. Someone who was that into planning something like that would have done the research to know ingesting the ricin probably wouldn't kill you. It doesn't make sense, unless someone was either toying with you for their own sick amusement or trying to manipulate you somehow."

A small crease formed between Shay's hay-colored eyebrows. "I want more protection on Iva."

"I'll bunk in her room and one of us will stay point with her at all times," Reyna replied.

Weller nodded. "We'll stick closer to Iva at all times, but I will become your constant shadow for now, Shay. And, Reyna, I want you to call our friend, Detective James, and see if he can coordinate a little extra police attention on the hospital until we can get out of here. We'll need his help, especially in watching out for car bombs."

Chapter Twenty-three

A Nearer Menace

He couldn't believe his luck. Shay Greenaura was admitted to his hospital. He felt a rush of excitement ripple through his nether regions. The urology unit was empty this time of night and he knew there were no cameras monitoring the courtesy phone there. He ducked into the building from the non-carded front entrance and waited several minutes to make sure no one was near before picking up the plastic handset with a gleeful anticipatory grin.

He settled the stethoscope around the back of his neck so that it fell below the neckline of his blue scrubs before dialing the direct extension to Shay Greenaura's room.

The phone rang three times and then her voice answered with a breathy note of curiosity. "Hello?"

He couldn't help but laugh. "I'm going to kill you, bitch. I'm going to fuck you over so hard you'll finally realize you know a real man before you die." He placed the handset back on the phone's base and walked back out the door whistling "Stairway to Heaven" with perfect pitch.

†

Shay's face was deathly white and her lower lip trembled. She hung on to the bedside phone's handset.

Weller stomach clenched. "Shay, what is it?"

Shay held the phone toward Weller. "A death threat."

Weller grabbed the phone and pressed it to her ear, but the line was already silent. She looked to the caller ID but only an internal hospital extension showed. She dialed the extension and waited until an automated greeting informed her, "You have reached the Cook County Surgical Urology Department. Our normal offices hours are . . .' before hanging up the phone.

"Shay, what did they say?"

Through tears she replied, "He said he was going to kill me. After raping me."

"He?"

"Yes. A guy's voice."

"Any accent?"

Shay shook her head vaguely. "No. I don't know. Nothing I noticed."

"Could you hear any background noises?"

Shay shook her head more firmly this time. "No."

"I'm going to step into the hall and talk to Jye before I call Detective James. I'm going to ask to have you moved to another room too. Just as a precaution. Okay?" Weller studied Shay's face carefully, but Shay only stared blankly back at her. She picked up Shay's free hand—the one without the IV taped to it—and held the smaller woman's cold slender fingers in both hands to warm them.

Shay's eyes finally met Weller's. "Okay, but you'll be just outside the door, right?"

Weller nodded. "Right. I'll be stuck to you the whole time. No one comes through that door but me right now."

Shay nodded her consent and Weller let go of her hand.

†

"Jye." Weller waved him over from his post by the nurses' station while keeping the back of her heels pressed to the closed door of Shay's room.

Jye placed a hand near his concealed weapon and walked briskly toward her. "What's up?"

"Shay just got a threatening phone call from an anonymous male. It appears he was calling from an extension within this hospital's surgical urology department."

"Shit."

"Yeah. I want you to explain to the charge nurse on duty why we need her in another room as soon as possible and ask the nurse to be sure this room is left empty for 24 hours. I don't want any new patient getting threatened or worse by mistake."

"You got it, El Jefe. I'll arrange the change and let you know when we're coming into the room to do it."

"Use our codename identification protocol from here on out. You escort every visitor or healthcare provider that intends to open that door."

"Yes, ma'am. Do you want me to update Drew and Reyna?"

Weller took a deep breath and let it out slowly. She nodded. "I'm going to call Detective James and get some officers to the Urology department. Hopefully, he'll also give us a detail on the floor."

"Copy." Jye turned smartly on one heel with his hand still near his concealed weapon and walked away in search of the charge nurse on duty.

Weller pulled out her phone and dialed the mobile phone number she had programmed in for Detective James. He answered on the second ring and Weller decided that he must be outside from the windy background noise. "James here."

"Hello, Detective, this is Addison Weller from Shay Greenaura's protection service."

"Addy, I can't imagine you have good news."

"Shay's still at Stroger Hospital and she is recovering, but we just received a threatening phone call direct to her patient room. The caller was male and the call appears to have been made from the hospital's surgical urology department on the first floor."

"You're with Ms. Greenaura, right?"

"I'm in her room and we have someone on duty at the nurses' station. I was hoping you could send some officers to investigate the source of the call."

"Done. I'll be behind them as soon as I finish here. What else?"

Weller could hear the soft scuff of something rough, like maybe his stubble, over his phone's microphone. "I'm having her room changed as soon as they can and asking them to leave it empty for twenty-four hours."

"I'll put a detail on the room for twenty-four hours then, in case he bites again, and I'll alert officers in the hospital of the situation so that they know who you are and stay sensitive to anything you might need for the next few days."

Weller smiled contentedly at the Detective's kind competence. "Thank you, Detective James."

"My pleasure. I'd love to collar this sick bastard. Anything else?" Something banged in the background.

"Just one more thing. I don't think the ricin and the phone call match. I can't tell you why exactly, but I think there are two threats."

"Angry male rapists don't usually assassinate by poison. I trust your instincts." He chuckled.

"Yeah, something like that," Weller replied. "I just wanted you to know I'm going to hire someone to trail Mitch Dane."

"Iva's father, right?"

"Yes, sir."

"Let me know if you find anything interesting then. I'll keep you posted on what I come up with in urology, and I'll let you know who the patrol leads will be at Stroger for the next few days."

"Thanks."

"Later."

"Bye." Weller heard an ambulance siren before James hung up on his end.

Chapter Twenty-four

New Year's Eve Regrets

"This is Tom O'Bannon with WGN-TV reporting live from the New Year's Eve Rock and Roll Ball in Rosemont. With a little less than two hours to go before the countdown, things are really hopping here as you can see by the crowd around me." Shay watched as the TV reporter sidled up to a middle-aged woman in a pink-sequin sheath dress and black combat boots. "This is one of the many fans waiting to get back into the overpacked Montrose Room at the Hotel Intercontinental to see the next act. What's your name?"

The woman rolled her eyes and smiled. The reporter held his microphone toward her. "Amy, and I'm here to see Black Tragedy rock this house."

Tom turned back to the camera and laughed.

Shay heaved a massive sigh and gave Weller an exasperated look.

Smiling, Weller lifted the remote and gestured at the

TV. "Do you want to watch something else?"

"Not really."

"Ah. Anything I can do?"

Shay shook her head, but Weller muted the TV anyway.

"Addy, I'm sorry."

"For what?"

"For being the reason you're not out celebrating the New Year in style." Shay's shoulders slouched and she ran a thin white hand through her blond bed-head curls.

Weller, relaxing back in her chair with her feet stretched out in front of her, asked, "Where were you supposed to be? Probably something much more structured and public than our night here at the hospital, huh?"

"We were going to play Smart Queer's New Year's Eve Musical Showcase in LA."

"Right. Beni listed it on the travel schedule for this week."

"Yeah, he said they were nice when he canceled it. We'll make it next year instead." Shay tried to keep the disappointment out of her voice.

"But what?" Weller noticed that there was a silent concern still lingering.

"But who knows if they'll bill us as a headliner again. I hate losing our momentum like that because of this." Shay gestured at her bed.

"It's just the one gig, right?"

"Yeah. So far."

"Well, the doctor said you would likely be released the day after tomorrow if the labs come back right."

"Yeah, you're right. I'll be ready to rock before we can miss another gig, huh? I should count my blessings."

Weller shrugged and clicked off the TV. "It can't hurt to count them."

In the newly darkened room, Shay admired the dim multicolored lights of the ceramic Christmas tree lamp Syl and Iva had brought to the hospital for her on Christmas day.

"Do you want me to brighten the tree lights?" Weller reached toward the little lamp's click-wheel switch.

"No, it's okay the way it is." Shay smiled at the memory of Iva carrying the little lamp in with both arms wrapped around it.

"Do you leave Iva with Syl a lot?" Weller asked.

Shay stiffened, but searching Weller's face could find no hint of recrimination in the remark. Shay nodded. "Life on the road is no life for a kid."

"And?" Weller pressed the question.

Shay cast her stare out the window and into the distance. "And. And I'm afraid Syl is a better parent."

"Why?" Curiosity marked Weller's voice.

"Syl has more patience, more focus on what is going on around Iva, and what Iva needs. Syl is devoted to RobO. She hardly speaks to the rest of us, so I know she won't let any crazy assholes slip into Iva's life."

"And you might?"

"I did."

Weller's face showed her question.

"Her father." Shay shaped the answer with a bad taste in her mouth.

"He was abusive?" Weller asked.

"In the end…and worse." Shay sighed heavily.

Weller waited out the silence hoping Shay would elaborate.

"I told him I was leaving, I was taking Iva, and that we were done," Shay explained. "I expected it to make him mad. I wanted it to make him mad. I wanted to hurt him, to take his security away from him, the same way he disappointed me. I felt cheated when he turned out to be a lousy abusive drunk, just like my mother. I realized I'd schemed and struggled to fit into a relationship with him so that I could have Iva and give Iva a real dad. He was supposed to be a better parent than me. Not a dangerous leech."

"So you made sure he couldn't see Iva or collect any support from you?"

"Yeah. I followed him one day and I got a video of him buying heroin. Enough evidence for criminal charges, but not totally unforgivable in terms of recouping any of his parental rights. But then, he went to a library and snuck into the women's restroom. I followed after a while, wondering why he'd go into the women's restroom to shoot up." Shay paused, swallowing, and scrubbing her eyes.

Weller waited.

"He was molesting a little girl. A blond, about six years old. I started screaming and hitting him, but he grabbed my chin and threw me against the sink. My head hit the porcelain and it was lights out for several minutes. He ran out before the police got there."

"But the police caught up with him?"

"Yeah, but the little girl wouldn't say anything and the physical evidence wasn't enough to arrest him. And me, being his angry wife with a concussion, I wasn't a credible witness. The heroin was also a first time offense and my video was the only proof. Beni bluffed Mitch into signing the divorce papers as I put them forth, with all of that as a threat for pressing charges, but I don't know if it really would have stuck. Any of it." Shay looked up at Weller with tears in her eyes. "I made a mistake. A big one that I couldn't fix. I made that bastard the father of my biggest treasure on this earth and then exposed her to that kind of hurt. I didn't learn from my childhood. I didn't learn enough to even avoid putting Iva in the same spot I was once in myself."

Weller stood and walked over to Shay. "But you did. You learned to spot the red flags, to question Mitch's behavior, to investigate it, and then to protect Iva as forcefully as you could once you recognized the threat."

"But I should have recognized the threat way before then." Shay's tears flowed.

"Ah, hell, Shay. Hindsight is twenty-twenty." Weller put a hand on Shay's small shoulder and gave it a soft squeeze.

"You can't say that. You think the same thing about Secretary Brayson's death, don't you?" Shay placed her hand over Weller's and sniffled.

"Maybe," Weller conceded.

Shay pulled on Weller's hand not relenting until Weller sat down beside her on the bed.

Shay leaned into her and Weller took it as a sign that Shay needed a little physical comfort. She held the distressed performer in a loose hug.

Shay wrapped her arms around Weller's ribs and leaned her head against Weller's shoulder. "Some pair of sorry sinners we are," she whispered into Weller's neck.

The warmth of Shay's breath on the exposed skin at her neck gave Weller shivers. Weller sighed, settled into holding Shay for real, and rested her chin on top of Shay's blond curls.

Chapter Twenty-five

Down Beats

Her phone buzzed on her hip and Weller plucked it up to find Detective James was calling her. "Hi. What do you know?"

"I know you're really not going to like the news that I have for you. Any of it." His voice sounded thick and tired.

"All right." Weller, already resigned to bad news encouraged him, "So shoot."

"The easy one first. The call at the hospital was made from the courtesy phone in the urology unit on the first floor. There wasn't any video camera on the phone and the entrance to that area isn't controlled, even after the department closes."

"I suspected that much. I take it no one ever showed up to the room we abandoned?"

"Not a soul."

Weller poked her head back in the studio door to

make sure Shay was still contentedly showing Iva how to play bongo drums. She smiled at the two of them, surrounded by percussive instruments on the floor. "What else is on your mind?"

"Are you alone?"

"Enough not be overheard."

"When did Shay's bassist, Jane Smith, leave the studios today?"

The hairs on Weller's arms stood alert. "Around four."

"Was she alone?"

"Yes. She was on her Harley."

"Did she say where she was going?"

"Home. She has a one-room efficiency fairly close to here in an old apartment building on Coles Avenue near Rainbow Beach Park. Do you want me to get you the address?"

"No need, Addy. A commuter called in an accident in a tenant parking lot on Coles. Someone totaled Jane's bike and then apparently drug her behind some parked cars and beat the snot out of her."

Weller, cringing inside, worked to keep her face unemotional in case Iva or Shay could see her in the hall. "What's her status?"

"She is alive and awake, but muddled. Her nose is broken and she had to have multiple cuts stitched up. The ER doctor said she is in good condition and should be available to answer questions soon. I'll text you and let you know when they plan to release her. I really don't think she should leave alone."

"Yes, I agree. We'll come get her and keep her here with us from now on."

"I'm sure she'll like that better than a police presence."

"Probably. How did you get called in on this?"

James cleared his throat and sighed. "That's the really bad news. He left a note pinned to the front of her shirt that says, 'I'm getting closer, Shay Greenaura. I can't wait to fuck up your daughter Iva too. One, two, three…are you ready for me?' There's no signature. No one on the street saw anything or anyone."

"What about fingerprints?"

"We lifted some, but there isn't anything in any of our database searches and it will take weeks to get the more comprehensive searches back from Interpol. Assuming he's ever been convicted of a crime, or worked as a federal employee so that his fingerprints are registered in any of the databases we can legally access."

"Fat chance, but you never know. Information can come from any angle, or anyone anywhere, or at any time."

"Glad you're still an optimist." James laughed.

"I try." Weller sighed and rubbed the small of her back. "Jane might remember something about him."

"It's a slim possibility. The Harley was hit from behind and her helmet is caved in on one whole side. It looks like she was probably unconscious when he dragged her out of public view. She was brought in that way. She woke up in the ER."

"Hmm." Weller's hope for a clue to help them dwindled at that news and at the sheer hopelessness in James' tone. "Okay. Thank you for calling me first."

"You're welcome. I'll text you and let you know as soon as I find out when they plan to release Jane, and I'll let her know you're coming to get her."

"Sounds good. Bye," Weller ended the call and took a minute to gather her thoughts before interrupting Shay and Iva's play.

†

Fallow toed the kitchen tile with his green Chuck Taylor's and wiped at his tears with the sleeve of his rust-colored sweater. "So you think the guy who threatened Shay at the hospital is the same guy who beat on Jane?"

"Yes, we think so, and we think this guy is becoming more of an immediate threat." Weller answered, keeping her face bland and calm.

Shay nodded.

"You mean he is devolving and escalating?" Syl asked quietly.

RobO laughed and Shay looked at him quizzically.

Drew also chuckled softly. "Yeah, in TV land, that is what the psychic profilers call it."

Syl looked blankly at her husband, and then Drew,

before asking, "You mean the psychiatric profilers?"

"Jesus, Drew," Reyna hissed and then said directly to Syl, "Yeah, hon, he means behavioral analysts, like in the shows."

RobO laughed again. "It's okay, Reyna. It is funny. We all want to think we know how a madman behaves. We all want to think only a madman would do these kinds of things. We all want to believe there are special people working very hard to take care of all these madmen so we don't have to think about it. Right, Syl?"

Syl nodded and smiled. RobO put an arm around her shoulders and pulled her close to him.

Weller tried to gauge Shay's reaction to all of the news, but Shay remained quiet and still. "Detective James says Jane is awake and the hospital is ready to release her. Reyna and I are going to get her."

"Are you okay?" Shay asked.

Surprised, Weller answered, "Yeah, I'm fine."

Shay nodded.

Weller squeezed Shay's shoulder. "We'll be back as soon as we have Jane. In the meantime, will all of you guys stay together in this part of the dorms with Drew and Jye?"

"Yes, we will," answered Shay.

†

Weller and Reyna walked out of the dormitory doors and down the lawn to the secured parking lot.

"She's a damn loaded pistol," Reyna elbowed Weller, "and she's the first person I've met with the balls to ask you how you are when you're wearing your 'if-pissed-could-kill-face' without getting a silent glare in response."

"Shit." Weller shook her head and gave Reyna a sheepish grin as they approached their Chevy Tahoe.

"Get in the car, boss. I think we need to figure out a place to hide everyone."

"I know. We're going to charter us a flight to a back bay I know."

"Uh oh."

"What?" Weller pinned Reyna with a mock glare.

"I said, 'yes sir.'" Reyna grinned and lifted both brows. "Does this mean we're going into DEFCON 1?"

Weller thought back on Shay's small form, pale and lost in a hospital bed—frail and vulnerable—beyond their protection in that moment just as Elle was in her hospice bed. Then Weller thought of Jane's perky nose and shiny Harley, both trashed for no reason. Weller felt an unreasonable anger welling up in her chest searing her resolve. "I think it does, Reyna, or at least it means we're going DEFCON 2 from here on out. Everyone stays fully armed and ready to fire at all times. Let's get our clients on lockdown until we get this bastard isolated on our own target range."

"That means they will have to miss more gigs." Reyna cocked her head back toward the dorm building.

"Yes, it does, but I think Jane is all the convincing they need anyway. I'll talk to Beni."

Chapter Twenty-six

Bound

They wandered off the chartered jet one at a time into a bright humid day. Shay smelled grass, manure, and salt. Her Chicago winter clothes felt heavy in the balmy breeze that blew around the large, fabricated, metal hanger and offices in front of the jet.

"Where are we?" Fallow asked.

A laugh bubbled up from Reyna. "Weller has taken us all home to her grandpa."

Shay looked expectantly at Reyna.

Reyna wiggled her eyebrows. "Somewhere down in Texas on the Corpus Christi Bay."

Shay looked to Addy for confirmation and received a smile wider than Lewis Carroll's Cheshire cat. "Actually, on the San Antonio Bay."

"I thought San Antonio was a landlocked city?" Fallow asked.

Reyna grabbed two of their duffle bags from the jet's hold and handed them to Fallow.

"Let me help," Shay offered.

Reyna waved her off. "Fallow, it is a landlocked city. They just reused the name for the river than runs through it and goes on to this bay."

"Oh. Like Lake Chicago in Wisconsin," Fallow said.

"There is a Lake Chicago in Wisconsin?" Drew asked.

"Well, there was. It was a prehistoric, proglacial lake that helped form Lake Michigan," Fallow answered.

Addy took several bags and led the way toward the parking lot.

"Now I'm really confused. Lake Chicago became Lake Michigan in Wisconsin?" Drew asked. "Was the lake-making crew working drunk and confused like DC's road-paving crews do?"

Conversation ceased as Addy stepped into the arms of a very tall, tan, and weathered old man waiting in front of two chocolate-colored Ford Expeditions.

Shay sighed.

Jane wrapped an arm loosely over Shay's shoulders. "Got it bad already, huh?" she whispered.

"Why do you say that?" Shay hissed.

"Because you're emanating all kinds of expectant curiosity like a cheeky blond puppy." Jane's affected Cockney accent made the word puppy sound like she was saying poppy.

Shay bit her lip and then managed a tiny self-deprecating shrug.

Jane gave a hearty laugh, and Shay was delighted to see the bassist back to herself, despite the purple bruising still evident under both of her eyes.

†

Shay peered over Addy's shoulder from the backseat. She watched the Expedition with Addy's grandfather at the wheel traveling the flat blacktop road in front of them. The scenery was endless miles of farming fields. She tapped Addy on the shoulder. "Can we have some music?"

"How about it, boss?" Drew seconded.

"Okay with me."

Drew flipped on the radio and scanned the dial until he came to a thumping hip-hop beat interspersed with DirtyD's latest homage to his welter-weight grandfather's struggle for civil rights. Drew's head bobbed slightly with each bass note.

Shay mouthed the lyrics under her breath and watched more of the road fly by.

The song finished and radio commercials started.

Drew reached for the knob, but Addy's hand caught the larger man's mid grab. "How about something from the CD deck?"

Shay watched Drew's big head shake and his shoulders jiggle with laughter. "Aw, hell no, boss. Please. I can't take anymore of your Jimmy Buffett crap."

Addy replied, "Oh, really? That's not crap. That's classic."

"Classically snoozeville," Drew asserted.

"'Margaritaville.' Classically fun and relaxing. Besides we're headed for the bay. It fits." Shay could see Addy's smile in the rearview mirror.

Drew turned to Shay. "Please, famous musician, will you back me up on this?"

Shay laughed. "Well, I'm not a Parrot-head, but I am curious about what else Addy considers good music."

"See? That settles it." Addy pressed the button for the CD hopper on the steering wheel, and George Strait's 'Marina Del Rey' filled the speakers.

"Aw…no." Drew grimaced.

"Perfect." Addy relaxed back in the driver's seat.

Drew looked to Shay, Iva, and Fallow in the back seat.

Shay shrugged and sang along. Iva joined in, and Drew pulled a long face at Fallow.

"Well, we do like the Weller relaxed," Fallow said.

Drew returned his eyes to the road ahead of them. "Yeah, there is that."

†

The Expeditions finally rolled to a stop at the end of a long gravel road facing a swath of smooth green water that Shay supposed must be San Antonio Bay. Two piers jutted out into the bay, with four boats tied between them. She noticed one of the boats had the name *Addison*. The smell of fish and hay greeted her when she opened the SUV's door and stepped out. She reached a hand out for Iva, and her daughter took a firm grasp before spritely hopping out of the huge vehicle on her own.

"Where is this, Mama?"

"I think we're about to find out, sweetheart. It's Addy's safe place, I think."

As everyone else piled out into the yard, too, Addy waved them over to the shade of an exceedingly large oak tree. "Please allow me to do some introductions and a little coordination before we unload everything and get settled in."

Shay quickly glanced over the big tin-roofed ranch house behind Addy, and the white-washed cabins flanking both sides of it.

The tall old man stepped very close to Addy and squeezed her in a one-armed hug before he started speaking. "Hello. I'm Lucas Fermo, Addy's maternal grandfather. You can call me Lucas or Grandpa as you see fit. Welcome to my hunting and fishing ranch—Addison's Retreat."

Shay couldn't pass up the opportunity to tease. "Wow, Addy, it's even named after you."

Laughing, Lucas shook his head. "Actually, Addison was my wife's maiden name. The retreat and Addy are both named after Loraine's family. She insisted."

Addy's smile was so broad that Shay could see that even her bottom teeth were straight and white. "Yes. What Grandma Lolo wanted, she got, and whatever she wanted to give, you got."

"Yes, ma'am. No strings attached. That woman gave more love than most people can hold in one lifetime." Lucas had a broad, sheepish smile.

Shay noticed the hard nicked-and-gnarled skin on his knuckles. He used one broad hand to swipe a short gray wisp back from his tan forehead.

Iva let go of Shay's hand to go tug on Addy's shirt hem. "Is this a safe place, Addy?"

Warmth spread through Shay's chest as she watched Addy bend down and pick up Iva with a smile. "Yes, little bit, this is a safe and fun place. Grandpa Lucas tells the best jokes."

Iva wrapped her chubby little arms around Addy's neck and turned her head toward Lucas. "Will you tell me one?"

Lucas cleared his throat and tapped one finger on his chin for several beats before asking, "Did you hear about that container vessel that sank near Cancun?"

Shay shook her head and watched Addy eye him with mild suspicion. "No."

Iva interjected, "What's a contained vessel?"

Addy answered, "Grandpa meant a boat that carries stuff."

Lucas reaffirmed, "Yep, I meant did you hear about that boat that sank near Cancun?"

Iva shook her head.

"It was loaded with millions of dollars of mayonnaise.

It was the saddest Cinco de Mayo ever."

Iva looked lost and the rest of the group groaned collectively before a giggle escaped Shay. "I now see where Addy gets her arsenal of bad puns and goofy jokes."

Lucas' face lit up with mirth. "Yeah, she gets her wonderful sense of humor from me."

Reyna snorted a laugh. "And her habit of keeping that karambit knife in her right hip pocket. Don't let their mild manners fool you, Shay. Those two are dangerous old sea-wolves."

"Wolfish maybe, but loyal," Lucas admitted while looking at his granddaughter with a lopsided smile.

"Yes, very loyal too," Reyna replied.

Shay watched Addy closely and noticed the hint of a blush crawling up her neck.

Oblivious, Iva yawned and put her head down on Addy's shoulder.

RobO yawned. "Sorry to be a spoilsport, but as wonderfully entertaining as this is proving to be, which of these nifty cabins should I head to for my nap?"

Addy adjusted Iva higher in her arms and stood taller. "Right. We're taking the four cabins clustered together on the south side of the big house. They all face the sunset over the bay."

"Now that's what I'm talking about." Fallow excitedly bounced up and down on the balls of his feet, rubbing his hands together.

Shay laughed at his delight and Addy continued.

"Hopefully that will encourage everyone to do a whole lot of contented porch-sitting. The two ground rules are: first, that no one goes anywhere alone, even on the property, and second, that no one leaves this property without an armed guard with them. Shay, Iva, and I will take the three-bedroom cabin closest to the main house. The rest of the cabins are all two bedrooms. RobO, Syl, and Drew will take the second cabin closest to the main house. Jane and Reyna the third, and Fallow and Jye the fourth. That will give you all a guard in the same cabin with you without making anyone feel too tight for private space."

Lucas added. "The rest of the cabins are locked and empty. They will stay that way while you all are here for added security. Your kitchens are all stocked with staples so you can make your own meals, but you're also welcome to join us at the main house for lunch or dinner."

Shay bit her lower lip and hesitated to say anything. She noticed Syl watching her nervously. Addy leaned over and whispered, "Don't worry, Shay. I sent Grandpa the details about everyone's dietary preferences. Your organic and vegan staples are already on hand."

"Oh, you're good."

"I know it." Addy winked and beamed back at her with a lopsided smile that Shay noticed mirrored Lucas's smile very well.

Chapter Twenty-seven

Slap Iron

"Yeah, you'd be surprised how hard it is for a full-grown man to stand his ground with one of these two little women," Drew said to RobO and gave a great guffaw. He gazed somewhere over Shay's head toward the morning sun rising steadily over the ranch house.

"No shit," Jye added when RobO pulled a skeptical look.

"Aw, c'mon man, you want us to believe that a former NCAA tight end and a former NCAA catcher can't handle one barely-over-five-foot Latina?" RobO continued ribbing the two guards while they lingered in the yard after a leisurely coffee.

"They're both too fast and ferocious." Jye, with a somber face, gave him a mild shrug.

"Yeah, what she and Weller lack in bulk they more than make up for in snake-like grace and meanness. Sparring one minute with either one of them is like trying to hold off a thousand angry King Cobras in a four-by-eight-foot prison cell for two days," Drew explained.

"You should have seen what she did to the Wimberly twins." Jye pointed at Reyna who was helping to clear the breakfast table on the porch.

Taking the bait, RobO asked, "What?"

"She wanted to spar with two 'aggressors' at once, so being too new to know better, Josh and Jason volunteered. In the first thirty seconds, she had them both on the ground. Josh was holding his knee and keening like a baby, and Jason was in an arm bar trying to tap out for all he was worth. Jason had to ice his thumb for a week."

RobO looked blank. "She hurt his thumb?"

"She's a judo artist. Fifth dan," Drew said.

"Is that good?" Shay asked.

Jye shrugged and nodded. "It means she has been promoted five times since she earned her black belt ranking."

"And Addy?" Shay asked.

Drew smiled. "Weller has no ranking that we know of. She just has a damned uncanny ability to use absolutely anything as a weapon."

"And she is impossible to hit," Jye added.

"So they could teach someone my size to defend herself?" Shay inquired.

"Shit, Shay, I know you're tenacious and Lord knows you can do mean, but even Reyna is built like a fire plug. They probably can't work miracles, sis," RobO answered.

Shay stared down at her fine wrists and general lack of significant muscle with dejected acceptance.

Drew tapped Shay on the shoulder and she looked up at the big man. “I bet they could teach you enough so that you could help yourself out of a lot of bad situations. It’s mostly mental awareness and rapid decision-making. The smaller you are, the sooner you need to be aware of threats, so that you can make a more rapid decision to attack your aggressor before your aggressor becomes aggressive enough to disable you. Your size gives you less room for hesitation is all. Both Reyna and Weller know what that is like, and they can help you learn what advantages to watch for and how to use them quickly.”

Shay felt hopeful. It was something she needed to know. Something she needed to be able to share with her daughter one day.

Weller cleared her throat from behind Shay. “Yes, we do know what it is like to be small and female in a tight spot. You are capable, Shay, of learning a whole lot of stuff about how to defend yourself. Besides, who doesn’t like bad-ass ninja rock stars?”

Shay spun around and gave Addy her thousand-watt stage grin. Addy’s brown eyes were warm and smiling back as Shay asked, “So when can we start already?”

“No time like the present. Jye, you’re with me and Shay. We’ll take the old Jeep over to Grandpa’s range for some target practice. Then we’ll switch out with Drew and Reyna, so they can get in a few practice rounds, too.”

The guys nodded and Jye started toward the Jeep.

Startled, Shay threw both hands up. "Whoa-whoa. I didn't mean self-defense by firearms. I still don't believe in those damned things."

Addy gave her the lopsided smile. "I know you don't, but that doesn't mean the people who threaten you won't believe in them."

"Can't you just teach me to disarm them?" Shay pleaded.

"Christ, Shay, she isn't Wonder Woman and she can't make you into Cat Woman." RobO gave a big rolling laugh that visibly shook the belly under his Stretch Armstrong T-shirt.

Shay toed the ground and furrowed her brow.

Addy tapped her shoulder. "Listen, I know you don't condone these things, but I stand a better chance of teaching you how to anticipate a firearm threat situation, and avoid it altogether, if you know a little something about firearms and the reality of using one."

RobO winked at Shay. "So you're not trying to convert us all into Texas Republican NRA enthusiasts like you?"

Shay was shocked at her brother's uncharacteristic snarkiness until she noticed him and Addy grinning at one another. "Well, are you?" Shay asked.

"Well, I am a Texan, but I'm not Republican and I don't support the NRA, so…" Addy answered with a small shrug.

"What's that? You're saying you don't fit your stereotype?" RobO cupped a hand to his ear.

Shay felt herself pale a bit, as she caught the justified reprimand.

Addy put her hands on both of Shay's shoulders and bent down until Shay met her eyes. "Seriously, I believe strongly in gun control. I don't think citizens need automatic weapons or even a semi-automatic handgun to defend themselves from their own government. I mean there are plenty of military, paramilitary, and law enforcement officials and retirees with the weapons and, more importantly, the knowledge necessary to resist a military coup, which would resist and side with the populace. And, you can't tell me a zombie apocalypse is any real concern. And, most people don't get sufficient training or practice to use that kind of firearm in any of the truly life-threatening situations they claim to be worried about. And, in an all-out resource war, the real survivors will probably be those who run the farthest and fastest into the wildlands away from everyone else. And well, you get the picture."

Shay smiled sheepishly. "I'm sorry, Addy. RobO is right. I've been plugging you into my stereotype of you for too long now. Hell, of the two of us, I'm the one who fits the stereotype better."

"There's a stereotype of a liberal lesbian hippie vegan folk singer?" Addy teased.

Shay grabbed Weller by the hand and pulled her off toward where Jye waited with the old Jeep running. "Come on, Tex, and show me how to slap some iron."

†

The HardiePlanking of the pier was warm under Weller's jeans even in the weak January sun.

"Lucas makes an amazing black-bean burrito." Shay swung her legs back and forth.

Weller kept the folded karambit knife held out in the palm of her hand. "Hu-unh. He does."

Shay stared out over the placid water. "Does that run in the family, too?"

"Yes, but you're dodging the question."

"This isn't truth or dare." Shay gave Weller a frustrated glance.

Weller gave a half shrug and the lopsided smile she hoped would entice Shay to play along. "It could be. Tell me the truth and I'll take your dare."

"I can't ever see myself using that knife, Addy."

"I hope you never do, but it's easy to fit in a hip pocket and if you ever do find yourself in trouble, it gives you more to scratch with than fingernails." Weller let her concern show on her face, and when Shay finally met her eyes, she held the contact.

Shay looked down at the knife in Weller's outstretched hand and let out a small shaky breath. "Is this important to you?"

Without hesitation, Weller replied, "Yes." She knew it

was important in her gut, even though she couldn't logically explain why Shay, carrying a knife, her knife, made such a difference to her peace of mind.

Shay reached out and claimed the knife from her palm. Her slender fingers tickled as they brushed the palm of Weller's hand. Weller smiled.

Shay leaned back enough to tuck the knife into the right hip pocket of her jeans. With a taunting lift of her eyebrows and small smile, she said, "Okay, but fair is fair."

Weller shrugged. "It sure is."

"Truth or dare?"

Afraid of the question that might arise if she chose truth, Weller answered, "Dare."

Shay paused to think for several seconds before her face lit up with obvious mischievous intent. "I dare you to teach me how to two-step. If I'm going to go all cowgirl, I might as well know how to go the whole act."

Straight-faced, Weller stood and extended a hand to help Shay up. "Right. Let's go then."

"Now?" Surprise widened Shay's blue eyes.

Weller noticed they were bluer than the bay shining blue around them. "Yep. Iva's already with RobO. I'll let Jye know to cover Fallow and Jane until we get back, and Reyna and I will take you to two-step."

"Uh. We have to go somewhere?" Shay accepted her hand up.

"Not too far. Why? Are you having second thoughts?" Weller couldn't stop the broad grin from spreading over her face. "I thought this was truth or dare, and I'm pretty sure you just dared me."

"But I thought you could teach me here." Shay looked pointedly down at the pier's wide uneven planks.

"It sort of requires a sawdust floor to do it right, and I know just the place."

"But is it safe to leave the ranch?" Shay twisted her hands together.

"Yes. It is the early afternoon of a weekday. Taking you to the closest two-bit bar with a sawdust floor, with two armed guards flanking you is safe enough. Safe enough that I'm not worried about doing it to make you regret daring me." Weller grinned wide and hoped Reyna would see the point of building this trust.

"Yeah, about that. Oh, what the hell? Why not?" Shay bit her lower lip before leading the way up the pier toward the cabins.

†

Weller stopped in the open doorway of the bar, looking it over before waving Reyna and Shay in the door and pulling it firmly shut behind them. On a Wednesday afternoon, the Backwoods Bar was mostly empty.

"Here?" Shay rubbed one elbow and chewed her lower lip.

Reyna chuckled under her breath. "Would you ladies like anything to drink?"

Weller smiled. "Dr. Pepper, please."

Shay's eyes widened. "You drink soda? I've never seen you drink anything but water or milk."

"Well, you did say this was supposed to be fun, right?"

"Hmm." Shay smiled and loosely nodded at a head-cocked angle.

"Anything to drink for you, Shay?" Reyna half-turned toward the bar.

Shay peered toward the tap heads and squinted. "I'll try a draft of that beer with the blue star on top."

"One Lone Star and one Dr. Pepper. I'll hold them at the bar for you until you're ready." Reyna walked directly up to the bartender.

"Until we're ready?" Shay asked.

"You did say you wanted to learn to two-step."

Shay looked around the bar.

Weller reached for Shay's hand. "This way." She nodded toward a small empty space behind two pool tables and in front of a digital jukebox. The warmth of Shay's hand in hers ran up her arm, leaving a nerve tingling pleasantness in its wake. She squeezed Shay's hand and pulled her toward the dance floor. "Don't worry. I promise I'll be gentle."

"I'm sure you will." Shay's blond curls shone a deep gold in the dim bar lights.

Weller swiped her credit card and flipped through the digital jukebox, quickly selecting five dollars' worth of songs with an easy two-step rhythm. She turned back around to find Shay standing very close and trying to peer around her at the jukebox.

As the first notes of George Straight's "Ocean Front Property" started to play, Weller held both of her hands palm up.

Shay placed her hands on Weller's and lifted both eyebrows. "Now what, Master of the Dance?"

"I'll lead. We'll dance apart like this so you can see the step at first. Next song, I'll make you look up at me."

"Sure." Shay grinned. "I'm a professional musician. I can play without looking."

"I'm counting on it." Weller quirked her lips. "We'll start the step on your right foot. It's just like walking to a quick, quick, slow, slow beat. On the first beat, you'll quickly step back with your right foot one step, then quickly back one step with your left foot on the second beat, then slowly back one step with your right foot on third beat, and finish on the fourth beat by stepping back with your left foot. That's all there is to it."

"Okay."

Weller listened to the beat of the song for the right downbeat. "Now," she announced as she stepped forward.

Shay watched their feet intently for four full counts and then looked up with a smile. She started keeping pace without looking before the second song even started.

On the third song, Shay let go of Weller's hands, placed her right hand on Weller's shoulder, and pulled her body in closer. As Mickey Gilley's "Lonely Nights" played on,

Weller found herself forgetting that Shay ever needed any instructions.

"Are you a natural at everything to do with music?"

Shay's face tilted up and she gave a thoughtful frown. "I don't know. I mean no one besides RobO has ever called me a natural at anything. I think he is as biased to think well of me as I am to think well of him." Her brow creased.

"Shay, you don't need anyone to verify that you're a natural at something, that's just something you know."

"How so?"

Weller smiled kindly at the smaller woman in her arms as they glided around the dance floor silent for a few steps. Shay's shampoo smelled of peppermint and patchouli. Addy softly cleared her throat. "Well, it's like this feeling that every time you do this thing it's just right. You don't have to think about doing it. Everything just flows and time has no meaning. That means you're a natural."

"Oh. That definitely happens when I write songs, usually whenever I play guitar, and sometimes when I sing." Shay grinned.

"And when you dance?" Weller guided them through a quarter turn and her right hip briefly rubbed Shay's.

"Maybe. You?" Shay asked with a smile.

"Good question. I guess I don't know." Weller smiled faintly.

Shay's blue eyes darkened. She leaned closer to Weller and her face was serious. "What are you a natural at, Addison Weller?" Shay placed her hand on Weller's forearm. They continued dancing.

Ignoring the warm electricity of Shay's touch on her bare forearm, Weller tried to clear her head and think about the question honestly. She blinked and licked her lips. "Fighting."

"Fighting?"

"Not like boxing. I mean fighting to survive. Fighting to protect others. It requires athleticism and an intelligence that I don't have to work at. It just flows."

Shay squeezed her forearm. "It requires a warrior."

"Maybe."

Shay smiled broadly. "But what about dancing? Are you a natural at that?"

Weller shook her head. "I learned to two-step when I was a teenager. When I was old enough to date on the lesbian scene, the only place really to dance in Dallas was Sue Ellen's, a country bar. So I've spent so much time dancing this dance, it's automatic."

"You knew you were a lesbian as a teenager?" Surprise painted Shay's face with strawberry highlights.

"Yeah."

"Before you left Dallas?"

"Yeah."

"But Beni said you were a naval officer. You went to Annapolis."

"Beni says too much."

"Can't argue that, but still, doesn't that mean you went to Annapolis knowing you were a lesbian during the

'Don't ask, don't tell' phase of rules?"

Weller nodded.

Another song, Brad Paisley's "Ticks" started playing. Shay stopped in mid-motion and pulled Weller over to the side of the jukebox by a battered old upright piano with yellowed keys.

Reyna brought the drinks they had ordered, an almost cold can of Dr. Pepper and a mug of Lone Star, over to them.

"Thanks." Weller reached for her soda and took a long swallow.

Shay tentatively sipped her beer. "Thank you, Reyna."

"You're welcome. All done with the lesson?"

"No, not yet." Shay answered, looking at Weller.

"Just a break. Shay was asking me about the 'Don't ask, don't tell' experience at Annapolis."

Reyna smirked. "Ah yeah, Weller and I started at Annapolis the same year the policy went into effect. They gave us training guides in the form of comic books to help us figure it out."

"No shit?" Shay almost sputtered her beer.

Weller laughed from her belly. "No shit. The year before we went civilian they had us play a video game, choose your own adventure style, on how to avoid getting involved in human trafficking."

Reyna barked a laugh. "Oh yeah, that was a good one. Imagine, you enter a basement in a bar in Eastern Europe and find an Asian female chained to the boiler. Should you:

A) leave immediately and return to base, B) try to free her and take her to the closest US Embassy, or C) seek out the bar manager and inquire what is going on?"

"B," Shay answered firmly.

Addy whispered, "Turns out the answer was A."

"Wow. I see why you went civilian."

Reyna watched Weller dance Shay around the floor again.

Weller held Shay at a respectable arm's length, but Shay stepped in closer and rested her head on Weller's shoulder.

A burly cowboy two stools down from Reyna started shit-talking with his buds about the lesbians on the dance floor needing a real man or three.

"Let it go, Jim," one of his lanky friends advised.

The cowboy turned all the way around to face the dance floor, squaring off his shoulders and sucking in his beer gut.

"I can't let that go on. That tall one's got her hands all over the li'l one. Someone needs to teach her some manners," Jim barked, a few decibels too loud.

Reyna met Weller's eyes and tilted her head at Jim.

Weller spun on the floor, cradling Shay in light arms until she was between Shay and the cowboy. Shay cuddled in closer oblivious to anything else but the dancing.

Jim took a clumsy step forward and clenched his fists.

Reyna leaned back with both elbows on the bar and

projected her voice at Jim. "You better bring your big friends."

The oversized shitkicker looked down at Reyna leaning beside him and she watched his eyes struggle to focus.

"Wha' for?"

"Well, you're gonna need 'em."

"Wha' for?"

"I don't think you want to swap fists with the tall one. I've seen her jack some pretty big beef right into the county emergency room. She is a former federal agent, too. You know what they say about how law enforcement sticks together." Reyna feigned studying her fingernails. "I've seen her go crazy over less. Her patience is pretty thick, but once you piss her off…well, let's just say that if she wants to, she probably could rip your limbs off and beat you with the bloody stubs."

"Oh yeah? Well, who the hell are you?" Jim leveled a big stubby finger in Reyna's face.

Reyna tilted her hips enough to show the butt of her FN 5.7 jutting beneath her shirt. "Another former federal agent with a temper and a license to carry in this state."

Jim shoved his fist into his pockets and turned back around to face the bar.

"Bartender, would you please give that man another beer, on my tab?" Reyna asked.

"Sure thing." The bartender pulled a drafted beer and set it in front of Jim.

"Smartest thing you've done all week, old man," said the cowboy next to Jim.

Reyna returned to watching the room, smiling to herself, as Weller still held Shay close on the dance floor. She wouldn't have chosen Shay to remind Weller that forming attachments could be a good thing. Maybe Shay wasn't the best candidate for bringing Weller out of her self-imposed grief fest, but Reyna was glad that someone might thaw some of the ice that had frozen her best friend's emotions solid for so long.

Chapter Twenty-eight

Release

RobO and Syl sat in the two Adirondack chairs outside Shay's cabin, sipping Shiner Bock beers. Weller waved at them and listened with increasing joy at Shay's excited tone "Hey guys, you should have seen me two-step."

RobO cracked a wide smile and waved his beer. "Nah, we were too busy listening to actual silence and sampling these suds."

"And what's your ruling on the suds?" Weller asked.

"Pretty good stuff, but you know, I'm not sure what the difference is between a bock and an ale," RobO replied.

"Me neither," Weller confessed.

"How's Iva?" Shay asked.

"Curled up asleep on the bed in her room already," Syl answered.

"Yep, she declared her intent to wait up for you and then fell over like a sack of potatoes after Lucas gave her a cup of chamomile and honey tea. He told her a really long story about Tarpon migration patterns," RobO said.

Shay gave a questioning look.

"Tall fish tales over warm tea is the cure for all that ails you," Weller said.

"Sort of creepy in that perfect, familial, love-and-care sort of way," Shay replied.

Clouds rolled over the early moon, dimming the ambient light on the patio.

RobO clanked his empty bottle against the arm of his chair and he stood. "Well, sis, we're outta beer and we're outta here. See you gals in the morning."

"Yeah, goodnight, guys. Thanks for tucking in Iva," Shay said as RobO and Syl walked hand in hand the fifteen feet to their own cabin.

Drew waved to Weller from their patio before following them inside, and closing and locking their door behind him.

The rain started in earnest just as Weller pulled open their cabin door for Shay to enter.

†

"So you think we're all safe for the night?" Shay asked Addy. They stood in the living room just inside the tiny cabin's front door.

"Yes." Addy turned on a lamp and wiped away the raindrop that had caught her square in the forehead before they made it inside.

"Thanks for tonight, Addy. I felt human again. I felt free and alive and I didn't worry about any of it."

Addy smiled. "You're welcome."

Shay turned to go to her room, but stopped mid-turn and spun back to face Addy. "How do you feel?"

Addy cocked her head. "I feel fine. Thanks for asking."

Shay felt her nerves butterfly in her stomach. "Ah, no, I'm sorry. I mean how are you feeling? What do you feel? Were you upset, happy, worried, or what tonight?"

Addy rubbed her chin. "I had fun. It was nice to see you laugh."

"But how did you feel?" Shay insisted.

"Does it really matter?" Addy asked softly.

"It matters to me." Shay watched Addy's lush lips.

Addy drew out a long low sigh. "I felt all sorts of things. Happy. Wistful. Worried. My feelings were a big useless, conflicted, untrustworthy mess."

Shay thought about this for several seconds. "You trust your instincts."

Addy nodded.

"But you don't have any faith in your feelings?" Shay asked.

Addy shook her head and shifted her weight back and forth over the balls of her feet.

"What's the difference between feelings and instincts?" Shay stepped within inches of Addy, purposefully breaching her personal space. Her feelings and her instincts told her they needed to care for one another, provide each other a deeper level of security than their contract allowed. She realized that she needed Addy to hold her and maybe even to love her. She knew down to the rock-bottom of her soul that Addy was someone who loved unconditionally.

As Shay stood close, Addy became very still. Eventually, she replied, "The difference is that instincts save your life, help you notice important but subtle facts before your mind has time to articulate you've noticed them. Feelings, however, obscure your common sense, make you blind to the most obvious threats, and get you hurt."

"Instincts are sometimes wrong. Can't they lead you to worry about things that turn out to be unimportant?"

"Sometimes." Addy's eyes shifted around.

"And sometimes feelings are right and lead you to pay attention to what makes you want to live. Right?" Shay pressed the issue and watched the pulse visible in Addy's neck quicken to a three-quarters time tempo.

"Maybe."

Shay stepped even closer to Addy, until their bodies were touching. She demanded, "Kiss me."

Weller watched the green and gray flecks play like kaleidoscope bits in Shay's blue eyes. She wanted to just say no to the demand, but her hands moved of their own accord. Shay was shockingly small, soft, and warm in her arms. Then the touch of their lips snagged all her attention into a roaring wave of heat and something that tasted just like home.

When the roaring tide of sensation ebbed a bit, Weller finally ended the kiss by drawing her head back a fraction of an inch. She could not find the strength or the heart to separate the press of their bodies. She tried to take a full breath and give Shay the space to reconsider where this should lead them.

"Please, again," Shay whispered.

Weller smiled and cupped Shay's heart-shaped jaw in her hand. She brushed her thumb reverently along Shay's cheek before kissing her forehead, her cheek, the edge of her jaw, the soft spot just below her ear, and finally her mouth again.

Shay's hands wove through her hair in response and gently clutched the fine curls at the base of her neck.

Weller felt goosebumps rise up her ribcage and an aching want blossomed up through her chest. The tip of Shay's tongue traced the edges of her bottom lip and then fluttered around her tongue coaxing Weller's body to respond. An instinctual gasping need gripped her stomach. She instantly remembered what feeling with real intensity was like. It was something she had lost in the fierce grief spent fighting a sickness that could not be beaten during the many months before Elle was actually gone.

Shay slipped one hand into the collar of Weller's shirt, tracing her collarbone to the strap of her bra. Her hand stilled there and she knew Shay was asking and wanting permission for more without a word.

The rain outside became an incessant patter that matched Weller's pulse hammering in her ears. Drawing in a quick breath full of Shay's peppermint and patchouli shampoo mixed with the comforting twang of sawdust from the bar, she was surprised to find that her libido lived. Her desire to hold a woman close definitely had not died with Elle. The ache of wanting to make love to Shay Greenaura was like a hand squeezing her heart, full of urgency to live, to hum with the hope of love again. She extended all her senses outward in the space of one long breath. She discovered her instincts sang with an urgency to give Shay the security of their intimacy, screamed of an imperative to love in this moment, regardless of all the hitches that might cause.

"Please, Addy, I need you now."

Weller turned Shay around and cradled the smaller woman in front of her as she walked Shay toward the bedroom.

Shay turned to face her when they reached the edge of the downy double bed with its blue-denim quilt.

Weller ran her hands slowly down Shay's arms. "You are beautiful."

"You make me feel beautiful." Shay's voice came out husky and low. She pulled Weller's shirt free of her jeans and slipped her hands nimbly along the skin of Weller's belly.

Weller brushed a soft blond wave of hair away from Shay's jawline and left a path of kisses along the slender column of her neck.

Shay retaliated by unbuttoning all of Weller's shirt

and leaving a hot whisper of breath at the cleavage just above her black silk bra before tracing kisses along the top of each breast. She pushed Weller's shirt back and off.

The *whumpf* of her shirt hitting the floor was loud to Weller. She felt dizzy with want. She sighed at the sudden coolness of the room's air against her bare torso.

"Sweet Jesus, but you're beautiful, Addy." Shay openly gazed Weller up and down with evident appreciation.

Weller was at a loss to answer for a minute. She swallowed against the emotion welling in her throat. She gently lifted both hands and turned around to show Shay her back. She deliberately pulled loose the paddle holster with her gun and set it on the side table.

Shay used the moment to unhook Weller's bra and slipped it off her shoulders. She placed a kiss in the middle of Weller's back. The hotness of her mouth was inspiring the muscles there to twitch and jump.

Weller turned back around and lifted Shay's slouchy T-shirt off in one fluid motion. All of her nerves stood up at attention and then the world exploded into warm sensation as the bare skin of their breasts and torsos pressed together. She took her time, letting them both savor the long kisses that followed, until Shay's insistent hands tugged emphatically at the hips of her jeans, urging them off.

She complied and then stripped them both of every remaining article of clothing without taking her eyes off Shay's. Again, she paused, giving Shay the chance to reconsider where this was leading them, and then smiled.

Shay pushed her onto the bed. Accepting the whole weight of Shay's body pressed on top of her felt like entering a temple. The heat of their skin was as hot and sacred as the first kiss of the sun at summer's altar. Shay's breathing was musical, melodies inspired by the trace and patter of her hands, each note softer than the first as she ran her fingertips down the singer's spine and over the pert curve of her ass.

Shay's tongue thrust into her mouth and the communion of their want released a groaning gospel deep in her throat. Her hips jerked upwards of their own accord, seeking pressure, wanting to touch more, and she felt Shay's slickness slide hard against her inner thigh. She hooked one leg over the top of Shay's and twisted them over so that Shay was looking up at her.

"I knew you were a top."

"I'm no such thing."

"Oh?" Shay kissed her chin.

"I'm an equal opportunity employer. I will do what I need to do to make you feel loved." Weller placed attentive kisses over each of Shay's areolas, delicately tongue-lashing each nipple until it hardened to greater attention.

Shay's eyes dilated, her body twitched, and her breath quickened. "I need to touch you, Addy. I want to be inside you while you're inside me."

Weller smiled and lifted her body enough to allow Shay's hand to slip between them, her touch slipping past Weller's tender folds to play softly syncopated strokes against her thrumming clitoris. "Oh God, Shay." Weller's body jolted and she focused on not falling over the edge before she could bring Shay the same release.

"Please, Addy. Please." Shay caught her eyes and Weller almost froze in the intense vulnerability and adoration she found in the gaze.

"My pleasure, Shay," she answered before trailing her whole open hand down Shay's belly, lightly over the tiny thatch of curls between her legs, and then over the wet velvet folds of her vulva, to push and pull two fingers teasing into the tensed softness of her vagina.

Shay sang as she pushed her hips unabatedly against Weller's hand, inadvertently bringing Weller to the crest of her own orgasm. Wave after wave of orgasm caught them up into one spiraling net of ecstasy. They thrust against each other over and over before the last shattering release in the deepest hours of the night.

Chapter Twenty-nine

To Catch

Weak sunlight flowed through the gauzy curtains and painted a faint square on the whitewashed pine floors of the cabin's small bedroom. Shay snuggled deeper into the warm length of Addy and the cocoon of covers around them.

Addy squeezed her a little tighter.

Shay moved the palm of her hand in a lazy glide down Addy's long oblique muscles, toward the small of her stomach and over the graceful arc of her hip and back up again. She watched Addy's eyes spark to her touch.

Addy softly palmed Shay's jaw and brushed the pad of one thumb along the plane of Shay's cheek.

Shay leaned into the touch and smiled. "I've got to go check on Iva, but I'll be right back. Please don't move." She placed a kiss on the perfect column of Addy's neck near the glossy brown waves of hair just behind her ear.

Addy's eyes went very wide and her breath rocketed

out as she bolted up to a sitting position.

Shay was almost distracted from Addy's obvious agitation by the very white sheets cascading down her lean torso to reveal a beautiful play of early sunlight on skin. "What? What's wrong?"

"Iva. I never checked on Iva. I've been distracted for hours" Addy's face flushed white.

Shay tilted her head, confused, and placed her hand on Addy's forearm. She spoke softly, "Honey, it's okay. I'm her mother. It is my responsibility to check on her and I would hear her if she woke in the night. She would call for me."

"Not if someone snuck in and did anything to her. It's my job to keep the bad stuff away from you two." Addy stood and pulled on her jeans and shirt.

Shay stood before pulling the top sheet off the bed and winding it around herself.

Addy, staring at her, froze in place.

"Come on, we'll peek together." Shay extended one hand to Addy.

Addy took her hand and led the way across the hall where they peered in the open door of Iva's room. Iva snored softly, tucked up against the line of pillows between her and the side of the bed that opened toward the floor.

Shay watched Addy's eyes track to the small window across the room. Nothing was disturbed.

Addy rubbed the slight hitch at the bridge of her nose.

Shay smiled to herself and tugged Addy's hand until the taller woman was facing her. She pressed herself into the circle of Addy's arms and whispered up into the crook of Addy's neck, "See? All is okay. Your job isn't to stop the bad stuff. No one can do that, Addy. You give us one more level of awareness, one more layer of care to wear as we walk through the rougher patches."

Addy's arms tightened their hold a little. "I can't be this distracted, Shay. Caring is one thing, but loving you so much right now is too much risk of losing you."

Shay's breath hitched in her throat and the word "loving" echoed in her head repeatedly. She tilted her head back to look into the infinite depths of Addy's dark eyes. "Love?"

Addy nodded. "But not like this." Addy kissed her heatedly for emphasis. "Right now, I either need to bow out as your protection lead, or put the development of this love on pause until you're safe again."

"And if you bow out, you can't stay with us?" Shay swore she could feel her heart skip a beat at the thought.

Addy answered, "I don't know. You'd need another guard and the team would probably suffer if I tried to stick around while distracted like this...especially if I tried to stick around as the boss."

Shay's head drooped forward until her forehead rested on the broad plane of Addy's chest and she let go of a long shaky breath. "Okay." She kissed the warm hollow of Addy's throat and then stepped backward out of Addy's arms. She felt the loss of physical comfort caused by the removal of Addy's arms from around her like a shooting pain all the way from the heels of her feet to her scalp.

†

Long legs stretched in front of her, Weller nestled deeper into the cabin's couch and listened to the sounds of Shay giving Iva a bath in the small bathroom near the kitchen. Content that everything was ready for the next day's sunset sail, she decided to call the main office in DC and find out what her tail on Mitch Dane revealed.

Gina picked up after the first ring. "Hey, El Jefe. I'm glad you called. I have some news for you."

"Ah, so the tail on Mitch Dane turned something up already?"

"Actually, no. Mr. Dane appears to be a dud. So far, he's stuck to his touring schedule and hasn't had time to get into much trouble beyond a few small drug buys. His tail has seen nothing that appears relevant to Shay or Iva. It doesn't appear he has been near Chicago anytime lately."

Weller flicked at a conspicuous bit of lint near her knee. "So what's your news?"

"It's actually for Reyna. She asked me to look into Simone Saez's travel history as much as possible and I think I found something interesting."

"Good idea. What'd you find, Gina?"

"Maybe nothing but coincidences, but maybe

something. Ms. Saez was in New York City modeling at a Victoria Secret's show the day after Secretary Brayson was killed. She was also in Rio, modeling LUBLU clothing for a fashion magazine, the week Cardinal de Romani was assassinated last year. I correlated four more modeling gigs she's done with mysterious public official deaths."

Weller, frowning, took a long slow breath and released it silently. She rubbed her right temple. "That is interesting. Is there any consistency in the kills? Are they all bombs?"

"No, they're all different. One was an apparent drug overdose of sorts. Too much cold medicine while on a contra-indicated antidepressant."

"Any poisons?"

"No. The drug overdose is the closest to that."

"Okay." Weller chewed on her lip. "How confident are you that there is something meaningful about these correlations?"

Gina cleared her throat and clicked her tongue against her teeth. "That's just it. I'm not confident they mean anything. I was about to call you and ask if I should bother sending the information to Reyna."

Weller closed her eyes and listened briefly for her own intuition. Her palms tingled and she felt a slip of anger in the pit of her stomach. *But how much of that is just jealousy.* She remembered Simone caressing Shay's cheek in passing at the gala. She opened her eyes and shook her head. "I'll tell Reyna, Gina, but can you do me a favor and send an email summarizing what you've found to Detective James with the Chicago PD? His email address is in Shay's client file on the secure drive."

"Yes, ma'am. I'll do it right now."

"Wait, Gina."

"Yes, ma'am. For what, please?"

"Until the morning. It's late in DC and this will wait for you to have a real life."

Gina's laugh was loud and long. "As if you have room to talk."

"Goodnight, Gina."

"Goodnight, Weller."

†

Weller turned her face into the salty breeze as Reyna steered the Mako's 204cc engines wide of the marsh edges. After Reyna killed the engine near the base of a cut into the marsh on the bay's northwestern edge, Weller's grandfather fixed a scented-plastic mullet for bait on two rods and handed them off to RobO and Shay.

Weller stood at the back corner of the boat nearest to Shay and noticed the late afternoon sun glint on the water. In the distance, she could hear the low hum of other boats on the water, but only two smaller recreational boats were in the visible area. She studied the nearest, a small skiff, sitting about sixty feet farther north in the marsh, with one lone fisherman perched on the bow platform, dressed in baggy cargo khakis, large floppy hat, and sunglasses. The fisherman looked to be fiddling with a rig. Weller turned her attention toward the other vessel, a late-model light-tackle inshore boat with two young men who appeared well settled into fishing and drinking beer on what was probably their day off.

Shay cast a line out over Weller's field of view. "What are you going to do if you catch one?"

RobO laughed. "She's going to scream like a schoolgirl and dance around the boat trying to avoid it."

"I will not." Shay hummed some tune so lightly that Weller couldn't hear enough to put a name to it for sure, but decided it sounded like *nanny-nanny-boo-boo.*

"She's definitely not going to eat it." Fallow crossed his arms and leaned against the boat rail.

"You know something had to die to bait your hook, right?" RobO asked.

"Not so," Lucas replied, "I baited your hooks with synthetic mullet."

"Oh. Cool." RobO's tone conveyed genuine wonder.

Shay cocked one hip and rested the base of her rod against it. "And I won't scream like a girl. I'll get Lucas to help me release it."

"Unless it's one someone else wants to eat, right?" Weller crossed her arms over her piqued aqua polo shirt.

"Right. Although if it's cute then I reserve the right to release it anyway."

Weller was about to tease Shay about the improbability of a cute fish, when she saw a beer can hit the water sixty feet off the bow of their boat. She looked up and out over the water, following the can's most probable trajectory, toward the two young men she suspected were the source. She heaved an aggravated sigh and just then the percussive boom shook the boat beneath her feet.

Weller's ears were ringing and her eyes were watering from the salt spray, but a quick glance around showed everyone was present and accounted for, even if in a state of shock.

Dead fish popped to the top of the water in scores.

Reyna was already moving toward the boat's engine console to move them out when a second can of beer hit the deck of the boat near the engines. Weller only had time to realize the can came from the opposite direction from the first before her body reacted instinctively. Grabbing Fallow and Shay by the shirt collars, she dove off the boat, pulling them into the water with her.

†

Lucas grabbed the machete from its sheath beside the fish cooler and, in one fluid motion, brought the blade down on the fuse, severing the still burning wire from the beer can before it could reach the contents. As he bent down to pick up the can, he called out to Addy. "I've cut the fuse. You should get back in the boat."

He shoved his pinky into the mouth of the can and felt the end of what he thought was a professional-grade M-

80 firecracker resisting his touch. He pulled out his pinky, and stuck the can under his nose so that he could take a good whiff of its contents. He smelled tannerite. "Reyna, key the engines. We need to get out of here."

He dropped the can into the leg pocket of his cargo pants. He headed over to the rail to help his granddaughter back on board the boat.

Reyna keyed up the engines.

Lucas pulled Shay on board first and then Fallow. He pushed them to sit just in front of the console, next to where RobO was already huddled, wide-eyed and silent. They dripped endlessly on the white deck. He returned to the rail to reach a hand down to Addy.

Weller gave her grandfather a conspiratorial glance and shook her head.

He barely nodded.

She pushed off the bow. In a silent frog swim she went toward the marsh and the other vessel at a wide angle. A backward glance proved Lucas must have understood as she saw him miming pulling her in with his back to the lone fisherman's skiff.

Soon she heard Reyna drive the boat toward wider and deeper water.

As she neared the lone fisherman's skiff, Weller felt the marsh ground sloping up to meet her. She crawled closer as quietly as the water allowed, but to no avail.

The fisherman turned toward her approach.

Weller froze in place and listened to the breeze softly sawing through the sea grasses that were too short to provide total cover for her.

The fisherman reached down to the skiff's deck and pulled up an AR-15 rifle.

Weller stood on shaky legs in the muddy marsh and drew her FN 5.7, cocking the soggy firearm.

The fisherman grinned a very bright, white smile and said in a surprisingly feminine voice, "Ah, poor, Weller, you're all wet and useless." Simone hoisted the AR-15 to her right shoulder.

Gunfire ripped across the bay in successive shots that rattled everyone on Lucas' boat.

"Fuck, fuck, fuck!" exclaimed Shay.

RobO muttered, "Oh God."

"Why the hell is she out there?" Shay pinned Reyna first and then Lucas with her glare. She waited for an answer that never came.

The bullet hit Simone square in the muscle of her right shoulder. The AR-15 dropped, bounced on the edge of the skiff, and slid into the water. Simone grinned. She reached her left hand up to put pressure on the small hole left by Weller's FN 5.7 round.

Weller muttered a small clichéd rhyme under her breath, "Thank God in heaven for the amphibious FN 5.7."

"Now what, wonder girl?" Simone asked with a

predatory look.

"We wait for the Coast Guard." Weller kept the FN 5.7 trained on Simone's chest. Weller hoped they would arrive before twilight finished its slide into the deepest shadows of the sunset and blinked into night.

"Ah, but you cannot wait that long. You would have to kill me and you don't have the hunter's instinct, Agent Weller."

Weller stiffened at Simone's use of "Agent.".

Still smiling, Simone continued. "You see; I know you will not shoot to kill unless I'm an immediate threat to someone you protect. That means that I can restart this engine and drive this boat out of here as long as I head away from Shay."

Weller eyed the deck of the skiff and calculated her odds of approaching and crawling over the side to subdue Simone.

Simone laughed and moved toward the console.

Weller fired seven rounds in quick succession. Each round put a nickel-sized hole through the Honda BF90 outboard's all-weather hood, as near to its small sealed starter as Weller could guess.

Simone keyed the engine, and nothing happened.

Silence played over the water for a few seconds, and then Simone let out a long, full, belly laugh and launched toward Weller from the boat like a giant panther.

Weller dodged Simone's clutches at the last moment, taking the brunt of Simone's knee against her left hip. She whipped the butt of her weapon at the base of Simone's skull in a backhanded swing and Simone splashed into the shifty marsh to the left side of her. The one and half pounds of her loaded polymer weapon worked well enough to fire wet, but it wasn't heavy enough to put a debilitating dent in Simone's head.

Simone shook it off easily and turned, surprisingly quickly in the muck and the mire.

Weller threw a hard right palm across her body straight at the bridge of Simone's nose.

Simone's left arm swung up and knocked Weller's strike askew before Weller could find any satisfaction in making the model's career a little tougher.

Weller followed the momentum of her thwarted palm-strike down Simone's arm and managed to make a clean grab around Simone's wrist. Before Simone could fully start her next swinging punch, Weller had already twisted behind her, dragging Simone's arm up into a pin behind the model's back.

Simone struggled to throw her free elbow back at Weller, but Weller pressed the muzzle of her FN 5.7 into the small of Simone's back, dead on to her spine.

"I have no qualms about making you a paraplegic," Weller hissed between gritted teeth.

Simone went still. "Fine. This is your round then. But you won't beat me. You couldn't beat me when it mattered to Brayson and you can't beat me now either." Simone tilted her head and shifted her eyes toward the spot where the AR-15 had slid into the marsh. “There is no evidence.”

In the distance, Weller could see the sweeping lights of a Coast Guard Defender boat.

With a brassy laugh, Simone asked, “How does it feel knowing I am going to get away again? That I can enjoy the hunt as much as I want, leaving poor little incompetent government servants and misfortunate accidents to blame? Don’t worry I will put you out of your misery soon.”

Weller didn’t have time to answer before the Coast Guard Defender boat directed blazing floodlights toward them. An armed seaman stood on the boat’s bow with a mounted M420 machine gun pointing their way. The boat’s pilot used the speaker to demand they put their arms in the air.

Weller held her FN 5.7 by the muzzle and raised it skyward in the light.

Chapter Thirty

Legalities

Rubbing tired eyes, Weller pulled the Coast Guard's gray woolen blanket closer around her finally dried clothes.

"Would you like more coffee?" Sergeant Investigator Rosa Esperanza of the Calhoun County Sheriff's office asked Weller. Detective Sergeant Scott Selley from the city's police department had stepped out of the interrogation room to take a phone call.

"No, thank you."

"Selley already put in a call to Detective James. Hopefully, that's who is calling him now." Esperanza tapped a chewed pencil on the legal pad in front of her.

"Right. I hope so."

"We also have some folks out looking for the AR-15."

Weller sighed, knowing the probability of finding the gun in the dark was low at best, but nodded.

"And, while Saez is claiming that you shot her for no

reason and is asking to press charges against you, having her under our protection at the hospital goes both ways. She can't leave until we escort her in to make a statement."

"Yeah."

"I've also already checked your business licenses, security certifications, and weapon registrations. They all check out. So you know what I'm saying, right?"

Weller studied the slightly overweight woman in khaki tactical pants and a black sheriff's polo sitting across the table from her. From the expression on Esperanza's face, Weller supposed the woman was empathetic. She shook her head to answer Esperanza's question.

The investigator gave a gentle smile. "I'm saying I believe you."

"And you need evidence to justify the arrest."

"Yes, but you know that."

"I've told you my side. Have you found and questioned the guys in the other boat yet?"

"We've identified them and sent officers out to locate them. We'll take their statements and I promise you we'll follow up on those statements. Your grandfather also turned over the can. We'll process it, but as I'm sure you've probably guessed, there is a nonconsumer-grade firecracker and a significant amount of tannerite packed inside it."

Weller nodded and stared down at the crack in the table's cherry-wood laminate.

Esperanza tapped her pencil again and it made a pleasing *thwatt, thwatt* sound in the silent room.

Detective Sargent Selley stepped back into the room and clicked the door shut behind him. Weller watched Selley smile broadly at Esperanza before he pulled out his chair and sat down again. He placed his pale skinny forearms on the tabletop and clasped his hands together before leaning back in his chair.

"Well, ladies, very good news to share. That was Detective James returning my call. Ms. Weller, he wanted me to share with you that the forensic team processing the gala evidence found positive trace of ricin in the room Ms. Saez used to get ready that night. Based on that finding, the FBI is already in route to her home address in Miami, and we've been asked to detain Ms. Saez for questioning by federal investigators."

Esperanza smiled widely, revealing a full set of clean but slightly crooked teeth. "That is good news."

Knowing Simone would not be able to weasel out of custody long enough to put Shay at further risk left Weller relieved enough to finally smile herself. "That *is* good news. Thank you."

"You're welcome." Selley directed an anxious look to Esperanza. "But I'm not sure we can release you yet."

Weller almost laughed at the young Detective Sargent's anxiety, but held it in.

Esperanza cleared her throat. "I think we can, Detective. We have Ms. Weller's statement, and Ms. Saez has not officially reported anything except her desire to press charges. As far as we know right now, it is a self-defense incident."

Selley's smile returned. "Yes, ma'am."

"Good, then we're all agreed. Ms. Weller, would you like me to drive you back to Addison's Retreat, or would you prefer to call someone to come get you?"

"I would love a ride if you have the time."

Esperanza smiled and stood. "My pleasure."

†

They pulled out of the painted white-brick of the county sheriff's annex in an unmarked Lincoln Continental that Weller guessed to be a 2010 model. Weller was content to ride quietly, keeping her thoughts to herself for the hour-long trip. She was surprised to find the investigator seemed determined to share her own thoughts.

"Now that it is clear you're not an assault-with-deadly-intent suspect, I can tell you that we found the two men in the other boat shortly after the Coast Guard delivered Ms. Saez to the hospital."

"Was there anything to corroborate my charges against Ms. Saez in their statement?" Weller decided to try to keep the investigator talking in hopes of learning more.

Esperanza made a right-hand turn and used the opportunity to show Weller a friendly smile. "Yeah. They admitted they wanted to try blast fishing in shallow waters. They said they ran into Simone Saez while buying Might Putty at AutoZone. Both guys independently claim Simone invited them to come along with her to some likely spots on the bay, saying she was interested in the same thing. Apparently, she laid on the charm well enough to convince them that she thought illegal fishing methods were incredibly sexy."

Weller snorted a chuckle. "Yeah, I'm guessing that wasn't a tough charm. Supermodel meets refinery workers already bent on playing with fire."

Esperanza laughed wholeheartedly. "You said it, sister. Anyway, I'm guessing she used the opportunity to try to get at you or your client. Any ideas why?"

"Nothing useful." The night passed by in nearly complete darkness. Weller watched the city lights give way to farmland. Her reflection in the car's window looked noticeably bedraggled and tired. She could see crow's feet radiating out from her eyes with greater clarity than normal.

"But this isn't the first attempt. I mean the ricin bit, right?" Esperanza pushed for more information.

"It's definitely not the first attempt. I've no hard evidence, other than the ricin, that it might be another attempt by Simone Saez to do harm."

"Is she after your client or you?"

"That is a good question. I hadn't considered that possibility before now, honestly." Weller rubbed the hitch at the bridge of her nose. "But I think she is after my client. She had no way of knowing Vigiles Security or I would take a contract to protect this client before we did so. My client experienced real threats before we were ever hired."

"Hmm." Esperanza drummed her fingers thoughtfully on top of the steering wheel.

"You're hoping for a motive," Weller said.

"Yes."

"The only thing that makes sense to me so far is the assassin angle I mentioned when I suggested that you contact Detective James."

Esperanza nodded and left off drumming her fingers. "Yeah. Someone could have hired her to harm your client."

Weller scratched the scalp above her left ear. "But that doesn't really make sense either. Who would pay a likely very expensive assassin to exterminate a modestly popular lesbian folk singer?"

"That's the rub all right. I sure know some out-of-work thugs and wanna-be gang-bangers who would do the job on the cheap around here." Esperanza shrugged, keeping one hand on the steering wheel. "Do you want to listen to the radio?"

"Sure."

†

"I'm hooked, Lucas. These last ten days of kicking back at Addison's Retreat, after the sunset cruise snafu, have been the best ten days of our year." RobO pulled Syl close. "Right, buttercup?"

Weller watched Syl give a shy nod.

"I don't think I've ever had a vacation." Fallow took

another sip of his Corona.

"I know I've never had a vacation." Shay twisted a finger through Iva's curls as she rested with her head in Shay's lap.

Jane, stretched out next to them on the grass, lifted up on her elbow enough to give them all a glance. "Not that I don't appreciate the vacation, but I could have done without my prior beating and your near boat bombing."

"No doubt." Fallow raised his beer bottle in salute.

Weller nodded, and shifted her back around so that the old oak tree's rough bark scratched the itch between her shoulders. As she stilled herself again, she could feel the smartphone on her hip vibrating. Upon inspection, the caller ID showed Detective James' number. Standing, she excused herself before walking toward the the pier for some privacy.

James' voice had an edge to it that Weller didn't recognize. "Addy, I have strange news."

Weller bent her head toward her left shoulder and then her right, achieving a satisfying pop near the top of her spine. "Okay, I'm all ears."

"Are you alone?"

"Yeah. I can see the others, but I'm out of their hearing range."

"As the feds were leaving the hospital in Port Lavaca with Simone, two teenage Texas Syndicate Gangster recruits shot up the parking lot. Simone, two federal agents, and a local officer all died on the scene."

Weller stared blankly at the bay in front of her and

tried to process the news and its implications. "Who was the local officer?"

James hummed a second before answering, as if reading his notes. "A city patrolman named Nelson Tate. Why?"

Weller thought of Espinosa and Selley with relief and then sent up a quick prayer for the patrolman and agent's families. "Wait, this happened days ago didn't it? Why are you only telling me now?"

She could her James sigh. "It happened three days ago, and I wasn't completely debriefed myself until yesterday. I wanted to have some sort of feel for whether it was safe for you to bring the Greenauras back to Chicago before I called you."

"I see. Thanks, Detective. So what do you know, and how does it make you feel about the prospect of us returning to Chicago?"

"Well, first, let me be completely honest with you, it doesn't matter how I feel about it. The FBI has asked me to invite you all back to Chicago so I can take your statements, and then I am required to share my case file with them in its entirety."

"Makes sense." Weller nodded, even though she knew James couldn't see her.

"But back to what I know and then we'll cover what I feel."

"Okay. Go ahead." A cloud sailed over the sun above Weller before clipping its way farther west.

"First, about the parking lot shooting, Omar Morales, a Texas Syndicate crime boss known as Z-42, tweeted praise to both shooting suspects for getting the job done right and killing, I quote, 'that disloyal cunt he once trusted to execute his most sensitive targets.' What little the feds will tell me about the investigation at Simone's primary residence is that they did find out that she held an OpenBazaar account. It was used for selling obscured assassination services through a decentralized dark web market. They've traced some payments back to fronts for the Texas Syndicate and several other crime organizations around the world. So your paid assassin idea is a very popular theory at the moment."

"Hmm." Weller bit her bottom lip and rubbed her brow.

"Yeah. Hmmm. I know that doesn't give Simone a motive for killing Shay or any of the other assorted rape victims, but there is more in their findings that might. Simone had a really strange obsession with hunting in general. Her place is littered with mounted hunting trophies and exotic furs. She owned firearms and knives that could be consistent with the wound marks we found on our Chicago victims, but that wouldn't explain the semen we found on some of the victims"

He paused, ostensibly for a breath, but Weller heard an unspoken clause too. "And what else?"

"She had several textbooks on toxicology, the physics of explosives, black ops psychology, and such. She also had several saved press clipping about Brayson's assassination. A few of them mentioned you in particular. And…are you still alone?"

Weller sucked in a long breath. "Yeah."

"There were hunting photos on her computer with embedded encrypted data. Some of them hide what looks like a tracking log of Secretary Brayson's schedule and a plan for her assassination. Three of the photos hide a recipe for ricin, a full background report on Shay, and all of the press information regarding Shay and Mitch's relationship woes."

Weller stared out at the still blue bay in front of her as the word "hooked" scrolled boldly through her mind's eye.

James' gravelly voice finished. "That sort of vindicates your assertions about her."

She felt no moment of triumph or relief yet, only bland acceptance of the knowledge.

"Addy? Are you still there?"

"Yes. I'm here. Anything else?"

"No more than that on the assassinations, or at least no more that anyone would share with me. There was a cash payment of $30,000 in an envelope with RobO's fingerprints on it."

Weller could feel her face pale at the idea. "You think RobO paid Simone to kill his sister."

"No. I don't. It doesn't make sense. The car bombing almost killed his wife and niece, not Shay."

"If he really paid her, maybe RobO didn't know exactly what kind of help he was buying. Maybe he just thought something limiting would be done to Shay and Shay alone. Maybe Simone just got creative all on her own?"

"Maybe." James cleared his throat. "Car bombs and other random harassments were her style. She obviously did vary her services and obfuscate her tactics."

"Taking an assassination for only $30,000 doesn't sound like it was her style." Weller glanced briefly toward the sound of the bay lapping at the moored hulls of her grandfather's boats.

"No, it wasn't her style, but maybe the money was only a hunting trophy of sorts. She didn't deposit it. In fact, the envelope was still sealed as if she didn't even count it."

"So what? You think she took this contract for kicks? To pilot a new hunting passion?"

"I don't know. It's possible the high-dollar assassinations weren't supplying her enough thrill for the kill anymore. Right?"

"Maybe," Weller supposed. "And the prospect of thwarting me twice, with Brayson and then Shay, was just an unexpected bonus to her new hunting pursuits."

"Maybe." James voiced the rest of her thought, "But we'll probably never know for sure."

She nodded at the empty bay before turning her back to it to stare at the group still lounging under the large oak tree on shore. "Right. So now how do you feel about our safety in returning to Chicago?" Shay smiled in her direction. Weller swallowed the lump of apprehension growing in her belly.

"Well, the one outstanding question that gives me

immediate stress is why RobO gave her the money."

"Me too." She studied RobO laughing by the oak tree, and even from this distance, she could see the love in his eyes when he looked toward his sister and niece. Her stomach settled a little. She realized she didn't suspect RobO was that good an actor or inclined to hide his true feelings from anyone. *But it is always possible to be fooled.*

"I think you're just as safe returning with them all as you are doing anything else though." James clicked his tongue against his teeth lightly.

"And what does your gut say?" Weller asked.

"My mind says it is possible that Simone waged psychological warfare on Shay, by raping and killing other women who looked like her, hoping to frame some celebrity-obsessed slob for all of it later. And maybe the victims we found with semen on them were wrongly attributed to this case and really belong to some other murdering rapist, like my FBI colleagues are suggesting. But my gut doesn't believe it."

"Mine either."

"At any rate, the feds want you all back in Chicago."

"We'll be there before nightfall tomorrow, James. I'll text you our arrival details as soon as I schedule everything, and I'll call you when we touch down."

"I'll be waiting. Thanks, Addy. Safe travels."

†

Shay fidgeted with her hands and resisted the urge to push her chair closer to Addy's. She stared at her brother and her sister-in-law across the precinct's conference table. She looked up at Reyna, standing watch by the door, who offered her a slight smile.

A knock sounded and Reyna opened the door to let Detective James usher Beni in.

Everyone looked to Beni. His signature lavender tie was very askew and the top button of his shirt was undone. "Hello."

Addy shifted forward in her seat beside Shay. "Hi, Beni. Thank you for coming. We thought it best that legal counsel was present for the family."

"Yes. Thank you for insisting. Have any charges been filed against RobO yet?"

"Wait. What? Why would I be charged with anything?"

Shay watched her brother's eyes go wide and the blood drain from his face.

Panic and fear was the only thing evident on his wife's face beside him. Syl's mouth hung open.

Shay started to talk, but Detective James put a hand on her shoulder, beseeching her to silence before he walked to the head of the table. He pulled out a chair and sat down, laying his hands to rest on the tabletop. "Among Simone Saez's possessions was an envelope containing a $30,000 cash payment with your fingerprints on it, Mr. Greenaura."

Her brother blinked repeatedly at Detective James

before croaking out a strangled, "What?"

Shay's heart breathed a sigh of relief in that instant as she saw the pained confusion plainly on her brother's face.

Detective James persisted. "The envelope, with your fingerprints on it, contained $30,000 in cash. Did you make any payments to Simone Saez at any time for anything?"

RobO shook his head slowly. "No. I never gave Simone money for anything. Not even a soda pop."

"Why did she have an envelope with your fingerprint on it?"

"I don't know."

Detective James tilted his head and gave RobO an intense glare. "I don't believe you."

RobO was silent but his bottom lip trembled. He looked from Detective James to Shay.

With a slap to the table, Detective James repeated, "I don't believe you. What did you pay Ms. Saez to do to your sister?"

RobO's head jerked up. "Nothing. I didn't pay Simone to do anything." His whole body started shaking and he cried, "I never carry cash."

Shay had the words to back up her brother's claim on the tip of her tongue but found herself swallowing them.

Detective James stood and exclaimed, "Bullshit. No one carries that much cash around anyway. That has nothing to do with your ability to pay Simone Saez to kill your sister."

Just hearing the accusation spoken aloud yet again caused Shay to flinch. She remembered to keep her own composure only because Addy placed a warm hand on her shoulder and left it there.

RobO was openly crying and repeatedly murmuring, "No, no, no, no. I didn't."

"He has only ever done everything that he can to protect me." Syl glared at Detective James and her voice dripped bitterness.

"And he has profited nicely in return." The grimacing grin Detective James gave in reply sent a shiver down Shay's back.

Standing, Syl clenched her fists at her sides and turned her focus to Beni. "Make them leave RobO alone."

Beni wiped his hand over his face. "I can't, Syl. This is an acceptable line of questioning. We need to know what happened."

Syl's chin fell toward her chest and she barely pronounced, "Make them leave him alone. I paid Simone."

Shay felt like a brick smacked her in the middle of her chest, and she had to gasp to get a good breath of air.

"You what?" RobO asked in a tone dead of any emotion.

Syl went pale and she crumpled back into her chair. "Oh God, Shay, I didn't know. I promise. I didn't, I wouldn't…"

"Hire someone to kill me?" Shay's shocked hurt quickly fired into startled anger.

"I didn't know she was a hit woman… I didn't hire anyone to kill you. I mean I didn't ask for that." Syl placed her hands over her face and sobbed.

"What did you ask for?" Addy stood behind Shay and placed both hands on her shoulders.

Shay took the cue to remain calm and forced herself to lean back in her chair.

Beni passed Syl his snow-white handkerchief and, as Syl took it, he encouraged her. "You need to answer the question, Syl. What did you ask Simone to do in return for the payment?"

Syl's sobbing calmed. She wiped her face. She clenched Beni's handkerchief tightly in both hands. "We were just chatting about her wanting to make the Brazilian folk album. I told her I was frustrated that RobO never got the chance to shine, to make whole projects happen." Syl hiccupped and stuttered, "H…he…he deserves that, Shay. He's got that talent too."

"I know," Shay said.

"But you don't help him do it," Syl accused. "I offered Simone the $30,000 as a bribe to her so she would ask for RobO to have the producing lead alone on her project. I wanted him to have sole production credit for something."

In the span of silent seconds, everyone was processing that information. Shay could hear the clock ticking on the wall behind her with a startling loudness. She was sure her world would visibly have started spinning out of control if Addy's touch hadn't grounded her to the room.

"Just on the album. The one album," Syl clarified.

"It looks bad." Addy's voice was calm as it passed

over Shay's head. "Simone only took money for professional hits."

"But $30,000? That's pocket change she didn't need for a kind of target she's never bothered with before," Reyna said from her position by the door.

"That might help in court," Beni said.

"It might?" Shay sighed. "Jesus, Syl." She noticed that RobO's mouth had stopped opening and closing like a fish as he stared directly at his wife.

RobO repeated, "Jesus, Syl," before adding, "where did you even get $30,000 in cash?"

Syl studied the table intently. "Extra grocery money. I over budgeted and saved some for years." She shrugged. "I'm sorry, Shay. Not everything was always as organic as I said it was."

RobO was shocked silent again. Shay asked the next question that she knew was plaguing them both. "Why did you think you needed to do that, Syl? You know that I love you and RobO. Right?" Shay's eyes teared up and got so blurry she had to wipe her sleeve over them to see Syl's face clearly.

Syl dropped her head to the table covering it with her hands. This time her whole body shook with her sobbing.

†

Weller stood with her back to the closed door of the conference room, trusting Detective James and Beni to work out what was the best way to let the Greenaura family wait out all the legal inquisitions to follow. She sighed and turned her attention to Reyna. “Chicago PD thinks this is case closed.”

Reyna nodded. “And Detective James?”

“Not so much, but his hands are tied.”

“And he’s getting pressured to leave it to our fine federal alphabet soup.”

Despite herself, Weller laughed at the old joke. “Yeah, apparently the NSA is interested in Simone now too.”

“Not surprising. So what about you? What do you think?” Reyna crossed her arms and leaned against the wall beside Weller.

“I’m still not sure it’s over. Not everything fits yet.”

“I trust you completely. What do you want us to do?”

“I want you and the guys to go home.”

Reyna’s posture stiffened. “What? But if you think there is still a threat…”

Weller gave her old friend a reassuring smile. “I don’t think—I feel like there is still a threat to Shay.”

“Good enough for me,” Reyna asserted.

“Maybe, but not a good enough reason to keep a whole team wrapped up in a protection detail here. Especially not when you could be starting that contract in Norfolk next week.”

“It’s a business decision?” Reyna’s brows quirked in a look of incredulity.

Weller shrugged. “Yes, it is a business decision to

make the most of our labor hours. I think I can sufficiently protect Shay well enough to determine if there is more threat. Don't you?"

"Yeah." Reyna gave half shrug. "But don't you think you're too attached?"

Weller shrugged. "Maybe that is a good thing."

"Maybe." Reyna smiled. "I can't say I ever really bought into that zero attachment philosophy of yours."

Weller tucked a strand of errant hair back behind her ear and tightened her ponytail. "Yeah, well, I have to admit that this isn't just a business decision. I'm attached to you, too, and I understand that Jerome's boat is in this month."

"If I take the guys to Norfolk, I can see my husband." Reyna's smiled widened.

"Yep." Weller grinned back wholeheartedly.

"You might be okay after all, El Jefe."

"I love you too, Segunda al Mando."

Chapter Thirty-one

Alternate Plans

"You heard, Beni, Shay. Syl can't really leave Chicago yet. Do you really want to leave Iva in her sole care while we're all away?" Weller watched the struggle to decide playing out on Shay's face.

"It's hard, but yes, I do. I have to trust Syl again sometime. She loves Iva and Iva loves her. We're family."

Weller kept her face blank. The early days of March had not yet brought any signs of spring to Chicago, but she was still glad to be sitting on a bench in the sun with Shay. Iva played in her newly constructed playhouse.

"What did Detective James say?" Shay finally asked.

"There haven't been any new rape victims paralleling your looks since Simone's arrest."

"And we haven't received any other threats. I don't think I can put off doing our shows any longer. Aside from the fact that I've always wanted to play in Denver's

Paramount Theatre, our smaller acoustic show that Friday night is something we've been promising our dedicated fans for months. They paid steep prices to get in and the charity for the ice-storm victims is depending on our earnings for that show."

Weller looped an arm over Shay's shoulders and hugged her in closer. "I know."

"Do you think Iva and Syl need more protection?" Shay looked up.

Weller resisted the urge to place a kiss on Shay's pert nose and focused on answering the question. "I think the new security staff is sufficient as long as they stay here, but I'd feel better if someone besides just Syl was with Iva at all times. Especially if they leave the convent grounds."

"Like Sonny or Duval?"

"No, we'll need them to drive the bus to Denver and help out there."

"What about Jane's sister?" Shay suggested.

"I think so. She won't finish her criminal justice degree until May. She'll still have to go through the application process, do all the testing and physicals before she can start in a police academy anywhere. So she'll be available for at least another six months, and she's done some basic security guard work already."

"And Iva knows and likes her." Shay smiled.

"And she knows and likes Iva." Weller looked back to the playhouse. Iva laughed delightedly at the rolling chime of her playhouse's warbling doorbell. The beautiful blond child pressed the button again before slipping inside the house to answer the door for herself.

†

He backed his truck into a spot in the public parking lot so that his license plate faced the adjacent building's brick wall. He looked over the whole intersection and the bus stop on Wazee Street and determined that the only camera around was the one facing the people waiting at the bus stop. Coors Field loomed in the distance and the Friday afternoon traffic was building up half an hour before five o'clock.

He took his new 9mm Beretta out of the glove box and pushed the gun into the oversized hip pocket of his boot-cut carpenter jeans. He buttoned his mock-neck wool cardigan over his dark-green 'Greenaura is for Girls' T-shirt. He unbuckled his seat belt and patted the show tickets in his right cardigan pocket and the capped dropper of Intensol in his left cardigan pocket. The clipping of his cousin's obituary he had taped to the dash fluttered in the wind created by his movements and caught his eye. Renewed rage soared through his veins.

"I'll get the bitch, my brother, don't you worry. I'll make her suffer."

He reached into the plastic Walmart bag on the passenger seat and dug out the two-roll pack of mini duct tape, popped it open, picked out one, and put it into his left cardigan pocket with the Intensol. He dug out the baggie of zip ties, selected his lucky number of five, and put those into the ruler pocket of his carpenter jeans. Finally, he checked that his beautifully sharpened buck knife was safely tucked inside his right jackboot, and adjusted the legs of his jeans squarely over his boots until he was sure no one could see even the hint of any bulges.

He stepped out of his black truck and checked his hair in the rearview mirror. Satisfied his handsome blond coif was still combed into place, Guy Dane gave a wide smile, and spritely sang, "Tonight's the Night," to the tune to his cousin Mitch's best song.

Guy walked up the block to 17th Street and took a right toward the Magnolia Hotel. He knew he would have to be patient and wait for his chance to show Shay Greenaura that he was her biggest, angriest fan. It would be a long evening, but he was confident he could find a way to make it an even longer night, full of beautiful screams begging for his mercy. A tingle of excitement thrilled warmly through his lower belly. He took in a big appreciative breath of the crisp city air.

"It's just good to have the whole weekend off and something fun to do," he announced. The crowd around him had all stopped at the corner and waited for the street light to change.

"Amen to that, buddy," said a good-looking, red-haired guy standing near his elbow.

†

Guy was patiently waiting at Harry's Bar for the post-show fan meet-and-greet to start when Shay herself walked in and approached the bar beside him. His fingers twitched on the Intensol dropper in his pocket and he uncapped it. He tried to keep calm.

She smiled at him and he smiled back before she waved down the bartender.

He could only pray that she ordered something that would work well with the Intensol's orange color and wintergreen taste. He liked his chances of getting her alone and compliant if she did. Guy was so wishfully patient that he almost didn't hear her order her hot herbal mint tea with a drop of honey and a squeeze of lemon.

A tall dark-haired woman in a gray suit stepped up to the bar on Shay's other side and eyeballed him briefly. He smiled shyly at her and did his best to feign nonchalance. He turned his gaze to the white wine in his own glass. He watched with his peripheral vision. The tall woman turned away from the bar looking over the crowd behind them.

The bartender informed Shay her tea would take a few minutes but offered to bring it over to her when ready. Shay replied something that Guy didn't fully hear, but it sounded polite and affirmative. She then walked toward the small crowd of fans eagerly waiting around the bar's biggest booth. The tall woman followed Shay.

His heart was hammering so loudly that he could barely hear the gentle thud of the coffee cup on the bar top.

The bartender placed it down and opened a mint tea bag. Guy pulled the open Intensol dropper from his pocket, but kept it fully cupped in his hand. He deliberately slowed his breathing and closed his eyes briefly as he recalculated his estimate of Shay's weight and worked through the dosing directions in his head again just to be sure.

He opened his eyes again, assured that, within twenty minutes of finishing her tea, Shay should need to pee and be sufficiently suggestible without being in an obvious stupor. A swell of confidence washed down his back and his mouth went dry with hope as the bartender poured hot water over the tea bag and then strode back toward the kitchen. Guy downed his white wine and then pushed his glass toward the cup of steeping tea. A surreptitious look to each side and up at the mirror showed him the room behind him—no one was paying him any attention. He moved his right hand from the empty wine glass and squeezed the Intensol dropper dry as his hand passed over the steeping tea, before sticking both hands in his jeans pockets and leaving the bar.

†

As Addy trailed her out the bar door toward the bathroom, Shay felt nearly giddy with contentment. "I can't believe how good it feels to be singing and interacting with fans without all the fear and apprehension."

"It's good to be engaged in your calling." Addy chuckled. "So would you say you're a natural now?"

Shay stopped and turned to face Addy on the carpet in the empty hallway. "Yes. This is my natural. I know it's nearly midnight and we've been busy since the wee hours of the morning. I'm exhausted, but it feels like I earned my exhaustion. I'm happy. I'm a natural at this." She stood on her tiptoes and kissed Addy on the cheek. "Thank you for helping me get back to it."

Addy blushed. "You're welcome."

"Now, I really have to pee." Shay set off for the nearest restroom.

†

Guy chewed his fingernail. He watched the two women conversing down the hall. No iteration of his plans included dealing with the tall woman in the gray suit. He couldn't shoot her. The gun was mostly to intimidate Shay, if needed. After spending only a dozen or so hours at the range to qualify for his permit, he wasn't sure he could even hit anything with it. It would make way too much noise and attract attention, leaving him with too little time to get Shay isolated, bound, and extracted to his rented hideout in a loft next door.

"Patience," he whispered the reminder to himself, and left off chewing on his fingernail.

Shay kissed the cheek of the tall woman and an idea dawned on him. He rushed farther down the hall toward the restrooms ahead of them.

†

"Well, hell." Shay laughed. She eyed the out-of-order sign taped to the women's restroom door. She could hear more than one toilet running on behind the door and there was a stink of sewer peeking through the brighter smell of industrial cleaners. "I've really got to pee. Any idea where the closest working restroom is?"

Addy laughed and looked pointedly toward the door to the men's restroom.

"Right." Shay pushed open the door to the men's room. "Hello. Is anyone in here?" There was no reply. The urinals were all empty so she stepped in and peered quickly under the walls of the two bathroom stalls to find no feet.

"Looks good." She turned to Addy and asked, "Will you make sure the guys stay outside for a minute?"

The furnace kicked in and the hum of industrial heating sounded above them. "Yes, ma'am." Addy stepped outside pulling the door closed.

Shay hurried to the closest stall and pulled open the door. Surprised to see a handsome young man sitting on the toilet, she immediately apologized, "Oh, I'm so sorry."

She took a quick step back and he stood, leveling a small, very dark handgun directly at her heart. He raised a finger to her lips, gesturing her to be quiet, then grabbed the collar of her shirt, and pulled her closer. When the tip of the gun pressed directly to the skin above her heart, he whispered, “Say something to make her go away for a few minutes and I won’t shoot you.”

She could tell he meant it. His eyes were a bright dark-blue and his other hand grasped the back of her neck gently but firmly. “Now, please.”

“Hey, Addy, can you, uh, go ask RobO to find our give-away guitar and bring it down to the bar for the fans? I need a few more minutes in here than I thought.”

Shay heard the door push open.

The man with the gun to her chest mouthed the words, “Be still.”

Addy’s voice sounded a touch skeptical. “Are you sure you want me to abandon the door? Someone might come in.”

The gun pressed harder into Shay’s chest. “Yeah, I’m sure. I don’t want to keep the fans waiting just because I ate more fiber for lunch than I should have.”

“I don’t want to leave you alone,” Addy insisted.

The man glowered and gritted his teeth.

Shay swallowed and managed to choke out a giggle she hoped sounded convincing. “I think I need to do this bit alone, Addy.”

Addy gave a dark laugh. “Yeah, okay, I get it. A little too protective, huh?”

“Yeah.” Shay wondered at the calmness of her own voice. She thought she should feel panic but all she felt was slack fear. Her limbs felt limp and helpless.

“Okay, but I’ll be back in five minutes,” Addy called

as the door closed behind her.

Shay and her captor stared at each other for several breaths before his hand let go of her collar and he pulled something silver out of his cardigan pocket. She noticed his *Greenaura* T-shirt inside his cardigan.

He held the silver thing out to her. "Tear off a piece and put it over your mouth."

She took the small roll of duct-tape from his hand and followed his direction before she could really figure out why she was going along with everything so easily. She struggled to think about what she should do to save herself, but her foggy feeling of disinterested calm persisted. Her knees felt increasingly liquid.

He pushed her out of the stall. Raising the gun to point at her head, he stepped around behind her. He pressed the gun to the base of her skull. "I'm going to keep this pointed at you at all times. If you do anything other than what I say, or make any loud noises, I'm going to shoot you until I'm sure you're dead."

His left hand gripped her left shoulder and pushed her back into the stall. "I want you to climb the toilet and pull yourself up into that vent above it."

Shay noticed the open vent four feet above the old toilet tank for the first time.

"It's a tight fit, but we'll crawl down it with you in front of me to the first opening on your left side, and then we'll get out. No big deal, if you do what I say." His tone was kind like a nurse telling her what to expect before administering some treatment.

Shay nodded and breathed deeply through her nose, the tape over her mouth already itching. She clambered up the toilet and into the surprisingly roomy airshaft. She was glad to be a small woman as she crawled on her belly toward the first opening on her left.

She found the vent out to her left was already open. She peered out of it and noticed the top of a large, empty, utility shelving unit stood less than a foot below the opening. She felt his hand tighten briefly on her ankle and stopped in the opening.

"Crawl to the top of the shelving unit and then straight down it. The shelves are sturdy enough to hold your weight if you place a foot on each one. When you get to the bottom, step back two steps, and wait for me there. If you move more than two steps from the shelves, I will shoot you until I'm sure you're dead."

She found herself feeling sleepy. Her limbs were so heavy, but she did her best to comply with his directions. As she reached the ground, she took two steps back and looked up so she could watch him climb down. To her great surprise, he was already setting his second foot on the floor. His gun aimed directly at her.

"Very good, Shay Greenaura. I'm impressed."

She wanted to give a smartass retort, but the tape over her mouth wouldn't allow it anyway. She just huffed out of her nose and glared at him.

He smiled broadly and she couldn't help but think he

would make a good department-store-catalogue model. "Nice to meet you face to face. I'm Guy Dane, by the way."

The name surprised her and it took several heartbeats for her to figure out that his last name matched Mitch's. She didn't remember ever meeting him though. She blinked rapidly trying to fight off the sudden urge to yawn.

He laughed. "I know we never had a chance to meet in person. I'm Mitch's favorite younger cousin. We didn't get to see each other much over the last few years, but he was a real older brother for me after my parents divorced and my dad split. I really looked up to him. I was pretty stoked when he called and said you made him a dad." Guy shook his head and his grin turned to a glare. "I was a big fan of yours anyway. I always managed to get laid at more of your concerts than I did at Mitch's. I was excited when Mitch said I'd probably get to meet you and Iva the next time you were all in Chicago, but then he called to tell me how you fucked him over before that could happen. You destroyed the only family I had left when you framed Mitch and took away his kid."

Shay felt the start of panic finally fill her belly.

Guy gripped her shoulder again and pulled her close. He rubbed the tip of the gun over her chin and up her cheek to her temple. "You fucked up when you fucked him over, Shay. I don't know what possessed you to get Mitch hooked on heroin and arrested for the possession. I guess some women are just evil she-devils, huh? I guess I just need to exorcise your ass. Eradicate all of you cunning cunts from our lives so that we can have a chance to be real men."

Shay shook her head and held her hands out in a mea culpa gesture. She knew she needed to keep him talking if there was any chance out of this. She knew she had to find a way out of this. Through her fogginess, she tried to think about everything Addy had taught her about being held at gunpoint during their brief lessons at the retreat. Thoughts of Addy jolted her fuzzy mind into remembering the karambit knife tucked into the hip pocket of her jeans. There was a chance, she thought, if she could get him to point that gun away from her for just a second.

He flexed his shoulders. "I don't really want to shoot you though. Don't worry. I want to make you feel our pain." He smirked. "Mitch just wanted release, you know?"

Shay nodded despite the gun placed against her temple. She was hoping to keep him talking.

There was a sudden loud banging on the door of the utility room and Shay could hear Addy's voice.

Guy kept the gun pressed to her temple and smiled. "Good thing the door is locked and no one can hear us over the utilities. I guess she'll have to come back later with a key to see if you're here. Shame I'll have to hurry this along so we're finished by then." He released her shoulder from his iron grip and reached his hand toward the ruler pocket on his carpenter jeans.

As Shay watched him remove several long gray zip ties, the door behind them emitted a cracking scream.

She saw his eyes go wide and felt the gun leave her

temple.

Time slowed for Shay and all her senses suddenly came to life with amazing clarity despite the foggy haze clinging to her muscles. She could smell a drift of gun oil as she watched Guy point his gun at something over her left shoulder. She slipped her hand into her hip pocket and opened the folding karambit with her thumb as Addy taught her as she drew it out.

The Addy in her memory insisted, "It is something more to scratch with than your fingernails. Go for the femoral artery or a jugular with all of your might. Don't hesitate to make the killing blow when you're outgunned. It might be your only chance."

Shay made the decision. She cocked her arm back before pivoting into the sweeping knife swing Addy showed her. The blade neatly sliced through Guy's jeans, and skin, and tendons before clipping deeply into the muscle at the apex of his leg.

His gun fired twice beside her ear.

Shocked, she dropped to her knees. The sounds percussed her ear temporarily deaf. She watched Guy look down at her. His lips twisted into a grimace, his eyes darted over and around and back to her with a giddy looseness. He dropped the zip ties and made a feeble grab for her.

Blood spurted at Shay from the hole in his jeans and quickly coated the front of her shirt with its wet warmth.

Guy's hand twitched in midair, deathly white, and then fell limp before he could touch her again. He crumpled to the floor in front of Shay.

His face showed only surprise and he looked very young to Shay. He said something that she couldn't make out and then his grip on his gun relaxed.

Shay kept the karambit gripped tightly in her right hand and reached out her left to pick up the gun.

Guy convulsed and another gush of blood pulsed out from the cut Shay had created. She watched his gaze flick toward the ceiling and then glaze over.

She put the gun and the karambit down on the floor beside her knees and noticed the blood spattered over her bare arms and dripping from her shirt front—but was surprised to find her hands clean of it. After pulling the tape from her mouth, Shay turned from the sight of her would-be killer, dead in a sea of blood, toward the door behind her.

Addy was slumped against the doorframe with her head lolling and a wound on the right side of her chest pooling blood.

"Oh, God. No. Please, no," she begged. She stood on her liquid legs and rushed to Addy's side. Shaking, Shay reached for Addy's smartphone and dialed for help.

Chapter Thirty-two

Healing

As Weller opened her sticky eyes slowly, dull red light and the blanketing silence gradually gave way to piercing fluorescents and a screaming pain that ran from her sternum down to her right elbow. The smell of antiseptics and pure oxygen from the tube tickling her nostrils convinced her she was definitely alive. Her need for water was so strong that her mouth felt full of prickly pear cactus and sand, but her tongue refused to shape the request. She squinted, trying to bring anything into focus, and saw a small dark shape come swimmingly near. Her heart raced. She remembered using the emergency fire axe to pry open the utility room door at the hotel, seeing Shay at gunpoint, drawing her FN 5.7, and then nothing more.

A hand touched her left forearm as gently as a butterfly. "Weller?"

She blinked, wiggled the fingers on her left hand, and

then blinked again trying to clear the sticky film blurring her vision. Slowly she managed to clear her focus enough to make out Reyna.

Her need for water completely forgotten, she croaked a plea, "Shay?"

Reyna sounded relieved. "Shay is perfectly fine." She barely completed the words before another small form appeared, blurry, behind her.

"Addy, I'm okay."

Reyna stepped back and Shay came forward into the space, placing her fine-boned fingers underneath Weller's. Weller cupped her hand to grip Shay's and rested for several seconds.

Eventually she remembered to ask for water.

"Ice chips first." Reyna spooned three into her desperate mouth. After repeated spoons of ice chips, the pain that was spreading across the right side of her chest was weighing down even harder on her. Her vision cleared and her mouth achieved some blissful humidity to combat the dry oxygen feeding into her nose.

Her voice clacked but worked enough to ask, "The rapist?"

Shay's blue eyes grew very wide and her hand felt colder. Weller watched Reyna put a reassuring arm around Shay's shoulders. "He's dead. Detective James is here handling everything."

Weller read the body language of both women and decided that later would be a better time to ask for more details. One thought clamored to be spoken. "Tell James I recognized him, from Stroger Hospital. Saw him in the elevator there in scrubs."

Reyna nodded. "His name was Guy Dane. He was a charge nurse at Stroger."

Shay's voice was small and hollow. "He was Mitch's cousin."

Weller's pulse quickened. "Did Mitch send him?"

Reyna smiled and shook her head. "No. Mitch overdosed on heroin in Rochester last week. It's over, Weller. Shay is safe."

"We're safe," seconded Shay.

Reyna gave Weller a knowing smirk. "Now what about you, El Jefe. Don't you want to know if you're going to live?"

Weller wanted to laugh, but just the thought of doing so sent a jolt of pain up her sternum. "Yeah, okay. Will I live? Can I walk? Do I have all my limbs? Cause things on my right side sort of feel like a five-alarm fire right now."

Reyna did laugh and it echoed with relief. "I've told you a thousand times you're too damn tall. You make too easy a target, but you did luck out. That bastard got off two shots."

Weller interrupted as she remembered, "I didn't shoot. He was behind Shay."

Shay nodded and sniffled.

Reyna cleared her throat. "Yeah. Well, anyway. One of his shots hit you under your right clavicle, and the force of the shot pushed you backwards into the doorframe. You had a concussion, but maybe that worked in your favor since they've been keeping you in a bit of induced coma lately. The emergency physician was ecstatic the bullet passed above your lung and didn't cause a tension pneumothorax. That's the good news."

"And the bad news is?"

"You've got a hole in your scapula and your deltoid muscle. Both are going to hurt like hell for three to six months. Meanwhile, you can't do jack shit except look pretty and do the rehabilitation treatment like you're told." Reyna gave her a fierce look.

"Hmm." The fire in her back almost convinced her that the injury was as serious as Reyna stated.

"Don't 'hmm' me. We don't want your ass in our DC office until you've got a full medical clearance for active duty from a military physician." Reyna smiled with saccharine sweetness. "Company policy, as you know, El Jefe."

Pushing herself was one thing, but setting a bad leadership example was unacceptable to Weller. She just silently scowled acknowledgement of her already-defeated retort.

Reyna continued, "Your apartment in DC is too pathetic to convalesce in. You'll go out of your mind there. Do you want me to call your parents?"

"No. Definitely not that. I'll never hear the end of how dangerous and stupid my work is for the next twenty years. I'll call them."

"And leave out ninety-five percent of the details."

"Of course." Weller did manage a smile.

"What about your grandpa? Do you want to go to the Retreat?"

Before Weller could acquiesce, Shay interrupted, "I want Addy with me. We've got plenty of room and she can look pretty helping me hire all the staff Beni has been nagging me to hire. It'll keep her from losing her mind with boredom. Right?" Shay's words were anxious and hurried, and in her oversized "Girlz Rock" hoodie with her mussed hair, she looked closer to twelve than thirty to Weller.

"I'd really like that." Weller smiled directly into Shay's blue eyes.

"Great idea. I bet Vigeles' employee insurance will cover a home-health nurse for our finest target in Chicago just as well as anywhere else."

Shay smiled wide and her eyes shone. "We'll heal her right up."

†

"Addy?" Shay's breath was warm on her naked collarbone.

"What, sweetheart?" Weller traced her fingertips from Shay's temple to jaw and then brushed back an unruly curl of Shay's honey-blond hair.

Shay didn't make eye contact. "Do I remind you of Elle?"

Understanding dawned on Weller. She looked over the downcast profile of her delicate lover. She thought it over. Elle was darker skinned, dark eyed, dark haired, curvier, more likely to smile at anyone for no reason, and a thousand times more patient than either herself or Shay.

"You don't look anything alike, you know," Weller pointed out.

Shay mumbled, "I know. I googled her image and found a picture of the two of you together, at one of her exhibit openings. She was tall like you, and classically beautiful, like you, with perfect olive skin and a killer smile. She was your equal."

Weller's eyes wandered over her blond-headed lover, taking in the lurid green swirl of tattoos traveling up Shay's right arm, culminating in a tracery of leaves and branches on her shoulder, and spilling over onto her back to spell out "Art is the Heart of Earth." A wide grin cracked Weller's face. She continued to admire Shay's wiry musculature, small hips, and pale skin—her skin was so pale it made her blue eyes crackle and glow by comparison. She placed two fingertips reverently under Shay's heart-shaped chin and pressed upwards lightly until Shay's eyes met hers.

Shay's eyes were bright, vulnerable, and searching.

"Shay Greenaura, you are beautiful. You are loved. I love you, for you and for the things that you are willing to share and discover with me. You have caught my heart, entirely against my will, and not because of how you compare or don't compare to Elle. You do not have to earn this. Remember? We create our love together."

"Thank you." Shay sighed and curled tightly into Weller's unwounded side. Weller wrapped her arm over Shay and closed her eyes, content to rest awhile longer.

†

"I'm recovered, Shay. I can't stay here forever." Addy put her black duffel on the foot of their bed.

"Why not, Addy? Aren't we in love?" Shay crossed her arms.

Addy paused in the middle of pulling out the top drawer of Shay's dresser. "Absolutely. You know I love you."

"I love you, too. So what is the problem?" Shay didn't like the idea of Addy's sweaters leaving her dresser drawer, let alone Addy leaving Chicago.

"We have careers to manage. I need to be in DC now. We have a client load that requires Reyna and I both to take leads in different places for several weeks." Addy pulled the two sweaters from the drawer, leaving three behind.

"Okay, so it's just a few weeks." Shay sighed.

"No, Shay, that's not what I meant. Even after that, you and I both still have careers to manage." Addy placed the sweaters into her duffel before turning her attention to the sock drawer.

"Bullshit. You and Elle had careers to manage and you made it work."

Pausing with two pairs of socks in hand, Addy only

eyed the ground.

Scared, Shay clenched her fists at her sides. "What is it really, Addy? Why can't you stay and protect me? I can pay for your security services as well, or better, than any diplomat."

Addy tossed the socks into her duffel and stood still. "I can't be objective anymore. I don't want to be objective about you, and I can't protect you this way."

"This way?" Shay waved a hand back and forth between them.

Addy nodded, red-rimmed eyes sullen toward the ground, and cradled her right arm in her left.

"Addy, this is the only way you can protect me. The only protection I want is to be loved by you."

"I do and I will love you, Shay, but I can't stay here doing nothing real, nothing meaningful. I can't personally provide your security services just to have a reason to stay with you. It would slowly kill us both, even if my lovesick distraction didn't allow something stupid to hurt you."

"And I can't follow you around and actively manage a record label."

"No, you can't." Addy's brow creased and the hitch on the bridge of her now whitened from the tension.

Shay bit her lip. "So we're going to be rational adults about this, and we're each going to go on with our respective careers?"

"Yes."

"Shit, Addy. So I get to love you, but I never get to see

you?"

Shaking her head adamantly, Addy held up both hands. "No. You will see me. I will be on a flight to you every week if I have to. We can manage long-distance dating until we figure out something better. I know we can."

Shay cocked her head to one side and gave Addy a mild glare.

"I know it is inconvenient, Shay, but is it really any different than the way RobO and Syl were having to live their marriage?"

Shay snorted. "Yeah, well, you see how well that worked for them. Syl still gets to serve four years of probation for conspiracy to commit a class D felony after she finishes serving her time next month."

"Aside from triggering a serious case of soup-sandwich-crazies in Syl, it seemed to work okay. They still love each other."

"You have a point there." Shay gave out a light huff, stepped forward, and pressed her face into Addy's left shoulder. She slid her hand inside Addy's suit jacket and grasped the strap of the shoulder rig running around Addy's left arm. She knew this moment was inevitable. She couldn't really just catch and make Addy a captive love slave forever, under the pretext of letting her recover from her wound.

Addy wrapped both arms tightly around her and cradled her close. "Neither of us is the same kind of crazy as Syl, so maybe it won't trigger anything awful. Anyway, we could try. If you want?"

Shay sighed. "Do you mean like some sort of perpetual catch and release program?"

She could feel Addy shrug. "Yeah, I guess. It sounds like a dumb idea, huh?"

"No, Addy, it sounds like a great idea. It's a chance for us to be free enough to make our dreams happen and still be together, even if it is complicated."

"I give you my word, Shay. I will return to you. It's better than just a chance that we will be together."

"Even if it is just a chance, I'll take it. I want to be loved and cherished by you. Hook, line, sinker, and then released. You can save me every time."

"You can save me, too, Shay. You do save me."

Holding Addy close, Shay whispered, "I've got ideas though, you know, if this dating thing progresses into more between us."

"I bet you do." Addy stepped back and granted Shay a wry smirk.

Shay's insides went warm and shaky. "No, really, I mean you could head security for the whole label." Shay felt bereft without Addy's arms around her.

Addy shook her head and smiled ruefully. "Not really my style."

Shay looked down. "I suppose not."

"But I want to give Reyna the DC office, and open a second location in Chicago."

Shay went very still. Her stomach did a hopeful backflip. "Really?"

"Yeah." Addy smiled broadly, put her hands in her pockets, and blushed. "So I can be next to you every day, as your lover, as myself."

Shay grinned, squealed, "Woohoo," and launched herself into Addy's arms.

Addy managed to catch her, and Shay rewarded her with a shower of kisses.

Chapter Thirty-three

Release the Catch

Weller walked through O'Hare airport toward the exit with her black duffel in hand to find Duval standing in front of the black Chevy Tahoe waiting for her.

"Just in time, Addy. I think they were about to chase me off for parking here two seconds too long."

She shot him a smile as they piled into the SUV. "There was a weather delay in DC."

Duval shifted into drive and they pulled out into traffic exiting the airport toward uptown. "Don't worry. I'll get you there before their first set is over."

"Thanks, Duval."

"You're welcome. I'm just glad this was your last commuter flight, so to speak."

"After six months of flying back and forth, I'm glad Chicago is now 'home sweet home' too." Addy slid her hand into her pocket where her karambit once rested, and touched the rose-gold and emerald Claddagh engagement ring she had bought Shay the day before.

"I can think of a few people who will be very happy to know you see it that way. Welcome home." Duval flashed her a bright smile in the vehicle's dim interior. He turned on the satellite radio. "They're broadcasting Shay's show live from the Metro tonight. At least you can listen to the start until we get there."

As Duval drove onto the interstate north, Shay's voice filled the SUV's interior.

"I'd like to share a new song with you tonight. I know I don't normally write songs about love and all that fluffy stuff, but what can I say, love makes the world go round. This song is called 'Two Kinds' and it's about how learning to share yourself saves your life. I hope you like it." The approving crowd roared and then a trickle of guitar notes picked out the song's opening pattern.

Addy sang along to the broadcast, softly harmonizing with Shay's voice. "What is truth? You're afraid you have to have some definition, supported by a rational argument. You want the practical, definitive answer over the hogwash abstractions. The truth is. Truth has two faces, two kinds, and only the blind one ever faces reality. You wonder if you're worth it, but the truth is two kinds. The truth is relative. Your lips against mine and your tongue a soft quick pearl. The scent of cardamom and cinnamon near your skin. The bells of your laughter. Truth is assembled. We gather the facts. Your hand nesting entwined in mine or perched sparrow seconds on my shoulder in passing by. Our arms entangled in a holding pattern, frustrations scattered. Two wills connected. Truth has two faces, two kinds, and only the imagining one is afraid of what it might be missing. Truth is discovered, not caught. Love is released, not earned. We are freed by consensus and the telling of words too kind."

†

Shay hugged Addy tightly to her, breathing in and holding onto the familiar smell of Addy's clean cologne and dry-cleaned suit.

Addy hugged her tightly back as they stood alone in the Metro's green room, content to be holding one another as the crowd filed out of the theater before they would head home themselves.

"I can't believe I get to keep you," Shay mumbled into the heat emanating from Addy's neck.

Addy pulled back and smiled at her shyly.

Shay narrowed her eyes. "What? Don't tell me I don't get to keep you."

Addy's eyes widened and she shook her head. "Actually, I was going to ask you if you would keep me as your wife."

Shay felt her mouth hang open.

Addy smiled again and held out a rose-gold and emerald Claddagh ring in the palm of her left hand. "Will you marry me, Shay Greenaura?"

Shay glanced back and forth from the ring to Addy's sparkling brown eyes. "Oh, yes, I will marry you and keep you safe."

About the Author

Lacey Schmidt

Lacey lives in Houston with her wife. She holds a doctorate in industrial-organizational psychology that has afforded her many opportunities to learn how all kinds of interesting people help make the world go around, and many of these heart-warming and heart-aching experiences continue to influence her writing. Previous publications include a poetry book called *The Nightshade Lexicon*, a short story called *Love's Luck*, and the lesbian romance novel, *A Walk Away*, published by Affinity eBook Press NZ. You can find Lacey on Facebook, Twitter, Sound Cloud, or Google+ if you're so inclined. She also accepts any and all implied praise or encouragement directly by email at LaceyLSchmidt@gmail.com.

Lacey's Internet presence:

http://laceyschmidt.blogspot.com/
http://www.amazon.com/Lacey-L-Schmidt/e/B00P71M0QO
https://soundcloud.com/lacey-schmidt
Twitter: Lacey Schmidt @shrinky_schmidt
https://www.facebook.com/laceylschmidt
google.com/+LaceySchmidt

Other Books from Affinity eBook Press

Ready for Love by Erin O'Reilly
Kylie Wilcox's life dramatically changed with the death of her husband. Dr. LJ Evans, a renowned archeologist, needed and wanted nothing but her work for her happiness. Their worlds are about to collide and lives will be altered forever.

Neptune's Ring by Ali Spooner
In the sequel to *Venus Rising*, Nat and Liz, owners of Venus Rising, invite Levi and Vanessa to join them in a venture for a new club on another island. They find the perfect place in an unfinished resort Neptune's Ring. While on the island, Levi is drawn into a mystery involving secret compartments and a murder. Join the characters in this page-turning adventure, filled with steamy romance, intrigue and an unsolved murder.

The Ultimate Betrayal by Annette Mori
Lara is a successful, beautiful, charming, financier. She is also a total control freak, so whatever Lara wants, Lara makes sure she gets. Rachel is Lara's fun loving, charming, irresistible wife. Sophia's surprise visit to see Lara sets in motion a

number of life changing events for them all. Hell has no fury as a woman scorned.

It's in Her Kiss by Various Affinity Authors
A collection of various holiday stories dedicated to anyone and everyone that reads it. Young, old, lesbian, gay, bisexual, and transgender. We are all the same inside, and want the same things outside…love, happiness and that special someone to spend all of our holidays with.

Keeping Faith by TJ Vertigo
Join the antics of Reece, Faith, Cori, Vi, and even The Animal, one last time in *Keeping Faith.* Faith has finally made the big screen, but how will Reece handle her success? Will the love that they share be enough to save their relationship and soothe The Animal?

Bound by Ali Spooner
A rogue master vampire threatens the existence of the New Orleans vampire clan. Lord Jordan enlists Devin Benoit, sister of the Baton Rouge Alpha, and her witch lover, Tia, to assist with cleansing the city from potential disaster.

The Circle Dance by Jen Silver
Jamie Steele has moved to another town, trying to forget the heartbreak of losing her lover of six years. Sasha Fairfield finds her thoughts taken up with her ex-lover and thinks she

wants Jamie back. Follow this captivating romance as love dances through the lives of these women to its surprising conclusion.

Search for the White Moon by Natalie London
Kathryn Austin, a government agent, is given opera singer, Adriana Desi, as her new assignment. Their lives and futures are in danger as the White Moon terrorists hunt them. Immerse yourself in this fast-paced romantic thriller by debut author Natalie London.

Take Me As I Am by JM Dragon & Erin O'Reilly
When Jo Lackerly and Thea Danvers meet, an unexpected friendship develops, proving a catalyst for both women to change their lives irrevocably. Follow them on a journey of discovery that will have your heart smiling, blood boiling, and senses entangled in a wonderful romance.

Carved in Stone by Jen Silver
Join the characters from *Starting Over* and *Arc Over Time* in this final book from the Starling Hill trilogy. Ellie Winters thinks she might be going mad when the ancient queen wants a proper burial for herself and her consort. *Carved in Stone* has romance, adventure, a treasure hunt, and a happy endings for all, living and dead.

Anywhere, Everywhere by Renee MacKenzie

Catch to Release

Gwen Martin's life in the Ten Thousand Islands area changes irrevocably when Piper Jackson comes into her life. Without trust, can the budding relationship between Gwen and Piper survive? Or will the answers to the questions continue to haunt them?

Venus Rising by Ali Spooner
Levi Johnson arrives at Venus Rising, an exclusive lesbian-only tropical resort in the Virgin Islands and finds more than she expected—a sizzling hot love triangle. Torn between her attraction to two women, she struggles to choose the right woman to share her life.

The Devil's Tree by Ali Spooner
Torn between her love for the pack and her need to find what's missing in her life, Devin Benoit travels to New Orleans. Will the previous happenings at the Devil's Tree help or hinder Devin in the fight of her life, and the life of Tia, the woman who now owns her heart?

The Beggars' Coppice by Erica Lawson
Edda Case is a woman in crisis who discovers that things are not as they seem. Is it truly a message for her from beyond the grave or is something more sinister taking place? Can Edda solve the mystery of *The Beggars' Coppice*?

Locked Inside by Annette Mori

How much does the power of love matter to someone who must overcome obstacles far greater than most people face in a lifetime.

Line of Sight by Ali Spooner
Sasha and her lover Kara are back. Continue the thrilling adventures of this couple from the Sasha Thibodaux series.

Requiem for Vukovar by Angela Koenig
Requiem for Vukovar continues the Refraction series and the exploits of Jeri O'Donnell and her partner, Kelly Corcoran. In an epic siege largely ignored by the wider world, Kelly, who was prepared to give up comforts and certainties when she became part of Jeri's nomadic life, encounters more than physical danger. Her ability to maintain her core integrity is assaulted by the inevitable ugliness of war. For Jeri, the true battle is confronting her attraction to violence as she struggles against losing herself in the exhilaration of combat.

Against All Odds by JM Dragon
From award-winning and bestselling author JM Dragon, with significant updates by Erin O'Reilly, comes an original tale of romance where everything seems to be stacked against two women whose destinies bring them together. Life however takes a twisted path, setting both Steph and Louise in directions they never thought possible. Will love win out against all odds or will love be forever lost?

The Settlement by Ali Spooner
The outpouring of love and friendship toward Cadin helps her on her path to healing and learning to trust her heart to love once again. Join bestselling author Ali Spooner on this sensational journey that ends with a heartwarming romance.

Once Upon a Time by Alane Hotchkin
Raven only wanted to escape the blows that life had dealt her. She longed to be on the open sea and free. When she came upon a beautiful young girl sitting alone in the middle of a meadow, little did she know that her destiny would be changed forever. Will they become the pawns of the ancient vision or will both paths lead to the same port of destiny? Find out in this exciting high seas adventure that will capture your imagination.

Asset Management by Annette Mori
Follow the twists and turns to the explosive conclusion. Not everything is black and white. There are many shades of gray, and sometimes it's difficult to decipher who is good and who is evil. No one is all virtue or all malevolence, but sometimes love helps us rise above.

Do Dreams Come True? by JM Dragon
How do two people who really shouldn't get on end up in a relationship? Find out in this deliciously ordinary romance.

Return to Me by Erin O'Reilly
Will Salvation bring just that to Ellie, allowing her to find peace and happiness again, or will it have her questioning all that she believes in? A wonderful romance cloaked within an intriguing mystery.

A Walk Away by Lacey Schmidt
Sometimes chance brings you to the right person to help you resolve some of your baggage, and you learn to like yourself a little more. Kat and Rand are smart enough to recognize this chance in each other, but they also find that there is a catch to every opportunity—walking toward something is always walking away from something else.

Possessing Morgan by Erica Lawson
The investigation has barely begun when Andrea becomes the target of a nearly fatal hit-and-run. But was it really aimed at her? Can she and Morgan find the common ground they need to solve the case and stop the attacks, or are the gaps just too wide to bridge?

Affinity
eBook Press
NZ

E-Books, Print, Free e-books

Visit our website for more publications available online.

www.affinityebooks.com

Published by Affinity E-Book Press NZ LTD
Canterbury, New Zealand

Registered Company 2517228

www.ingramcontent.com/pod-product-compliance
Lightning Source LLC
Chambersburg PA
CBHW072052020726
47501CB00003B/565
* 9 7 8 0 9 0 8 3 5 1 9 9 2 *